Blood Promise

Holly S Roberts

Wicked Story Telling

<u>Animal Thrillers</u>
BREACH
SANCTUARY
RABID

<u>Crime Thrillers</u>
ONLY GIRL ALIVE
LOST LITTLE ANGELS
PRAY FOR HER

<u>Romantic Thrillers</u>
BLOOD PROMISE
HOTTER THAN HELL SERIES

Chapter 1

PART ONE: THE PACT

The rotund general who looked more at home behind a desk with a feast within grabbing distance, stared at me impatiently waiting for an answer.

His confusing question did little to settle my nerves. General Andrews was an uptight, yes-man, who now expected others to yes-man him. Somewhere in his sixties, his shortly cropped hair and shaved face, all the way to his shiny black boots, proved he had no business commanding a fighting force. He didn't get dirty, nor go without meals or a place to urinate or shit in privacy. This was his third appearance during the past year at an outpost he commanded. It was the first time I'd been ordered to his barely used office which was a tent larger than my sleeping quarters. The twelve by twelve canvas ruffled slightly. A single desk with a chair behind it and one in front took up most of the tent's interior. The general stared at me across his desk where he sat while I stood at attention beside the vacant chair.

Who exactly was I to be called in front of a general and not be offered the empty chair?

Tara Lott, at your service. I was the only civilian at the outpost and I desperately needed to stay under the radar for reasons I could not share with the general. With dull blue eyes, shoulder-length, thick brown hair, uninteresting features that no one called beautiful, and five two height, my looks allowed me to stay far below that radar. Now, the general was not helping matters.

Forty years ago, vampires and werewolves decided to make their presence known to humans. It went over like one would expect. If it was different than us, kill it.

All hell had broken loose because as it turned out, vampires and werewolves were hard to kill. It would have been easier if the powers that be had figured out early on that the two supernatural entities hated each other. Humans could have teamed up with one side or the other and possibly won. Nope, that's not how the elite human race worked. Monsters were monsters and needed to be annihilated.

Long story short, we still fought but the city was now the domain of Vampires and werewolves. I knew little about them in the isolated human military camp where I worked. Our human military's primary function was to keep humans safe. Rural areas were overpopulated with humans due to the surge from the cities. Not all humans lived rurally, but human street gangs ran the city and the people who lived there were a breed of tough individuals who could handle the new rules. This was all happening while vampires and werewolves continued fighting each other.

There had to be a catastrophic reason I was standing in front of the general. I was so stunned at what he'd asked me that concentration was hard. He also had a mole on his chin that had two long black hairs growing from it and no matter how much I tried not to see it, I failed.

"Ms. Lott, you haven't answered my question."

Oh right, there was a question. *Was I willing to help my country?* Why didn't he just pluck the hairs?

Andrews was the top commander in our military and he'd never liked me. He'd arrived at the outpost an hour before. The primary function of this camp was to give humans safe passage, though I saw little of that and had started questioning our real purpose.

I needed to focus and take the general's question seriously. I had to look him in the eyes, forget the mole, and say exactly what he wanted to hear. So why did I have such a bad feeling about this?

Doing as the general requested could gain me a military position. But, and that was a huge but, I had to keep a low profile. I'd managed to do so for years and a bonafide rank wasn't in my plans.

"How would you like me to answer your question?" I asked carefully, stalling for time so I could think this through.

The general sputtered. Andrews expected blind loyalty even from a lowly civilian. His incredulous gaze went to the other man standing in the tent, Captain Dickson. Dickson was medium height with a nice full head of military cut brown hair. His most stunning feature was his eyes that were hazel, with eyelashes most women would die for. I wasn't most women.

I, on the other hand, didn't want to catch anyone's eye and draw attention to myself. I didn't wear makeup or do more than toss my hair in a ponytail to get ready each morning. I wore clothing two sizes too large to hide my curves.

Nothing to see here; I'm a dweeb with a capital D. Dickson tended to ignore me and I was good with it.

The general's eyes said a lot as he stared at me. He didn't need to open his mouth. His contempt was clear. I glanced at the captain. His uniform wasn't anywhere near the pristine condition of the general's and his boots were dusty to the point you couldn't find the shine with a magnifying glass. He led tough men who killed if it was warranted, and he had their back when they needed him. You would never find him behind a desk.

A small electric current built at my fingertips and I pulled it back. Each day it seemed to get stronger and I wasn't sure why. If anyone discovered what I was hiding, I was as good as dead. Yeah, I admit it, I was one of the monsters. I wasn't a vampire or werewolf. I had no idea what I was other than nonhuman.

When I was a child, my father told me I was special, but he said no one could know how special. Objects moved around me and if I wanted something, it appeared in front of me. I was punished when it happened. No, not physically. My father would ignore me and isolate me from his love. It was a harsh lesson but as I grew older, I understood. To be supernatural when humans were still fighting the inevitable, was a death sentence.

My father instilled fear in me and I listened to that fear. After he died, I hid in plain sight. My job for the military was that of a kitchen grunt. I helped the military cook and had full cleanup duty.

The job sucked but I felt safe.

Now, for some reason, me, a nobody, was needed to do something very unsafe.

Then it dawned on me. I was expendable.

As minutes ticked by, General Edward's face went from red to purple. Neither was a good color for him. Had he expected me to jump up and down with joy?

"General, what Ms. Lott is saying is that she's willing to do whatever it takes."

The captain didn't look at me when he said this, but it proved he was a good bullshitter. He oversaw a group of half-crazy rangers who patrolled the outskirts of the city and helped humans escape. Although the captain kept his distance, a few of his rangers befriended me for some odd reason.

The general looked at me, his contempt dripping with the beads of sweat hanging off his chin and mole.

"What do you need from me, General Andrews?" I finally asked.

"This is top secret," he began and gave me his hardest stare.

I used my finger and made a crisscross over my heart, then laid my palm flat over it to symbolize secrecy. Maybe I should have made a shhh motion with one finger over my lips. He didn't look impressed with the heart gesture.

"A group of rangers disappeared inside the city," he said. "We need to know what happened to them."

"Rangers can't go into the city," I said foolishly.

Vampires and werewolves held the city boundary and had an agreement with the military that there would be no intervention within those boundaries. We monitored, or my friends did, the small rural towns that were the fallout for humans due to the war.

"Sometimes it's necessary to do things that go against the rules," the general said with a hard stare to accompany the words.

"I'm a civilian. What can I possibly do?" I asked next, the feeling of doom creeping closer and closer.

He tried to shred me with his eyes, but it didn't work. I stood my ground. As a kitchen grunt, I was accustomed to bullying by pretty much everyone. If it weren't for the group of rangers who semi-adopted me, my life would be hell.

"Frankly, Ms. Lott," the general said. "You are a nobody. The city is filled with people like you and no one will suspect you."

Oh the pain. Not! Most people didn't understand why humans stayed in the cities. They were almost considered traitors. I had lived there with my father until I was eighteen and I knew differently. Those who chose life among the vampires and werewolves were strong and they survived the new world without hiding. If it weren't for the gangs, I would have returned to the city years ago.

"Do I have a choice?" I asked, trying to keep my tone level.

His purple face darkened further. I might be blamed if his head exploded but the thought didn't bother me much.

Chapter 2

Unfortunately, the general's head stayed on his neck and there was no shredded brain matter to avoid.

"If you want a place to live in comfort and continue to skate through life, you don't have a choice," he said pompously, his large red nose tipping into the air ever so slightly.

That pissed me off. I worked from sunup until long after it went down. Some days my fingers were raw from scrubbing and my back ached so bad standing straight was nearly impossible. My sleeping cot barely stayed upright and my tent had holes in it. He should try getting off his fat ass for a few weeks and working kitchen detail before going home to a substandard tent.

I reined in my anger because it wouldn't get me anywhere.

"You want me to find the rangers?" I clarified.

"No, just information on their whereabouts," he said. "We'll give you something to take into the city and sell on the illegal market. That's where their last transmission came from. People are more likely to speak with you. Someone knows what happened to the rangers. Gather as much intelligence as possible. That's all we need you to do."

It was a big *ALL*. When I'd left the city, the illegal market was run by a single street gang with a very bad reputation. My father dealt with them often but that was my father.

"When do I leave?"

He relaxed slightly, his shoulders dropping.

"In two days, Ms. Lott."

I walked to the tent's flap and pulled it back. The captain was on my heels and bumped into me when I stopped. I glanced around him to the general.

"I know they're hard to come by but consider my tweezers yours after I leave, General."

Dickson hustled me from the tent with a small push between my shoulder blades.

"You have a smart mouth," the captain said with twitching lips.

I kept walking through the high desert terrain with its small bushes and skimpy trees that shot up toward the hot sun. It was my day off—the only one I had each week—and I needed a drink. The canteen offered free booze and a place to gather, play cards, or shoot pool during downtime. I turned and faced him.

"This is a suicide mission," I said angrily. "I can't defend myself," I lied. "How could I be the best person for this assignment?" I held up my hand when he tried to answer. "Stop pulling my tits. Forget the bullshit and tell me what's going on." Hanging with rangers taught me to always be direct.

Dickson gave me a long look and then did something that shocked me. He made an about-face and marched off to wherever captains went to hide their shame.

I had to face facts. The military didn't care if I lived or died. As a grunt, I wasn't just expendable, I was fodder. They had no idea I was capable of protecting myself. They didn't know about my magic, and they damn sure didn't know that staying hidden was all that kept me safe.

I threw aside the flap of the canteen and strode inside. I held up my hand when the bartender checked to see who entered.

"Tequila," I shouted over the noise. "Two." I held up two fingers and kept walking toward the table in the back. Said table was filled with my ranger pals. They watched me come in hot. Mule pushed out a chair with his foot. He was the shortest of my friends at five-eleven, with red hair, green eyes, and heart-stopping muscles. His smile was killer along with his handling of a M16 rifle. I had no idea how he got his nickname, but they all had one. Mine was a stupid nickname but no matter what I did, they wouldn't stop using it.

"Bad news?" Leo asked. He was a large Black man who didn't smile often. He had a bald cue stick head that made him look meaner. His angry disposition attracted women without even trying. I was immune but a girl could look and I'd looked my fair share with these guys.

"I had a meeting with the general. What do you think the news was?" I asked testily.

"It's bad," said Mule.

I rolled my eyes and resisted sticking out my tongue. Mule was a jokester and he teased me constantly.

"I'm being reassigned for the foreseeable future," I told them. "I have two nights to drink you shits under the table, and then I'm out of here."

The guys looked quickly between themselves. I almost asked what the hell was going on in their small minds, but Shep spoke before I could.

"Have you been moved to latrine duty?" he asked. His nickname fit because he looked like a lanky German Shepard. His eyes were blue, his hair always a tad longer than military short, his clothing slightly askew, and he had face stubble that appeared to be permanent. The dog analogy took nothing away from his sexy good looks that I tried not to notice.

It never made sense that the hottest rangers were the ones to adopt me into their group.

"That's one way to put it," I said, replying to his question about latrine duty. I was being asked to do shit duty; Shep had just put it in a nicer light.

I stood up to retrieve my drinks. I grabbed them off the bar and headed back to the table. I downed the first shot and put the empty to the side. I held on to the second, waiting for the burn to go away.

"You weren't joking," said Leo.

My eyebrows went up.

"Drinking us under the table," he reminded me. "I'm game. I'll go grab another round. You want one or two?"

"Two," I responded while lifting two fingers again.

The others gave him their drink orders and he went to the bar.

"Are they sending you to another camp?" Mule asked.

"Yep, and don't ask me which one; I'm not allowed to give details."

He reached over and rubbed my head.

"It's okay, kid. Can't be that bad."

There it was. The nickname they wouldn't stop using. Kid. Even if I did fall passionately in love with one of them, as the kid sister, they would tease me endlessly and not take it seriously. I'd had to come to terms with the fact they would never see me as an adult woman with needs.

"You make it sound like there's a top secret destination on the other end," Shep said. He looked at Mule and rolled his eyes. "She probably got demoted for the crap job she does."

"Is this a permanent assignment?" Mule asked, ignoring Shep.

"No. Couple of weeks at most." If I didn't return it would be because I was dead. I would never tell them that.

Leo came back with the drinks and I had my third. Things got fuzzy after that. I vaguely remembered shooting pool at one point. Dancing at another. Hopefully, I kept my clothes on.

"Come on, kid. You need your cot," Mule finally insisted.

I opened blurry eyes that saw double, no—triple. I was curled up on the pool table. Mule kept me upright as we made the short journey to my tent. He left me there, thankfully before I threw up on his boots.

I collapsed on the wobbly cot and watched the silver rods holding up the canvas do a dance. I tried to replay everything the general said but I was too drunk. A picture of my father swelled in my brain.

"The only chance you have is to stay hidden," he'd said before he died.

Up until now, I'd managed it. Going into the city was a suicide mission. I would be discovered and humans would kill me if the vampires or werewolves didn't do it first.

I barely made it outside before vomiting. I was too sick to brush my teeth and fell back in bed with a foul taste in my mouth.

My last thought was that I must have succeeded in drinking the guys under the table because I ended up on top of it.

Chapter 3

The problem with sleep, even after drinking enough alcohol to down a ship, was the dreams I'd had since my eighteenth birthday. This night was no exception. I opened my eyes in a bedroom I'd visited many times. The walls were covered in red brocade with gold embroidery. The huge bed took up the majority of space. The bed's cover had the opposite pattern from the walls with red on gold. I wouldn't have decorated any room this way, but I hadn't lived in the eighteen century or earlier. The bedroom reminded me of one of the historical novels I'd read years before.

Naked, I sat down on the bed. Sometimes I wore sexy lingerie but not tonight. My mystery man wanted me without clothing and I never argued in my dreams. Not that I knew it was a dream while I was in that strange room. I lay down and positioned my body seductively.

The man stepped toward me. He was dressed in tight formfitting black pants and a white shirt with long sleeves that flared at the wrists. On some men the shirt might appear feminine but on him, his masculinity was all I noticed. I couldn't see the tight ropes of muscle right now, but his onyx eyes, so dark they were pools of endless promise, let me know I would. Black hair fell to his shoulders. His face was equal parts precision and art. His jawline cut with sharp edges that blended into perfection. His flawless skin that I would soon have beneath me was lickable and I knew this because I'd licked every inch.

Nothing took away from his deadly persona. I was good with my sword, but this man would be lethal. Each of his movements was choreographed and I'd never doubted his ability to kill. It was written in every line of his body. He was a warrior like my father but definitely fiercer.

He gave me a smile that sent shivers across my flesh. He stripped off his shirt and my tongue circled my lips. Next came his pants. The striptease stopped my breath. I inhaled deeply when he moved over me and kissed my throat before his long exploration downward. When he kissed one hip, my thighs clenched. He murmured against my flesh and I forgot to breathe again.

"Open for me," he whispered, his breath hot and doing nothing to reduce the shivers he'd created.

"Who are you?" I asked.

"Your lover," he replied, and then he gently bit my inner thigh and spread my legs wider.

His tongue danced along my skin, avoiding where I wanted it most. I cried out in desperation, arching my back.

"Please," I begged to accelerate his favorite game of torment.

One of his fingers entered me and I gasped. I cried out when his tongue took its first sweep and two fingers were now gliding deeper. I bucked my hips harder but he was accustomed to my reaction and kept a firm grip on my thighs while his mouth continued the sweetest torture imaginable.

He drove me higher with his lips and fingers. My head went back and my neck strained in sexual agony. I wanted more. I wanted all of him, but he only gave me this and I'd learned to take what I could get.

I woke covered with sweat, my fingers desperately trying to bring release. I rolled and placed my pillow between my thighs, pressing myself into it until the orgasm rocked me and I found release. The room was spinning because the alcohol still had hold of me. I closed my eyes and passed out again.

The dreams began on my eighteenth birthday. I was too embarrassed to ask my father what they meant, and then he died and I had no one to talk to. We'd shared everything, but this was different. The dreams felt so real. Maybe I could have spoken to Mika about it, but what mortified me most was that I had two separate men in my dreams. Not multiple because it was pure fantasy but two distinct males who worshipped my body and filled my head with fantasies that came out of nowhere. I would dream of one or the other every night.

When I opened my eyes, I looked around the tent for a few minutes to gain my bearings. My head was no longer spinning but it pounded and I almost regretted the alcohol. I made it to the shower and vomited tequila into the drain. I hadn't eaten anything so it came up easily with just a touch of heartburn.

"Kid," Captain Dickson yelled into the shower tent a few minutes later.

He called me kid too. I was fated to be the irritating sister to every hot guy on the planet.

"Go away," I grumbled.

"I have clothes for you," he said from inside the large tent this time.

All that stood between us was a shower curtain. I stuck my head out and saw my old clothes over his arm.

"What are you doing with those?" I demanded without asking why I needed the clothes he brought this morning.

"You can't wear camo into the city. I'll have these washed and placed on your bunk when you return from your assignment." He didn't call it a mission because I wasn't a ranger. "There will be a backpack for you on the helicopter," he continued. "You won't be able to take anything identifying. Do you have any knowledge of the city at all?" He was distracting me from asking why I needed different clothing right now.

"I can find my way around. I lived there until I was eighteen," I answered and wished my head wouldn't pound with each word I spoke.

"Good. The side pocket of the pack will have a map. Study it then leave it on the chopper."

"Fine. Do you mind if I take the rest of my shower in peace?"

"You're expected on the helicopter in thirty minutes."

"I had two days," I practically shouted.

"Schedules change. Don't be late."

He left before I could throw a wet cloth at him.

I calmed down until I got out and tried on the clothes. I had been given a pair of jeans and a black tank top. They were formfitting and not the larger pants and shirt I wanted to wear. My usual clothes had a purpose. They covered my arm and leg muscles acquired from countless push-ups, sit-ups, and squats I did each night. The guys took advantage of the camp gym while I used my tent and my own bodyweight. The baggy clothing hid the results.

At least I was able to keep my boots. There was a black baseball cap in the bag and I pulled the bill low over my eyes to protect them from the sun. My head continued throbbing.

I went to my tent and grabbed two knives and slid one into each boot and pulled the jean legs over the top. I took an old beat-up case from beneath the cot and opened it. I removed the harness first and slipped it over my head and shoulder, then secured the buckles. Once it was situated, I pulled out my sword. It was a gift from my father. He'd taught me how to use it from the time I could lift it. I brought it over my head and effortlessly slid it into the sheath.

After exercising each night, I worked with the sword. It was all done in my tent away from prying eyes. I wasn't trained with a gun, but the sword and I were old friends. Trading on the illegal market required protection and even if the military expected me to be dead within hours of entering the city, I wouldn't go down without a fight.

My father took me to Hell's Market—as he called it—to buy things that weren't readily available from reputable sources. From the time I was eight, I wore my sword. My father had a reputation and he wanted people to know I was my father's daughter.

I was depressed knowing I was breaking my promise to him by going back into the city. He said I would know when my blood was ready to return. Maybe it had something to do with the tingling energy in my fingers, though I didn't think it the catalyst to enter the city and commit suicide.

Chapter 4

My headache worsened the more I thought about what I had agreed to do. I was not ready and I knew it.

I left my tent, upset that I couldn't say goodbye to my friends. I didn't think I would return. I wasn't sad about it; I was angry. They would quickly forget about me.

A gunship waited. There were five men on board. All were oversized Neanderthals with too many muscles said no girl ever. I was handed a headset. I rested it on my knees while I adjusted the flight straps. I put the headset over my ears and positioned the mic in case I was asked a question. Two men manned M61 Vulcan six-barrel rotary cannons, each facing an opposite doorway. I may not be a great shot, but I hung out with the rangers and listened when they talked guns and ammo. A third soldier stood in the middle to keep the ammunition rolling if it were needed. A pilot and copilot sat up front. I chose one of three empty seats directly behind them.

I hadn't left the camp since the first day I walked into it and asked for a job. I was a scrawny kid of eighteen. Captain Dickson took pity on me. I still had no idea why. I also didn't understand why he wasn't here to see me off. I shrugged his absence away, refusing to be upset.

Like the captain said, a backpack waited in one of the seats. It would easily slip over the sheath on my back. I opened the pack and discovered a change of clothes, including socks, a metal water bottle, and a large sack that took up most of the space. I opened it and saw smaller sacks. They were filled with black powder for bullets. Six bags total, about two pounds. They would sell for a small fortune. Guns were easy to come by, but bullets and powder were another story. It was a good choice for the illegal market.

I couldn't help wondering how the city had changed. From conversations I overheard, things had calmed down, but gangs ruled throughout the human sector. I had hoped the vampires and werewolves would remove them but so far that hadn't happened.

My father had made money by hiring out his sword to business owners who didn't want gang protection. He was gone more than he was home. When I was four years old, he no longer left me with a sitter. He said I was safer on my own. Looking back, I realized I'd had trouble containing my power and he was worried the sitter would notice.

Tears built behind my eyes. I hated thinking about the past because it inevitably led to thoughts of my father's death.

"They've found us and they're coming after you," my father said as he lay dying with a wound to his chest. He didn't say who had found us. "Hide outside the city. You'll know when you can come back. Say goodbye to Mika and Coop but don't linger. You will place them in danger."

Mika and Coop were our friends and the only people my father trusted.

He gripped my fingers tightly. "Promise me." Blood ran from his lips.

Those were his last words. He died within minutes, his hand going limp in mine. I barely remembered his face now. That saddened me. He'd been my world and he was the only safety I'd had. I thought my life was over. The only thing that kept me going was my promise to leave the city and wait for something unknown to happen. I'd waited six years and the only thing different now was the tingling of energy that wouldn't go away and was getting harder to hide. My limited magic, and that's what I'd started thinking that it was, didn't provide comfort. It scared the hell out of me.

I found the map Dickson mentioned. The rangers had last been seen in a very dangerous section of the city. It was my father's stomping ground and I was familiar with it. The businesses there might remember him and offer me a small bit of safety if Coop and Mika were no longer in the city.

My head throbbed to the whoosh of the blades. I leaned back in the seat and closed my eyes. We would arrive outside the safe zone in about forty-five minutes. It was enough time for a nap.

If I'd known the dream would come, I would have vetoed sleep.

My second dream man was the star of this one. He was wilder than the other, slightly disheveled but equally as dangerous. His chestnut hair was unkept and fell slightly past his shoulders. Where dream man one was hard lines of wiry muscle, these muscles bulged and I had trouble believing he could contain them under a shirt. He'd never worn one in the dreams so maybe I would never know.

I didn't name my fantasy men. I'd tried but nothing suited them. If they continued doing delectable things to my body, I was okay with their namelessness.

The dream took place outside. He had never taken me indoors. I hid in the tall grass beside the river, but he found me like he always did. I wasn't sure why I behaved like a scared rabbit until the moment he touched me. This man loved the hunt and finding me was part of his game.

I lay still, barely breathing when he leapt over a large log and landed feet from my hiding place.

"Come out, little rabbit," he said huskily.

I continued shaking until his hands lifted me by my arms. He held me up so I was facing him, his lips inches from mine.

"You can never hide from me," he said.

I couldn't and I wasn't sure why I tried other than he liked the game.

"Please don't hurt me," I whispered.

"Will you cry if I hurt you?" he asked with a smile that made my heart pound faster.

"No," I said. "You cannot make me cry."

"Oh, little rabbit, I will make you scream," he promised.

He moved backwards, carrying me like I weighed nothing. His back hit a tree and he lifted me higher. Using his teeth, he angrily tore my shirt so it hung open in front. In another move too quick for me to follow, my pants were gone with a small burning pain from where they ripped from my body. He forced my legs around his waist.

"Keep them locked or you won't like the consequences," he breathed against my skin.

I was braless and his lips latched on to one of my nipples making the other ache more intensely. He used one hand on my back to keep me in place while the other seared down my body. He wasn't gentle when his fingers entered me. They were large and rough. He nipped my breast and the sweet pain had me grinding against him. His other hand moved from my back and found my ass cheek, his fingers digging into my flesh.

A deep growl left his throat when I tried to unlock my legs. This too was part of the game. He released my ass and jerked my head back with fingers wrapped in my hair, exposing my throat. He added small nips with his teeth to the kisses. I groaned and pressed harder into his fingers.

"No," he said. "I control your body."

His fingers punished me and I writhed in unfulfilled need. I pulled his hair and he laughed. I bit him much less gently than he did me and he moaned. Tears trailed down my face but I remained quiet. His hand returned to my ass and one of his large fingers rammed inside me while two punished me relentlessly.

I screamed to the sound of his laughter and my eyes jerked open. I sat up straight and looked around. No one was paying me any attention. I was surprised I hadn't cried out in the small confines of the helicopter. The gunship landed. Sparks of power sizzled on my fingertips. I pushed it back.

I glanced outside. The area was sparsely filled with vegetation though a tumbleweed rolled past.

"Get out," said the captain.

I didn't need to be told twice. I grabbed the pack and jumped four feet onto the sandy dirt. The blades never stopped spinning and as soon as I was outside, the chopper lifted into the air and flew away.

Just great, I thought to myself as I looked at the barren landscape.

I had a long hike in front of me, so I took the water bottle from the pack. My headache had not improved. I took a few swigs and put the water away. After adjusting my baseball cap, I started walking toward the tall buildings in the distance. They were deceiving. I had at least ten miles of walking ahead of me.

The dust settled from the chopper blades and I noticed more spewing behind the low hills. It seemed strange that the guys in the helicopter hadn't noticed someone coming. Maybe the people ahead were here to accompany me into the city. It was a weak optimism.

I stared into the distance. Friend or foe?

Chapter 5

Moving forward, I heard them a minute later and then saw three motorbikes. I walked over the hill and they were driving straight for me. They didn't stop at first and I held my ground. Within minutes, they were circling about twenty feet around me. I waited while the dust spun up. It made breathing hard.

Assholes.

Finally, one drove closer and the others stopped.

"Fancy finding a piece of tail out here?" the biggest and ugliest said from a few feet away.

He was dressed in dirty jeans and a leather vest. No shirt to cover his overly hairy body. He had several thick gold chains around his neck and I wondered if they got caught up in his chest hair. His shaggy brown hair was oily and rivulets of sweat rolled down his dirty face into his scraggily unkempt beard. All I could smell were the bike exhaust fumes but I had a feeling they covered the group's body odor. I should be thankful. My eyes quickly scanned the other two. Triplets came to mind. They matched all the way to their bushy beards.

"I'm minding my own business. Leave me alone." It was pure bravado. Why had the chopper guys left me? The escort idea was gone now and I was staring at trouble.

"We got a live one, boys."

They were going to have more than a live one if they tried anything.

"What's in the pack?" the same guy asked.

"None of your business. I would suggest you leave." I'd deepened my voice because the last thing I wanted was for it to squeak.

They laughed more than they should have. I was a riot when I got going, but still.

I practiced with my sword in the tent but hadn't had a sparring partner since my father died. This didn't deter me. I watched as they lay down their bikes and moved closer.

I slid the backpack off and allowed it to tumble to the ground. They spread out.

"You know how to use that sword?" one of them asked.

"Why don't you be the first to find out," I said. The tingling in my fingers grew.

"You need to remove it in order to use it," the third one said.

They laughed at my expense.

"If I need to, I will. I don't think it will be necessary." I yawned for good measure.

The energy sizzled again but this time it ran up my arms, through my torso, and down my legs. I should be glowing but the idiots didn't say anything so I doubted I was. I didn't think it would stop me from defending myself but it was much stronger and I wasn't sure how it would affect me.

"Whose first?" I asked and smiled.

"What makes you think we won't all come together?" idiot number one asked.

"Where's the fun in that?" I asked. "Someone will come in first, I'll put him down, and the other two will come in together. You don't think it will go that way so the first will come in alone to see if my fighting skills are as smart as my mouth. I'm waiting." Talking too much when I was nervous was a thing with me.

Idiot one did the honors. I slipped his grab, bent low, and pulled the knife from my right boot. It was a slow draw because the jeans were tight against the scuffed leather of the boot. He was thankfully slow and missed me on his first charge. I had the knife in my hand and buried it in his gut when he came back for more. I twisted to the side when he went down, grabbing his stomach wound and groaning in pain. The other two charged just as I'd said they would.

I'd witnessed my father fight and kill and I had done the same, though not on his scale. His fighting was a thing of beauty. I wasn't bloodthirsty but I didn't turn away from violence. The thousands of hours my father spent training me came back. I could hear him inside my head.

Move, flow with the air, slice, stab, cut. Be one with your blade. He'd taught me to use both a knife and sword. Three minutes later, all three idiots were down. The first one was still alive. He was crawling away while bleeding out. He wouldn't get far but I couldn't take a chance.

"They chose death so never leave them alive," my father had told me repeatedly.

I walked over to the man, grabbed him by the hair, and sliced his throat. A short gurgle was my answer. I removed his bloody neck chains, wiped them on his jeans, and cleaned out his pockets. I checked the other bodies. They each had an assortment of gold and silver coins which went in the backpack after I placed a few in my pockets. The jewelry was stashed in the pack too. I wouldn't need to sell a small bag of gunpowder for a room on my first night in the city.

I examined the bikes and chose the best one. It had no identifying marks, which was a good thing. These guys belonged to a street gang and they wouldn't be happy that I'd killed their men or took their money. Spoils of war. They would have done far worse to me, including killing me when they finished.

My first kill happened when I was eleven. My father held me that night while my entire body shook. I wasn't upset about killing the bad man; I was upset that he almost got me. Now I'd had six years without hurting a fly. I was fortunate that the killing came back easily.

I hid the two bikes in a gully and dragged the bodies beside them. I was hot and sweaty by the time I'd finished. The container of water helped and I drank half of it.

I didn't ask for trouble but I didn't run from it either. If my father could forgive me for returning to the city, he would be proud.

I felt his presence.

"You're faster now," he said inside my head.

I'd noticed my speed while I fought. I hadn't felt rusty and I knew where the strike was coming before it landed. I'd blocked them all. My father had that ability but it was a first for me.

I tucked the jeans into my boots so my knives would be easier to grab if I needed them again. No, *when* I needed them. The day was still young and I may not have a place to sleep. My father's friends could be long gone.

I made it into the city without being stopped again. I was pretty good on the bike. It was something else that came back quickly. The map stayed in the helicopter but I knew the way. I would go to the illegal market the following day, but if I wanted to last more than ten minutes, I needed to give them a name they knew.

I wasn't sure if it was wise to give my father's name. I needed to scope out the situation first.

If Mika and Coop were still around, I could use their name if they were willing to back me. I drove through the streets which were narrower than I remembered. It could be the cement barricades blocking the entrances to buildings along the route. Street urchins scrambled up and over the short cement walls and ran in and out of traffic. There were no cars, just motorbikes and horses. I saw oxen towing a wagon.

It was the city I remembered. It claimed my mother and father's lives. I might be next on the list.

Chapter 6

I found the hotel. The outside was run-down but no more so than the last time I'd seen it. This was where I'd gone directly after my father died.

I opened the thick wooden door and entered. It was cooler inside with the Spanish tiled floor exactly as I remembered. A familiar woman stood behind the counter. She hadn't aged.

"We're booked," she said without looking up. "Try the rooms down the street."

She told everyone this.

"Mika?" I asked.

She looked up and examined me.

"Who are you?" her eyebrows lifted inquisitively.

"Tara."

It took her a moment to accept that I was who I said I was. She walked from behind the counter and drew closer. The biggest smile broke across her face and I was wrapped in her ample arms and pulled against her wide body and bulging breasts. I couldn't breathe for a moment; her hug was so tight.

She released me and held me at arm's length.

"We thought you were dead."

"Why would you think that?" I asked quizzically.

"It's been six years," she replied sternly.

Mika and her husband Coop were the only two people my father trusted. He'd said they would be in danger if I stayed with them longer than a night. When I came here after his death, Mika insisted I stay for the foreseeable future. I slipped out before daybreak the following morning. My father never said things he didn't mean.

"I've been busy but you're the first place I came."

She released me and wiped tears from her eyes, increasing my guilt.

"You're no longer a little girl," she said.

"I wasn't a little girl when I left," I told her with a smile.

"Your eyes are wise now," she said softly.

A small laugh slipped out. All I'd learned in six years was how to serve food and clean dishes. I was far from wise.

"I have money for a room. How much are they going for now?"

My father always paid. Even when I came here after he died, I left money on the nightstand for the room.

"Five silver pieces," she replied. "First night is free, though. It occurred to us after you left that you may not have had money to stay longer."

"It wasn't the money," I assured her. "I'm unable to speak about it." My father told me Mika and Coop respected the truth so that's what I'd given her. "I have something to sweeten the pot for the free night." I slipped the backpack off and walked to the counter and opened it. I reached inside and pulled out one of the smaller bags. "Here," I said and handed it to her.

She opened it and sniffed carefully just how I had done. Her smile lit up the room.

"Better than silver," she told me. "It gets you a week."

I wanted her and Coop to have some gunpowder, but I doubted they would take it as a gift so this worked great.

"Does food still come with the room?" I asked.

"Best food in the city."

"A week then. If I need more time, I'll let you know. Where's Coop?"

"He'll be home in time for dinner. Go upstairs and put the bag in your room," she said and handed me a key. "We don't usually have guests until the weekend. Take a shower and bring down your dirty clothes. It's part of the service." She smiled and hugged me again. "Coop will be so happy."

Room number four was the same room my father and I always stayed in. It was one of several with a private bathroom. I did exactly as Mika said and took a long shower. I'd wiped my hands after the gang attack but I still had blood beneath my fingernails and I wanted it gone.

The water was only lukewarm but better than the cold military showers. Mika's soap was better too. She made it along with lotions and other personal hygiene items. There was a building behind the main house that had her workshop. Coop sold her goods and offered his sword to anyone who could afford it. He and my father had sometimes worked as a team.

After the shower, I changed into new clothes. There was a little blood on the jeans I'd worn earlier but Mika wouldn't know what it was.

A booming voice traveled through the walls. I gathered the soiled clothes into my arms and headed downstairs to see Coop.

I was subjected to the same hug, though where Mika was large, he was thin and wiry. He had aged. It showed in the graying of his hair and added wrinkles. His eyes remained sharp. He was still a dangerous man.

"Mika said you can't talk about the past six years. Is there anything you can tell us?" Understanding showed in his gaze. He wouldn't ask uncomfortable questions unless it was absolutely necessary.

"I ran into three men on motorbikes," I said and left it at that. "I'm a bit rusty with my sword because I haven't had a sparring partner since I left the city. I'd love a good workout if you can find the time."

His smile was his answer.

"As soon as our food settles, we'll go into the back courtyard and give your arm practice. It may take a few months to get you back up to snuff but you're a quick learner." He turned to Mika. "What's for supper, woman?" he growled.

She swatted him with a dish towel.

"I had just enough time to make Tara's favorite."

My mouth watered.

"I've set up the dining room this night, but don't get comfortable. You'll be at the kitchen table with us when we have guests."

"I'd be honored," I told her, and her eyes filled with tears. When my father and I stayed in this part of the city, we always ate at their kitchen table, never the dining room where the guests ate.

"Escort Tara to the table," she told her husband.

The room was large and the table sat twelve. There were plants in the corners and on a shelf above the window so their leaves fell in cascades and blocked much of the sun. I swear I could feel the plants offering comfort inside my mind which was strange. The window faced the inner courtyard as did all the windows in the home. It was a safety issue and another reason my father stayed at their establishment.

There were chickens running around the courtyard and I could see the open barn doors. They kept several horses and a cow for milking.

"I need to move my motorbike off the street when we finish eating," I told Coop.

"It's in the barn. I hope you don't mind. Things don't last long on the street. As soon as Mika told me who our special guest was, I moved it."

"Thank you."

"Since we can't talk about your life, what if I tell you stories about your father?"

This time, it was my eyes that filled with tears.

"The guy was eight feet tall, weighed over four hundred pounds, and had only three toes on his right foot, but your father was determined to fight him."

This was the fourth story Coop told about my father and I only believed half of what he said. My father was never one to brag and neither was Coop, at least about himself. I hadn't laughed this hard in years and my laughter was done in between bites of the most delicious vegetarian tacos I'd ever eaten. I seldom ate meat products, really not caring for the taste, and Mika remembered. My father hadn't like meat either.

I didn't ask how Coop knew the man only had three toes if he was wearing boots because it would take away from the story and I was having too good of a time.

Dessert followed dinner. It was a chocolate torte to die for.

"I don't know if the food will settle tonight. It was so good and I ate entirely too much."

"For shame," said Mika. "You are too skinny just like my Coop. I think you both have a wooden leg you store the food in."

I rubbed my stomach.

"Please finish your outlandish story about my father's escapades while I silently suffer from a bulging stomach."

"Every word is truth," Coop assured me. "Your father was the greatest swordsman who ever lived. He taught me everything he knew so that title now stays on my shoulders, but I wear it with humility." He winked and finished the great adventure with the giant.

An hour passed and I didn't feel quite so stuffed.

"Are you ready to learn a thing or two?" Coop asked.

"I think I am but please go gently on me. As you said, I'll improve quickly, but right now I'm out of practice."

"We'll use the wooden swords and then switch when you improve. Let's go."

"I'll help Mika with the dishes first," I told him.

"No, tonight you are our guest," she said. "You did not pay for the room and you will work the extra energy off my husband so I can get some sleep tonight." Her eyes softened when she looked at him and he turned to me and winked again.

"I have more than enough energy for a sword lesson and a tumble when I'm done."

I blushed and they both laughed.

Coop took me to the library which held books and swords. He grabbed two wooden ones from a tall round container sitting in the corner. Half the walls held bookcases and half held mounted swords. I'd loved this room as a child and had sat reading in the corner chair for hours. Mika lent me books and we would discuss them the next time I visited. I hadn't read a book since I left and a familiar ache hit my chest. I missed my father but I'd also missed these two amazing people.

"Here," Coop said and tossed me one of the wooden swords. His eyebrows lifted when I deftly caught it and swiped the air to get the feel.

Chapter 7

The wooden sword was perfectly balanced, though lighter than a metal sword. Coop had his own metal forge and carved the wooden ones himself. I'd left my sword in my room. Coop made it for me when my father commissioned it. Coop said it was his best work. I looked at the swords on the wall and had trouble believing it. They were all beautifully detailed and made with love.

We went straight to the courtyard to the area where I'd watched him and my father practice. There were rises of different heights on all sides with sand traps between. I would listen to the clash of their swords for hours as they dodged, jumped, and charged.

My father never told Coop he took it easy on him but I knew.

Coop and I faced each other but neither of us bowed. Respect to your opponent was given after a fight. He came at me with a solid mid strike which he pulled and reversed the blade so it came upward, looking for an opening.

My fingers tingled and I dodged the move, knowing his intent.

"You have been practicing, Tara," he chided after my evasion.

"Alone in my room at night." I stepped into my swing that was aimed at his legs and he jumped back.

We parried back and forth for ten minutes but he was unable to get a strike in.

He dropped his sword to his side.

"You are doing exactly as your father did and disguising your talent. Did you think I wouldn't know?" He looked hurt.

"I am sorry. I truly have not sparred since my father died."

"He gave you his gift and you need to use it. Stop holding back and show me."

I answered with my sword. Coop managed to block, but after that my strikes came in hard and heavy. I killed him over and over. He kept fighting and never got angry. When I sliced his gut open, or at least showed the move that would do it with a real sword, he started laughing.

"You see her, Mika? She's better than Clay. The teacher has been schooled. I will be right back," he said and walked into the house.

"You have made him happy," Mika told me.

"I didn't mean to show him up."

Her smile was huge.

"He loved and respected your father. He felt like he failed when you left. No, do not feel guilty," she said at my expression. "You had your reasons and we respect them. Your father had his secrets. We respected him and he gave us the same."

Coop walked from the house carrying two swords. I stared in shock at the one in his left hand.

"Is that my father's?" It was. I would know that sword anywhere. My father didn't have it with him when he died and I never thought I would see it again. A cold shiver passed through me.

"Do not look at me that way, my child," Coop said. "A few months after you disappeared, I dispatched the man who had it. He wasn't too bright and he was not who killed your father. He was trying to sell it. He said it was a family heirloom when I asked. He died with his entrails on the ground beside him, begging me to kill him and make it quick. He wouldn't answer my questions and it took him a long time to die. I watched until he breathed his last."

"Thank you." It was heartfelt.

He handed the sword to me. I gripped the pommel, feeling the leather cord wrap against my palm. The guard was larger than the one on my sword and this one was heavier by about a pound. My father allowed me to use it for building speed. After I exercised with it, mine seemed lighter and it was definitely faster.

I lifted the point and my eyes traveled the blade's ridge. It was like an old friend and I wanted to cry again.

I looked at Coop. He was watching me with a serious expression.

"Can you fire it?" he asked.

I lowered it immediately, unsure if I'd heard him right but fearing I had.

"What?" I asked, trying to sound nonchalant. My father was very good at hiding his gift and he'd taught me the same.

"I watched him fight too many times to count," Coop said. "He didn't do it often, but if we were in true danger, he made fire dance on the blade. No one we faced was left alive if he fired it. I never mentioned that I saw it happen, but several times I killed good opponents because they were in thrall of the fire. So..." He stared into my eyes. "I'm asking as your father's friend. Can you make fire dance on the blade?"

I had never tried because of the fear my father instilled. It was diffi-cult to let go of his training and show someone what I could do. Hell, even I wasn't sure what I could do. It had been so long since I'd used my gift.

My fingers sparked, the energy running from them into the pommel. I didn't let the power have free rein, but I didn't hold it inside either. I lifted the sword again and a low blue flame started at my hand and traveled up the steel.

Coop came at me with his. I evaded him easily. His moves were fast but nothing he did got past my guard. Metal on metal rang throughout the courtyard. The sword burned and it felt glorious. I never attacked, only blocked. I also never retreated, though Coop tried to push me back. I pivoted when he did and used my legs without giving an inch.

"Left hand," he said.

I tossed the sword up and caught it in my left hand. We went through the drill again. The entire exercise was one I performed with my father many times, minus the flaming sword.

Finally, with a fine sheen of sweat on his face, Coop dropped his guard and stared at me.

"What are you doing in town?" he asked with startling concern.

"I have two reasons to be here," I said honestly. "One I cannot tell you, but the other is easy. I'm here to find the man who murdered my father and to kill him." I hadn't known this until I said the words.

"It is dangerous for you here," he said plainly.

"It's dangerous everywhere and as you've just seen, I can defend myself."

"You don't understand. There have been rumors for years that besides werewolves and vamps, there are other species besides humans. When I first heard these stories, I thought of your father. If I hadn't seen what he could do, I would have been skeptical. I know I am treading into your secrets and you may not be comfortable telling us, but what did your father say about your gift?"

My brain was screaming at me to give as little information as possible. My father loved Mika and Coop and he hadn't told them.

"He didn't tell me much," I said. "He said I was special and I had to keep my magic hidden. He said you and Mika would be in danger if I stayed with you." I looked at her with another apology in my eyes, then turned back to Coop. "He said I would know when it was time to return."

"Is it time for you to return?" Coop asked.

"I wasn't given a choice and I'm unsure if I should be here or not." I shrugged. "It's too late now. I'm here."

A look passed between Coop and Mika. She nodded.

"After you left," Coop said. "A package was delivered. It was addressed to you. It's from your father and you should open it. Mika, would you mind getting it for Tara?"

She turned without a word and walked into the hotel.

My heart raced.

"The sword is now yours," Coop said next.

I shook my head.

"No, it is yours. You were my father's friend and he wanted you to have it. The one he commissioned is in my room. It's an extension of my hand."

"I will save his sword for you. You may have need of it one day."

He was stubborn and I wouldn't win this argument.

"Thank you."

Mika returned with a package about the size of a book. It was wrapped in brown paper and circled with string. She handed it to me.

"Would you be offended if I open this in my room?" I asked softly. The feel of the package in my hands was bringing forth emotions that needed to be handled in private.

"Please," Coop said. He took Mika's hand. "We will see you in the morning."

Chapter 8

After they walked inside, I stood where I was for a few minutes, wondering if talking to them about the gift was something I should have done. I hated being skeptical of people who obviously loved me, but my father's training was hard to put aside.

I had to trust my intuition and it told me Mika and Coop would never betray me. I went upstairs to my room. My father's sword remained in my hand. I placed it on the chest of drawers before I sat on the bed. I held the package for several minutes, simply savoring it. When I was ready, I attacked the string first. It was knotted and had to be cut. I slowly removed the paper. Inside was a square wooden box about an inch thick. It had no seam to open and I wondered if it was simply a piece of cut, polished wood. My fingers tingled as I held it. The energy grew until it lit up the entire room. I allowed it to expand. The box recognized my magic.

Blue, purple, and green swirled around the room. I watched the wood change into something else entirely and I was holding a box. I lifted the cover and found several sheets of old paper.

My Dearest Daughter Tara,

Always know I love you. I may not be with you physically, but my energy walks beside you. When you close the top of the box, it will return to a piece of wood. After unlocking the key the first time, it will take a drop of your blood to reactivate. Use it to store your treasures as I have done.

Many trials await you, but I know you are the woman to overcome them. The necklace belonged to your mother. Wear it and feel her love.

I lifted the pages to my face and breathed in their scent. I wasn't sure if it was my imagination or if I could smell my father's unique fragrance that he always carried even after he returned sweaty and unwashed from his missions.

I turned to the next page.

Our kind—wielders—were poorly used by the vampires for generations. They did not deserve our power or our loyalty. They grew frightened of our abilities and tried to control us. My father was cast into servitude for one hundred years.

The werewolves destroyed us because of the power our blood gave vampires. They killed wielders on sight. My mother barely escaped with me. She was a powerful wielder. I never knew my father due to his servitude, but she told me he was also powerful. Their combined energy was passed to me. I married your mother, not because I loved her though love grew, but because of her great power. She understood this and felt the same. We were friends until we could no longer deny our feelings. When you were born, she held you for only minutes, then handed you to me and told me to take you away. She was dying and she knew it. She loved you as I love you.

Our families were part of the prophecy and we were raised knowing this. It caused resentment in me as it did your mother. We were never free. Before your birth, we agreed that you would be brought up without the responsibility of knowing your future. We planned to tell you when your power came through. It was foretold that a girl, the most powerful wielder in existence, would be born to us. That child is you, my darling Tara.

You will change the world for the better. It is written in time.

If you are reading this, I am gone and cannot guide you. It saddens my heart that you will be on your own. All I can do is tell you what little I know. One day your fingers will emit energy and you will have trouble hiding it like you did as a very young child. This will be a dangerous time for you. You must control it until the power changes everything you are. At that time, go out into the world and fulfill the prophecy.

Your sword will be an extension of your power. Mika and Coop are good people, but they are human and fragile. Coop knows a little of my magic and he still loved us. He and Mika are people you can trust.

Our power is tied to the earth. Charge your sword in sand or dirt after it has expended too much energy. Sink your hands into soil when you feel depleted. Plants are your friends and they will also recharge you.

You are the only survivor of our people. Magic is in your blood and cannot be taken away. Vampires, werewolves, and humans will one day live in harmony. You are the link that will bring everyone together again. Fulfill your destiny, and then, my daughter, live your life free and happy.

Your mother drew the image before you were born. You looked exactly like this when you were four. She said she dreamt of you.

With all my love in this life and the next,

Father

I turned to the next page.

There was no doubt the image was of me. My small hand held a ball of energy and my expression was that of accomplishment. I remembered this exact scene. This was the only time my father hadn't punished me when he caught me using my power. I'd forgotten I could form a ball of energy that way.

My mother's signature was at the bottom.

I ran my finger over her name and then traced the entire drawing. I pulled the pages to my chest and rocked with heartache and happiness that my father had left me this gift. When I was ready, I pulled the delicate chain from the box. It was gold with a locket hanging from it. I opened the small clasps to find a picture of my mother on one side and my father on the other. I bowed my head and lifted the metal to my lips as tears trailed down my cheeks.

I lay back in bed with the pages against my chest and the necklace in my hand. After several minutes, I read them again.

When finished, I itched to take out my sword. I was tired and needed a good night's sleep. I gently placed the pages and the necklace inside the box and turned off the light. I fell asleep with the box on my chest.

***

I woke to the sun shining through the window and the block of polished wood lying beside me. I smiled and placed it on the dresser. There was a vase of flowers on a small table and I put those on top of the wood.

I had to find the missing rangers and send word back to camp so I could start my new life. No more hiding. Kitchen duty was forever in my past. I dressed, then placed my knives in my boots and my sword on my back. I carried the backpack with the gunpowder.

I went downstairs and heard Mika singing. I stopped at the doorway to the kitchen and watched her cook and sing. She turned after another verse and her hand went to her chest.

"You scared me."

"I didn't mean to," I told her. "I missed you so much."

She smiled. "Were you able to sleep?"

"Yes, I'm rested and ready to start my day. I have more gunpowder and need to sell it in Hell's Market. May I use Coop's name to open doors?"

"Of course but take him with you for safety."

I wasn't sure if he should come. I worried for his safety more than mine. I was using his name, though, and if someone discovered who or what I was, he and Mika would be in danger.

"Is he here?" I asked.

"He's in the stable."

I turned to go out the back door.

"No, you will eat, and then you can find him."

"Yes, ma'am," I said with a wide grin. "It smells delicious."

"Pancakes with warm maple syrup. I've been saving the ingredients for a special occasion. I also have coffee, not that hickory garbage."

I laughed outright. I'd existed on that hickory garbage for years and it was better than nothing.

The pancakes and coffee were amazing. I ate quickly and washed my plate and cup as she'd taught me to do when I was a young child. My father brought me to their home every month. I loved to visit and hated to leave. Eating Mika's food brought back good memories.

"Is your garden in the same place?" I asked when finished.

"On the west side of the barn where the light is good. Your father also spent time in the garden."

I bet he did.

"My father mentioned it in his letter. After I finish in the garden, I will seek Coop."

I walked outside and went to the side of the barn where the large garden took up a good-sized strip of land. Mika and Coop's property was deceiving. It didn't appear this large from the street. Food was a necessity and fresh vegetables were frequently stolen. Coop's reputation had kept theirs safe for years.

I removed the backpack and dropped it to the ground. I then pulled the sword from its sheath. It sizzled in my hands, seemingly in anticipation. I walked a few rows into the garden and stabbed the point into the earth. A vibration traveled from my hand to my arm and punched throughout my body.

Chapter 9

I kept a tight hold on the sword, adjusted my stance, and held on. It glowed and pulsed. My father's instructions didn't say how long to keep it in the dirt or that I should hold it. I'd never had an affinity for plants, but now, the surrounding plants reached toward me. I carefully released the sword with one hand and touched one. Its energy caressed my fingers. I exhaled in wonder.

"Tara?" Coop asked.

I jumped and then turned and smiled.

"My father gave me a few instructions," I said excitedly. "Apparently, the plants and earth recharge my power. He never mentioned any of this to you?" It was a stupid question because I knew the answer.

"He told me it was dangerous for me and Mika to know too much and I took him at his word. When I first met your father, the war between the vampires, werewolves, and humans was raging. The last thing humans needed to know was that there were more supernatural secrets." He paused for a moment, picking his words carefully. "I was opposed to the vamps and weres and wanted them dead. Then your father saved my life. He got us out of a horrible situation because he was more than human. It took a few more interesting situations for my mind to change about the supernatural. I owe everything to your father and his gift. It made me wonder if werewolves and vampires were as bad as we'd been led to believe."

Coop continued. "Fear drove me. It's what drives humans. Things would have been better if we'd handled the vamps and weres differently. Treated them like neighbors, even friends. They told the world they existed and we paid them back with mistrust and hatred."

I had understood for a long time that humans would not accept my power, but I was not ready to jump into the corner with vamps or werewolves. I had a healthy mistrust of both, but then again, I felt the same about humans. I wasn't even sure that Mule, Leo, and Shep would have befriended me if they knew what I was and the thought hurt.

Coop wasn't finished giving me a short history lesson.

"In the beginning, the werewolves and vamps were killed without a trial. We also used them against each other. We're lucky they didn't eradicate us completely. Mika was raised much differently than me. She thought we could get along and find a way to peace. Humans destroyed that avenue. Most religions believed the creatures were sent from hell. I was in that camp."

He took a steady breath.

"Your father saved my life by killing a group of vampires with his sword fire. That probably wouldn't have changed my mind, but I was dying. He used that same energy to heal me. I never told him that I knew he'd done something to me that went far beyond human medicine. When you told me he was dead, I always wondered why he couldn't save himself." He shrugged. "Maybe it doesn't work that way."

Could my father have saved himself? I didn't believe so. His wound was fatal and the fact he lived long enough to get to me showed he'd tried. Maybe if I had more power, I could have saved him. Now it would haunt me.

Coop must have figured out that his words upset me because he changed the subject abruptly.

"How did it feel to recharge your sword?" he asked, smiling gently.

"Like I was hit by a bolt of lightning in a good way."

His smile dropped and he went back to the previous discussion.

"I'm sorry I was not with him the night he died and that I did not save him."

"No," I said. "We cannot think that way. My father wouldn't like it." The words changed my mood too. "My father would not want either of us to feel guilt over his death."

"How can I help you in your double quest?" Coop asked solemnly.

"I need to sell the gunpowder in Hell's Market and I need an introduction."

"Is this the part you can't tell me about?"

"Yes."

"Okay, I won't ask."

"My father said to trust you and Mika. He said you wouldn't ask questions and you don't. Why is that?"

The smile returned.

"I have my own secrets and your father never questioned me. We each had a line the other never crossed. We respected each other and I respect you."

I pulled the sword from the earth and walked toward him. He opened his arms and gave me a huge hug. He would read to me as a child while I sat on his lap. I was a grown woman now, but his affection made me feel like I did when young.

"When do we leave?" he asked.

"Just your name. You don't need to come with me."

He grumbled and released me.

"Two swords are better than one no matter how good you are."

"We leave in an hour."

We rode horses. Mine was a sturdy gelding buckskin named Dot. Coop's was a sorrel mare named Brandy.

"I owned Brandy's sire," he told me. "Some people don't like mares, say they're a passel of trouble, but I like a little spirit in my horse and my woman." He winked at me.

I preferred a motorbike, but if I had to have a horse, a gentle gelding was more my type.

Mika had washed my clothes from the day before but I stayed in the extra set. They were good riding clothes even though I still felt partially naked after years of loose material covering me.

We rode for an hour along quiet streets with only a few people milling around. The closer we got to the market, the more people I saw and the louder the area became. Weekends were worse or had been when I was here last. Humans from the outskirts of the city came to sell whatever they had or to buy and trade for what they needed.

There were guards at the entrance to the market which surprised me. Coop didn't look at me or them as we rode past. Overall, what I'd seen so far of the city was much tamer than what I'd expected.

"Who are you looking to sell the gunpowder to," he asked when we were far enough away.

We entered a row of booths.

"The gang. They'll have the information I need."

He frowned. "Somehow I knew this would be your destination, but I hoped you had better sense," he admonished.

"That's why I needed your name for an intro. Who did the guards belong to?"

"The werewolves. They are trying to cut down on humans being injured or killed."

"They care?" I asked.

"For years they let humans kill humans. Most likely as payback for how we tried to destroy them. That's changing, but slowly."

"What about the vampires?"

"They have guards on duty at night."

"The vamps and werewolves are working together?" I was stunned.

"Barely," he replied. "They have opposite shifts which helps keep the peace."

"I don't understand why the gangs still hold power," I said.

"They've worked with the vampires and weres for a long time. If they don't cross too many lines, the supernaturals leave them alone. It doesn't mean they aren't deadly. They don't like humans leaving the city and they skate the rules and cause trouble when they can." His eyes scanned the area as we left the market and entered what was known simply as Hell. "Be ready and try not to use your sword. Are you still good with knives?"

"Adequate," I told him.

"When you take the backpack off, they'll see the sword. It was a recent birthday gift and you're just learning to use it. You're my niece and your parents live in the west valley. Your family has hoarded the gunpowder but now they must sell it for necessities. Keep your mother's first name but change your father's name to Jim."

I couldn't help the burst of laughter that escaped me.

"Jim it is."

"Always stick as close to the truth as possible when you lie. The lies are easier to remember that way."

"You and my father were sadly remiss in parts of my education," I said with more laughter.

"You left before I had a chance so don't give me a hard time."

"Yes, Uncle Coop."

Chapter 10

"What are you doing here in the middle of the week, Coop?" a large man, unwashed and wreaking of alcohol asked.

"Get out of my way, Nelson. I have business and it's none of yours."

"Bastard."

"Drunk."

We continued our slow and steady pace until I noticed motorbikes, very similar to the one stored in Coop's barn, parked along a cracked sidewalk.

"They'll know where you got the bike so better off leaving it where it is and ride the horse if you come back. They'll also know how many of their men you had to kill too."

"It was three."

"Sword?"

"Knives."

He bit his lip. "You need no lessons in lying."

I followed Coop's example and got off the horse when he did. We walked them closer to a small group of men and Coop handed me his reins.

"Is Murdock around?" he asked no one in particular.

"Who wants to know?" The man who spoke was twice the size of Coop. He wasn't bad looking in a neanderthal kind of way. His shaggy hair reminded me of Shep. The man had recently worked on a motorbike and had oil covering his clothes and face or he hadn't bathed in days. I smelled oil not body odor so I settled on the former.

"Tell him Coop is asking." Coop turned slightly like he was checking on me but what he was doing was making sure the man saw the hilt of his sword sticking from the scabbard on his back.

It worked. The guy nodded and walked through an open door into the run-down building behind him. This was their clubhouse. From my position, I could only see a black hole beyond the door.

A man walked out a few minutes later. He wasn't as big as the other guy, but his nearly black eyes were shrewder, or more precisely, deadlier. He didn't smile. His skin was dark, his head bald, and he had an earring in his left ear, a large diamond. His face was defined by a heavy scar that ran from his eyebrow to the corner of his lip. He had knives, too many to count without staring. He carried them in a crisscrossed piece of leather that dissected his chest and held various sheaths. They were throwing knives which wasn't my strong suit.

"Coop," he said gruffly.

"Murdock."

"What do you want?"

"My niece has something you might be interested in buying."

Murdock sized me up. His shrewd eyes changed for a moment. I considered myself nothing special in the looks department and even in the tight jeans and skintight tank, my breasts were far from ample so I was unsure what caused his reaction. Maybe I imagined it.

"What is it?" The question was for me, but Coop stepped in.

"In private," he said.

"It had better be good." Murdock turned and walked through the door.

Coop gave me a look of caution that I wouldn't discount. One of Murdock's men took the reins to the horses. Thankfully Murdock only went into the shadowed entry about ten feet, then stepped into a room with a table and a small window about eight feet up the wall that let in a bit of light.

"It's my first time in the city," I lied and tossed one small bag on the table. "What do you think this is worth?"

He opened the bag, sniffed, then looked between me and Coop. He didn't say anything for a moment. Something was going on. I could feel it in my bones and I had to fight the tingling in my fingers. I hadn't planned what I said next.

"The military conscripted my brother Samuel. My parents found someone who would get him out for the right amount of money. I have five bags."

Coop went seamlessly along with my story.

"They took Samuel." He turned and gave me a hurt look. "Why didn't you tell me?"

I looked down and used the tip of my boot to brush the floor in apparent shame.

"I knew you would be angry and Mom said you would do something stupid."

"It might be stupid, but they will regret taking my nephew."

My eyes returned to Murdock to see if he bought the story. His expression hadn't changed. I was not feeling good about the situation.

"How much money do you need?" he asked sharply.

"I asked you first," I said with bravado.

"You're in my house. If I ask a question, you answer."

Coop stepped between us.

"I've always been fair with you, Murdock. You owe me. Stop pulling her strings. My nephew's been taken by the fucking military. She's on edge and now that I know, so am I."

Murdock looked between me and Coop. I saw Coop's finger move just a touch. He was ready to go for his sword.

"Five bags are worth more money than I have on hand, but I know a man who will pay," he said. "I'll arrange a meeting. Come to the city tonight at nine." He looked pointedly at Coop. "She comes alone."

"That won't happen," Coop objected.

"Then she won't meet the man and get your nephew out."

"I'll come by myself," I told him, ignoring Coop's sharp look. "I'll be here at nine."

"If anything happens to her, I'll kill you," Coop said.

Murdock only grunted.

We left quickly and mounted the horses.

"That entire conversation was bullshit on his part," Coop said. "Is there a chance they know who you are?"

"I don't see how but maybe they're suspicious right now because of what happened and why I'm here."

"This is the part you can't tell me."

"Unfortunately, true." I knew I could trust him but this was a military secret and telling anyone that rangers were coming into the city made it more dangerous for them. The next unit to *visit* could be my friends and I would take zero chance with their lives, especially with the werewolves and vampires patrolling the area.

I thought back to the general. My job was to find out what happened to the missing rangers. Chances were good they were dead and the general knew it. Not for the first time, I wondered if this was a setup. But why? What possible motive was there? Maybe I needed to confide in Coop. If two swords were better than one, maybe two minds were too.

"The fact you've gone quiet is worrying me," said Coop.

"I'm thinking."

"I won't pry but don't you think I could help you more if I knew what was going on?"

That gave me more to think about.

We rode in silence. It took me thirty minutes to make up my mind.

"I've been living in a military camp outside the city. They hired me to work the kitchen. It's what I've been doing for the past six years. Two days ago, the general came to our camp and sent me on a mission to discover what happened to rangers who disappeared a week ago. He gave me the gunpowder to sell in Hell's Market where the rangers were last seen. I didn't like it then and I don't like it now."

"Is it normal to ask someone who works in the kitchen to do something like this?"

"I'm the only civilian in camp. He said it was safer for me to try than it was for one of his men."

"That's bullshit and you know it," he said succinctly.

"I decided yesterday that I wouldn't be going back. That doesn't mean I can risk it if the rangers are alive and I could help them."

"If they were discovered in the city, they're dead. That I can promise. The vampires and werewolves are being fair to humans in the city, but they do not like the military."

I shrugged. "They leave us alone."

"Then there is a reason. Many of the military camps have been disbanded. I thought they all had."

I was closed off from the world outside the camp, but this still shocked me.

"No one said anything to me. I thought they were still helping humans to the rural areas."

"Humans are returning from the rural areas because they are worse. The city is growing and stabilizing. The biggest problem is the military conscripting boys who are barely teens."

Was that something Shep, Leo, and Mutt had been doing? I couldn't see it. Not my friends. I needed time to think. None of this made sense. My friends helped humans get to where they wanted to go. They'd told me so.

"Do not go to that meeting tonight," Coop said softly.

"If I don't go, the chances are good they'll come after me for the gunpowder. Your home is the first place they'll look."

"We'll leave. All three of us."

"The horses, the cow? What about them?"

"We'll take the horses and release the cow. Someone will take her in."

"And slaughter her. She's a pet more than food to you. You and Mika are not leaving your home."

He stopped his horse and grabbed my bridle.

"*You* are important to us." He was angry. "I owe this to your father. He told me once that you were special. Now I've seen it with my own eyes. Rumors have spread for years saying someone is coming who will put an end to the war between the weres and vamps. What if that someone is you?"

Chapter 11

The rumors were the prophecy my father spoke of in his letter. It made sense but still didn't help me.

"I'm not some great savior," I told him honestly. "I couldn't even help myself when I left after my father died."

He waved his hand in frustration. "You found a position in the military as a civilian which is unheard of. You've kept your power a secret and stayed hidden. You saved yourself with no help."

"I had no choice," I argued. "If it's different, kill it. That's the human anthem and why I'm in this mess. I'm—" I hesitated. "Different."

He stayed silent until we saw his home in the distance.

"You are not a monster," he said softly but with resolve.

I hadn't said monster but he knew I thought it.

My father said he and my mother were powerful but the wielders hadn't defeated the vampires or weres. Healing others, making a sword burn, and tingly fingers were one thing, changing the world, quite another.

Dinner was a quiet affair. Mika looked between me and Coop after she'd tried to start several conversations.

"Whatever is going on, don't you think we should talk about it?' she finally asked.

"I have a meeting in the city with the Hell's Market gang leader at nine tonight. Coop does not wish me to go alone but I am."

"I agree with Coop," she said. "You absolutely cannot go alone." Her stern look made me wince.

"I have endangered you both. For that, I am truly sorry. I must see this through; lives depend on it. Murdock said to come alone and that is what I will do. I'm worried about your safety. Please prepare for attack."

Mika stared at me in horror.

"I love you," I said. "You are my only family. You need to trust me. I can and will handle this."

We finished eating in silence. No one was happy and that made my sadness worse. I stayed in my room until I was ready to leave.

"I'm taking the motorbike," I told Coop. "I'll leave it in that pile of junk cars we passed before we entered the market. If I need to get away fast, that will be the best way."

Mika entered the room, carrying two backpacks. I almost started shouting.

"We own the building across the street and have a room prepared in it. Coop's business contracts are not always safe. We will stay there tonight."

I was able to take a full breath of air and release it. I threw my arms around her.

"Thank you. I will be okay but I was more worried about you."

"That is why we will be across the street. You worry about you."

She did understand.

Coop wheeled the motorbike to the front of the house.

"If I don't return, do not come looking for me," I told him.

"Sure," he said, and I knew he was lying.

"You didn't look for me six years ago. This is no different. If our paths are meant to cross again, they will. Keep my father's sword safe. I will come for it someday."

He clenched my shoulders and looked me straight in the eyes.

"You foolish woman. I never stopped looking for you." He shook his head gloomily. "Your father's sword will be safe. We need you to stay safe too." He kissed my forehead and released me.

I had to leave before I cried like a baby. It never occurred to me that he had tried to find me. I was okay with not being found, but there were times when I wanted someone to care about me. He and Mika did.

I threw my leg over the bike and started the engine. After a couple of revs, I headed to the market district. I drove as fast as possible. I had a need for speed and so did my magic. My hands sizzled on the grips. I zigzagged through the streets, avoiding obstacles, and sliding around corners. It was similar to using my magic to fight with my sword and allowed me to anticipate the turns. The stinging wind against my face relieved some of my anxiety. When I was a mile from the market, I turned off the bike's engine and pushed it so it made no noise. I hid the bike in the junk cars I'd mentioned to Coop.

I decided I didn't want to run into the vampire guards and took a back way into the market that my father had shown me. It was dark and I stumbled and tripped over objects under my feet that I couldn't see. I heard someone playing a guitar. Things like that didn't happen when I was here before.

I had trouble believing the vampires and werewolves were making the area safer, but I hoped I was wrong. The war should never have happened. The repercussions of war on the losing side were never easy. At least the vamps and weres hadn't wiped out humanity.

I pulled one of my knives and hid it in the sleeve of the leather jacket Mika gave me. The handle rested flat against my palm. I walked through the street with confidence I didn't feel.

The booths were mostly empty, the people manning some of them sat around burning fires. They stared at me as I passed.

A man stepped out and stopped me from continuing.

"You want to pass through here, you owe me a tithe," he said.

The man was short, maybe an inch taller than me. He wasn't armed but took quick glances at the people sitting at the fires. It seemed he was hoping for their approval.

"I want no trouble. Let me pass," I told him.

He grinned. Even in the near dark, I could see he had gaps in his mouth where teeth should be.

"What are you willing to pay?" he demanded, the grin remaining in place.

"I was here earlier today with my uncle and required no tithe. You may know him; his name is Coop."

His expression changed instantly, but before he spoke again, another man called out.

"Leave her be. We don't want no trouble with Coop."

The man in front of me melted into the dark. I smiled to myself, delighted that Coop was badass. I continued down the road without further hassle.

Two men were standing to either side of the door at Murdock's place. One ducked inside when he saw me. The big guy who spoke to us earlier stepped out.

"Come with me," he said in a deep, gruff voice that was slightly less antagonistic than it was before.

I was waiting to be searched or, at the very least, told to remove my sword. Neither happened. I did as he asked and followed him inside. The place consisted of long narrow hallways. I knew I would have trouble finding my way out after the fifth turn. At some point it had been a large warehouse store. The hallways were a good safety measure.

We finally entered a big room with no windows and only one exit, which was the door we walked through. At least the oblong table had chairs. Two men sat at the table. It was Murdock and someone else.

The man looked up and his eyes glowed with fire. I knew exactly *what* he was.

A vampire.

Chapter 12

I moved on instinct. My sword was in my hand and blue fire lit up the room.

"That answers my question," the vampire said. He remained seated, seemingly unconcerned that I was prepared to remove his head from his body. "I would suggest you take a seat. It wasn't easy to find you or get you here and we have much to talk about."

"I do not talk to vampires."

He smiled, showing fangs. His hand came up and he flicked his fingers. Murdock stood from the table and left the room with the man who showed me in.

This gave me a minute to observe the vampire. The fact he was the most gorgeous man alive shouldn't affect me, but it did. I had to remind myself that vampires were designed this way. They tempted their prey with staggering sexuality. I was not immune.

"You are coming into your power," he said.

He knew who I was. This was not good. I remained in my fighter's stance, ready for the coming battle.

"Tara." My name was a caress on his lips. "We have known who you are, what you are, and where you've been for six years. Your military could not have kept you from us if we wanted you. The loss of human life would have upset you. We didn't want that and left you be. Please sit down so we may talk. Your sword fire is quite blinding to my sensitive eyes."

He sounded so reasonable. I knew differently. My heart pounded in terror. The vampires played nice when they first came out, but they quickly turned into a nightmare. Humans had something to do with that, but I cast the thought aside. Vampires killed indiscriminately with pure malice. My father never said much about them, but I heard the stories in the city. When I grew older, new signs littered the streets that said Blood Bank. Desperate men and women entered the blood establishments. My father told me to never sell my blood. Once someone started, they never stopped. Giving blood to a vampire caused a high they couldn't resist.

I steadied myself and concentrated on the vampire in front of me.

"If you know my name, don't you think it would be polite for me to know yours?" I asked to delay.

"Drake," he murmured in a seductive tone that made my toes curl. It was the perfect name. Something softer than velvet traveled across my skin. "I am Blade's vampire at arms," he qualified.

Blade was a name I knew. He was the head of the vampire families and not someone I wanted to meet. That meant this man was almost as dangerous. I had no options. I didn't know if I could kill a vampire, but I knew he could kill me.

I lowered the sword. If he wanted me dead, I would already be lying on the floor in my own blood. No, that wasn't quite right. He would be drinking every last drop of my blood.

I slipped the sword into its sheath and allowed the knife that I'd pushed up the sleeve to fall into my palm. Knowing it was a bad idea, I walked forward and took the chair Murdock vacated.

I couldn't believe I was sitting beside a vampire. His facial bone structure was stunning. His long eyelashes swooped down over stark, incredibly dark eyes that flashed with a red-orange glow that looked like the purest fire.

"Why am I here?" I asked. Vampires had no need for gunpowder.

"You are here because this is where you belong." He looked around the room. "Not precisely here, but with my kind."

What the hell? He had to be joking.

"Why would I want to be with vampires?" I asked. His voice sent shivers down my spine and it wasn't all fear. I'd never felt this level of attraction. I had to break his spell but had no idea how.

"The vampires will teach you to use your powers. We have been waiting for you to come of age. This was explained by your father." He made it a statement.

His mention of the man I loved made me catch my breath. My father could do no wrong in my eyes. Anger brought me partially out of the fog I'd been cast into.

"What do you know of my father?" I demanded.

He looked at me for a moment.

"I know of him."

"You know what of him?" My heart was racing but the fear was gone. Only lust remained but anger helped dissipate that too.

"I know he was a good man who protected his daughter. He was a wielder as are you. At one time, our species lived fluidly with yours."

"What does that even mean?"

He regarded me for several long moments.

"It means your birth was foretold. When the vampires made our presence known to humans, it was because the weres had systematically destroyed your kind. Without you, vampires were forced to seek out human blood. Unless we killed the humans we fed from, we risked exposure. With modern forensics, it was only a matter of time before we were discovered. We went public and the werewolves were outed soon after. We needed human blood to survive." His smile almost made my heart stop.

He was devastatingly attractive and I needed him to stop making me think of warm nights and billowy sheets. I turned my thoughts to what he wasn't saying. Vampires had placed my grandfather in servitude against his will. His son, my father, never knew him.

"It is a pleasant experience for humans and we thought that would be enough," he continued. "After humans discovered the werewolves." A look of disgust entered his expression. "The weres stayed silent about wielders because they thought they had destroyed them all. We knew differently."

Vampires enslaved humans for their blood and for sex just as they had wielders. Werewolves were no better. They were violent. They killed whoever they came across. This was what I'd learned when my father took me to town. The werewolves and vampires were monsters. Any desire I felt for this man evaporated.

An explosion rocked the building. I was tossed from the chair and landed on the carpet.

"Werewolves," someone yelled from outside the room.

Drake grabbed me and I was suddenly on my feet.

"Do you know how to wield that sword or just make it burn?"

"I can use it."

"Someone betrayed me. You can rest assured they will die, but we must get you out of here first."

"I'm not going with you," I said stubbornly.

"Then you will die and I can't allow that."

A man and a wolf entered. The man was larger than the one who brought me to the room. The wolf, not the four-legged kind, but a stand on two feet, over seven foot tall, covered in gray fur with a mouth full of teeth the size of razor blades kind. They both stared at me.

"Drake," the man said and glanced at the vampire.

"Alaric." Drake's voice was no longer sensual. It was deadly.

"I want the girl. Give her to me and you walk free."

"You only know how to lie. You and your friend will be the ones who die."

Alaric growled and I had shivers running through me again. Fear was replaced by terror.

"I will enjoy tearing you apart and eating your dead heart," Alaric said with a continued low, steady growl.

The two men faced off.

Alaric was as good-looking as Drake in an entirely different way. Both men would stop women in their tracks. Where Drake was sleek, honed perfection, Alaric had hard swells of bulging muscle. His face could only be described as fierce in a Viking God kind of way.

His gaze moved from Drake to me again and I froze. I was the finest steak he'd ever seen, or so his eyes said.

"Run," he said softly which was far deadlier than if he'd shouted. I froze and he grinned. Large canines burst from his jaws. He threw his head back and what started as a laugh turned into a bone-chilling howl. His clothes shredded and a monster burst from his skin. The shift was so quick; if I'd blinked, I would have missed it.

Drake attacked and I drew my sword.

Chapter 13

"Do not kill her," Alaric yelled through large, distorted jaws that should have been unable to communicate.

Blue fire ran up my blade and I went into fight mode. The second wolf attacked. Sharp claws deflected my thrust, but power was building inside me and I moved faster than I had in the past two days. Removing chunks of fur and muscle made the beast roar so loud it hurt my ears.

Alaric was growling as he and Drake fought, but there was no time to check who was winning. Two more wolves burst into the room. They didn't interfere with the fight between Alaric and Drake. They came at me.

A claw raked my side, causing a burning pain, and I cried out.

Alaric roared at his men. "If you harm her, I will kill you."

I grabbed my burning side with my free hand and felt another surge of power when blood soaked my fingers. My blade burned brighter. I slashed across the first wolf's throat, almost severing his head.

The other two stopped for a moment and spread out. If Alaric wanted me alive, it gave me an edge. I slid my fingers into my blood again. Surprisingly, there wasn't as much and the pain lessened. Alaric flew over my head and slammed into the wall. The wolves looked at Drake. The vampire attacked one of them and he went down. I slid my sword into the heart of the other. A roar came from behind me and I knew Alaric wasn't dead.

This time it was Drake who went over my head in a leap I wouldn't have believed if I hadn't seen it. He landed on Alaric and I heard a horrible crack. The wolf went still.

"Come," Drake said and placed his hand out. "We must leave quickly. More will be here soon. Vampires are on their way to keep you safe."

I stared at his hand but didn't take it. There was another explosion and smoke poured into the room.

"Did I threaten you in any way? Did I make demands?" He didn't wait for my answer. "Alaric was taking you against your will and I am asking. He wasn't going to kill you right away, but you do not want to know what he would have done. Take my hand and I will get us out of here."

For two seconds I closed my eyes. When I opened them, I heard a growl coming from Alaric.

"He is healing. We must leave now."

I grasped the hand of a vampire.

I couldn't see through the smoke and breathing was nearly impossible. I held tightly to Drake's hand as I tried to cover my mouth with the sleeve of the leather jacket. I was suffocating without oxygen, but Drake kept running through the hallway's twists and turns until finally he threw open a door and we were out of the building in blessed fresh air. I couldn't stop coughing, choking, and gagging. He lifted me into his arms.

"Put me down," I tried to say between coughs. I might as well have stayed silent. I concentrated on breathing while tears poured from my burning eyes. I refused to let go of my sword.

I have no idea how much time passed when Drake came to an abrupt stop.

"Genesis, Adam with me. The rest, cover our retreat."

I could barely make out the outlines of the vampires through my tears. They didn't question him and Drake continued running with me in his arms. My head was against his chest and I learned something I hadn't known. Vampires had a heartbeat. Drake also smelled like nothing I had ever scented. We were running for our lives and I was turned on. Not good.

Several men had tried to hook up with me in the military camp, but the dreams kept me from temptation. I didn't care if the dreams weren't real. No man could live up to them.

After the rangers befriended me, the other men stayed away. Maybe my lack of a love life was just as much to blame for my desire as much as vampire pheromones.

Eventually my eyes cleared enough to see my surroundings.

"Put me down," I insisted.

"We are being chased and you will slow us down."

I had to admit I couldn't run as fast as him. Buildings zipped by at an incredible speed.

"Okay, but when I have a chance, the point of my blade will take a slice of your skin off your perfect face."

He laughed and kept running, drawing me closer. He wasn't even breathing hard.

"The wolf clawed my side. I think it's healing," I said when the thought entered my sexually fried brain.

"Your blood holds magic. Now hush. I need to listen."

He'd hushed me. What a jerk. I still wasn't sure that I should have come with him, but then again, what choice was there?

Drake slowed, then stopped and placed me on my feet. I wobbled for a moment. It was like having sea legs which I'd read about. He steadied me until he was sure I would remain upright.

I stared at Drake. He was much taller than I'd realized. His eyes were doing the red-orange flame thing as he gazed down on me.

"We're here," he said. "Blade's stronghold."

A huge double wrought iron gate with a gothic squeak was opening slowly. Two men and two women ran out. They were dressed in black leather from head to toe. I stumbled slightly when one of the women laid hard eyes on me.

"They are Blade's personal guard," Drake said.

"Use your manners, Lizbet," he barked at her.

She looked away but not before I saw something I hadn't expected. Jealousy. She wanted Drake.

Why would she be jealous of me? Even dressed in all leather, she was the most beautiful woman I had ever seen. I was a plain Jane and happy to be that way. She could keep her beauty and Drake for all I cared.

"Liar," whispered through my head. Drake's teeth could sink into my flesh whenever he liked. What in the hell was happening to me?

"Come," he said and took my hand again. His touch sizzled my skin and his dazzling smile almost had me jerking away.

But then my breath caught. We stepped through the gates into an oasis of trees and plants. I breathed in their essence and calm spread throughout my body. In the middle of the courtyard, a huge fountain had water surging thirty feet into the air. I'd never seen such opulent splendor in my life. Muted lights in different colors shone in strategic places, making it appear like a fairyland.

A large mansion—you couldn't call it a house—was fifty yards in front of us. Drake led me up the steps and stopped at a marble entry with two large doors. They opened at our arrival. Two men stood to the side and closed the doors after everyone was inside.

Drake continued walking.

"Hot tea for Tara," he said to no one in particular. "She was clawed. Bring Macos to me."

The vampires scattered.

Drake led me to a grand double stairwell that went down, not up. Inset lights came on every few stairs as we descended.

"Where are we going?" I asked.

"To your chambers," he said.

"No." I stopped. The stairwell continued down and all I could see was darkness.

"Tara. I want you checked by our physician. We must be sure your body expelled the poison from the wolf's claws. If it remains, the wound will fester and you will fall ill."

"I cannot stay here tonight. You don't understand," I said frantically.

"You can explain it to me after you have tea and your wound is inspected." His voice hardened. "I *will* keep you safe. You are over forty miles from the market and you have no way to return tonight without my help."

Reluctantly, I continued walking. At the bottom of the stairwell, lights flicked on as we entered a long hallway. The twists and turns reminded me of the gang's clubhouse, but that's where the similarity ended. The luxury was mind-numbing. It also smelled better, or maybe that was Drake.

More stairs continued downward, but he turned into another hall-way. Guards were strategically placed at each turn. Their eyes followed my every move but they didn't smile or acknowledge me. After multiple turns and passing at least ten rooms, Drake opened a door. He followed me inside. The room was amazingly large with a sitting area and a doorway to the side. White furniture filled the area. Green plants, some with exotic, colorful flowers, gave the room a breathtaking beauty. A strange sound whispered in my ear. I would swear the plants spoke to me. I reached out to one and a wispy vine slithered toward my hand. I wasn't afraid but it startled me and I jerked away.

"It was saying hello," a gruff, unfriendly voice said behind me.

I turned and came face-to-face with one of the ugliest creatures I had ever encountered. He was approximately four feet tall with a wide muscular body and short arms that ended in three dexterous claws. He had a mouth of serrated teeth that took up most of his face. His jaws didn't close completely and the teeth jutting out looked almost like tusks. He wore some kind of one-piece, earthtone jumper. I'd never seen anything like him.

Chapter 14

I wasn't sure of the protocol. Should I ask what species he was?

He spoke to Drake. "Dr. Macos will be here momentarily. He was delayed."

Drake didn't appear happy but he smiled at me.

"This is Hax. He is a guttybrew. You will see them throughout the compound. They stay underground and serve Blade."

The guttybrew simply stared at me.

I placed my hand out, which startled him. I kept it out.

"I'm glad to make your acquaintance. Thank you for explaining about the plant. It's not something I've encountered before."

He looked into my eyes, then at my hand, and growled.

"Hax, that was unkind. You may leave," Drake said from behind me.

Hax turned and walked out of the room.

"I've been put in my place," I said plainly.

Drake smiled and dimples showed on his cheeks. I hadn't noticed them before.

"My pardon. Guttybrew can be difficult. They are devoted to Blade and put up with the rest of us."

"I'll survive," I assured him.

"I'm not angry with the guttybrew. They can't help their disposition. It's in their DNA. Macos should be here to look at your wound. You are the most important person in the house and he should not delay."

I'd forgotten about my injury. My hand went to my shirt which was red with dried blood and I pulled it up. The claw wound was healed with only a slight line to mark where it had been.

"I don't believe a doctor is necessary."

Drake's eyes zeroed in on my flesh and he licked his lips, displaying a flash of fangs. It wasn't my flesh that got to him; it was the dried blood.

"Forgive me," Drake said uncomfortably and looked away from the blood. "If Blade discovers Macos did not check on your wound, there will be hell to pay." His voice remained slightly strangled.

"Is there a bathroom close by?" I asked carefully. He was a vampire. I had to remember who I was dealing with.

"Yes, through that door off the bedroom."

I didn't exactly hurry but I walked quickly. My opinion about Drake's beauty was waning by the minute. His desire for my blood was a total mood killer. He was the enemy. The wolves were also the enemy. My situation was not a good one.

The bathroom was huge and luxurious. It had a double sink, bathtub, and separate shower. I wasn't sure what all the holes in the bathtub were for; I'd never seen the like. Then there were three nozzles above the shower. I had trouble believing people lived this way. Mika and Coop had the nicest accommodation I'd ever been in. It was one of the reasons I loved visiting them when I was a child.

I'd lived with my father in a rented apartment that had seen better days. Even though he made money with his sword, we never had much. I didn't blame him because I knew where the money went. Two fatherless families in our building had apartments because my father paid for them. He'd had me take the rent to the landlord when he was unavailable. He never talked about giving our money to others; it was just how he was.

I removed a towel from a gold rack. It was soft and fluffy. I brought it to my nose and inhaled. Flowers of some kind. It didn't appear line dried. I wet it in the sink and lathered it with soap. I removed the jacket and went to work on my shirt. My skin was next and then the inside of the jacket until I was satisfied the blood was gone. I zipped the jacket to hide the wet stain on my shirt and walked out.

A man was standing with Drake and speaking in a low tone. He went quiet when I entered the room.

"Macos, this is Tara."

I knew immediately that he was vampire. Beautiful like Drake, but with a touch more refinement. His eyes were kinder and I hoped, as a doctor, he cared about people. He wore a white coat with pockets and black pants. His face was slightly thinner than Drake's, but his skin was just as flawless and his handsomeness something you would see in a prewar magazine that had young male models. Vampires didn't age after they were turned. Besides their violent tendencies and unquenchable quest for blood, it was one of the few things I knew about them.

"Forgive me. One of the guttybrew females was giving birth and there was a complication."

My hand went to my heart.

"I hope she is okay and you did not leave her to come to me. I'm fine."

"Do not let him off the hook. He should have come to you immediately," Drake snapped.

I ignored him. The doctor's mouth tightened ever so slightly.

"Please tell me of the new mother," I insisted.

"She and child pulled through. It was a boy," he said. His eyes had warmed while speaking.

I smiled in relief before I turned in Drake's direction.

"I think it would be best if you leave while he examines me," I told him.

His friendly demeanor was quickly changing. Fire flashed in his eyes.

"Drake, leave us. I will report to Blade when I am assured she is okay. I will also see her comfortable and settled for the evening." The doctor's voice held no room for argument.

"I can't stay the night," I said abruptly. "My friend will search for me and it will be dangerous for him."

"Write a note and I will have it delivered to your friend," the doctor said.

Coop wouldn't believe it was me. He had no idea what my handwriting looked like. I was ready to object but realized I could place something personal in it so he would positively know who wrote it.

"When you send the note, can that person wait for a reply?" I asked.

"Yes. Let's check you out first, though." He turned to Drake and raised his eyebrows.

"Good night, Tara," the vampire said and marched angrily from the room.

"Should I be worried?" I asked the doctor.

"My dear. We are vampires. You should always be worried." He gave me a sad smile.

I wasn't sure how to take what he said.

"I washed the blood from my wound, shirt, and jacket. It should be okay for you to examine me."

His smile grew warm.

"I smell only a slight trace of blood," he said. "But have no fear. I've trained myself to control my reaction. Drake has not and your blood is highly appealing. If you were not under Blade's protection, you would be unsafe with him. Most vampires do not control their natural instincts. I am not saying this to scare you. Blade's protection is the most valuable thing you could have. No one here will harm you, but things like blood, fear, and running from my kind bring out our natural instincts."

I shouldn't have come here with Drake but there was nothing I could do about it now.

"You will have my message delivered to my friends?" I questioned him.

"You have my word. Would you mind if I examine you now? Blade will want an update and he will give me an ass chewing for not immediately attending you."

"Why is that? I am fine."

He smiled. It was genuine but there was something in his eyes.

"You are The Promised. A wielder with unimaginable power. We have waited a long time for your arrival." His eyes flashed with a similar flame that Drake's had.

"I doubt it is me you were waiting for," I said, though I knew it was a lie.

"My dear, I felt your power when you entered the compound. Every vampire here did. There is no mistaking who you are."

I didn't want to admit to what he was saying so I changed the subject.

"Do vampire eyes flash with fire when they lie?"

He gave a short laugh.

"No, but you are very observant. Our eyes flash with hunger, sexual desire, and anger. When we lie, we can control it. I promise not to lie to you, but there are things I cannot reveal and I will let you know if we run into them."

Surprisingly, I believed him.

"Would it be easier to show you the wound in the light?"

"I can see perfectly in the dark so no. Wherever you are comfortable is best."

I removed my jacket and lifted my shirt. Macos walked closer and placed his hand out.

"May I?" he asked.

"Yes." I looked down before he touched me and the jagged line from the claw was hardly visible now.

"I'm going to poke and prod. It's something doctors are very good at. Tell me if there is discomfort."

His sense of humor was reassuring. He did as he said but I felt no pain.

"Would you explain why I healed so quickly?" I asked. "I've had other slight injuries, but this is the first time it happened."

He straightened and took a step back so he wasn't crowding me.

"You are coming into your power. Once it is fully realized, you will be harder to kill."

"I think Drake broke a wolf's neck during the attack. He healed. Will I be the same?"

"I don't think it will work to that extent but you may prove me wrong. My apologies, I need to give Blade an update on your wellness and get back to the mother and child. Could you write your note and give an address or directions? The reply could take several hours so you will not receive it until you wake in the morning. There should be pen and paper in the side drawer to your left."

It had to be midnight by now. I removed what I needed and wrote the short note.

I am safe. Do not look for me.

I will write or return as soon as possible.

Keep the pancakes warm.

Tara

Pancakes was a reference only Mika and Coop would know. I folded the note twice and wrote their address on the outside.

"Will my friends be safe?"

"I can have guards posted and guarantee their safety if you wish."

Coop would know and it would freak him out. He and Mika had stayed safe for six years without me. They would be okay.

"No, that won't be necessary," I said. "Thank you for doing this."

"You are safe within these walls. Your friends are as safe as they can be outside of them, I promise."

"Can I leave this room?"

His expression changed and I knew I wouldn't like the answer.

"You are protected by Blade and he makes these decisions. I am simply a doctor and I do not second-guess my liege."

"I'm a prisoner." It wasn't a question.

Chapter 15

"For tonight, you may not leave. Past that, I do not know," Macos said.

"I am still a prisoner," I said sharply.

"If that is how you wish to look at it."

"Was I set up?"

"I cannot answer this line of questioning, Tara."

But he *had* answered me. I handed him the note. My fingers shook slightly with anger.

"You must remain in the suite," he said. "Everything you need is here. Hax will check on you in the morning. If something is remiss, please tell him and he will do his best to take care of it. Good night."

"Good night." My tone was stiff and I felt bad after the door closed behind him. I also realized I should have questioned him about the plants. They swayed toward me as I paced around the large room. I checked the door and it was locked from the outside. My anger grew.

Energy shot through my body when a vine fell on my shoulder. Other plants extended their branches and feathered across my bare arms. I calmed internally at the same time energy filled me. A second before I pulled away, the vine withdrew and the other plants receded. They knew my thoughts and I was the tiniest bit freaked out.

I inhaled deeply. I was no longer angry. I wouldn't forget that Drake helped get me away from danger. Suffocation by smoke inhalation was not high on my list of ways to die.

I wandered around the front room a bit, poking in cabinets. The plants left me alone. Next was the bedroom where I searched through the drawers. Long sheer nightgowns and indecent underwear were in one. All my size. In another, there were T-shirts.

I took one of them into the bathroom to shower. There was no lock on the bathroom door, which bothered me and I grabbed a knife. If someone entered, I would see them through the glass and they wouldn't be happy. I turned on the water and shivered. It heated quickly and I had to adjust the knobs. I was unaccustomed to water that was too hot. I also discovered the multiple showerheads offered pure bliss on my sore muscles. There was delicious smelling soap, shampoo, and conditioner, which was a luxury. With a washcloth, I scrubbed my entire body and felt much better. I no longer smelled like the lingering smoke from the explosions.

I quickly dried myself with a soft towel, then placed it around my head to keep my hair from dripping. Lotion was on the counter and I saturated my entire body. Lotion was an illegal market item my father brought me for special occasions. It wasn't available in the military. I put on the T-shirt, wishing it was a bit baggier. At least it ended at my upper thighs and not my belly.

I removed the towel, found a comb and brush, and braided my wet hair. I was tired and didn't plan on waiting for it to dry before I went to sleep.

The covers were soft and inviting, and I snuggled in. The room was cool but the perfect temperature beneath the bedding. A million thoughts went through my head, including how the plants got enough light to grow down here.

At some point, I fell into an exhausted sleep.

***

"Miss," a gruff voice said from the doorway.

I scrambled out of bed, knife in hand. It was Hax. He didn't move closer.

"The reply from your friend is in the other room beside your coffee," he said.

"Yes, uh, thank you." I lowered the knife from a defensive position. I also realized I was wearing next to nothing and my face heated.

"There is a robe in the closet," he said grumpily, apparently reading my discomfort.

I wondered if anger was his normal mode or if it was me.

I kept half an eye on him and went to the closet. The robe was a revolting shiny pink material but felt amazing when I slipped it on.

"Do you know the time?" I asked.

"Ten."

"In the morning?"

"Yes."

"I can't believe I slept that long."

He grunted.

"Do you know how the woman and child Dr. Macos was with last night are doing?"

"They are well." He grunted again. "I will bring your breakfast in thirty minutes." He left.

I dressed first. My old clothes smelled of smoke and I couldn't handle the thought of wearing them. The closet had jeans and leatherwear. I put on the indecent underclothes first. I found a drawer with tank tops like the one on the floor of the bathroom. Somehow, they thought they knew my desired outerwear and the size. I guessed it was my style now because I no longer needed to hide my body, specifically my lean muscled arms. It didn't mean their knowledge of my clothing wasn't creepy. I tamped down my anger. It would serve no good. I needed answers.

I walked into the large room and went straight to the table.

Stay in touch or I will search for you. The pancakes and Dot are waiting.

K

Dot, the horse he'd loaned me, was his assurance that the note came from him.

I carried it with me and approached a grouping of plants. They reached out and I didn't shy away. The energy was soothing. One vine circled my wrist and the area on my skin glowed. I pulled slightly and it released me. I lifted my hand and ran my fingers over the greenery.

I had no idea how long I stood there. I laughed aloud when one of the branches tickled my skin.

"I need coffee," I told them and once more, they immediately pulled away.

I should have found this odd, but my father said in his letter that my energy was connected to the earth. We had no plants in the apartment of my youth and now I understood why. It would have been nearly impossible to keep me from using my energy if the plants made me feel better when my father refused to give me attention after breaking the rules. Thinking of this made me sad. A vine went to my shoulder and a slight buzz tingled on my skin. My thoughts settled and the vine moved away.

I poured coffee and added cream and sugar which was a delicacy. I had only taken two sips when a knock sounded at the door. Hax carried in a covered tray before I could answer. He took it to the low table in front of the couch.

"Thank you."

He grunted.

"Do you need anything more?" he asked gruffly.

"Freedom," I said.

With another grunt, he walked out.

It would take me an hour to find my way through the halls but I might need to escape and risk getting lost.

Chapter 16

The food was better than anything I'd eaten at the military camp and I finished it quickly. The room was much larger than my tent. I needed a workout and this area would do. I walked around the suite until my food settled then grabbed my sword from the bedroom. When I entered the main room again, the plants had pulled their branches and vines back leaving an even larger clear space than I had. Nope, that wasn't weird at all. I refused to freak out. I was trapped in the room with mindreading plants that had done nothing to harm me. It would be okay.

After a last look around the cleared area, I laid the sword on a table and began my warmups. The jeans did not have much give but if I needed to fight, I might be wearing them. I wasn't sure about the leather that remained in the closet. I would need to try it out but for now, I preferred the jeans.

When I finished the pushups, crunches, and lunges, I was ready to work with my sword. I lifted it above my head and began the drills that were seared into my muscle memory. As the sword moved faster and faster, unpleasant thoughts swirled in my mind.

What would have happened if I hadn't come here willingly? Would Drake have forced me? Was the attack by the werewolves a setup? I wouldn't be surprised. My brain was an emotional rollercoaster of doubt, fear, and anger. I missed a strike and messed up the drill so I had to start over. When I completed the complex dance, I stood inhaling and exhaling deeply.

A few minutes later, my arm rose again bringing the sword over my head. I pictured Drake, in all his sexy glory, as my opponent. His dimple flashed and he smiled but I didn't let it sway me from killing him. He might only be in my imagination but I swear I could smell his scent in the room. It gave me added incentive.

Downward strike and his right arm was severed. It fell to the floor. I removed his left arm at the elbow and it flew ten feet, landing in one of the pots. I systematically dismembered him until my final swing took his head. With Drake laying in his own blood, I went to work on Blade, the liege vampire who was really responsible for me being here.

I pictured Blade a little taller, a little paler, and a whole lot uglier. I eviscerated him in three blows. I then dissected his entrails into small pieces. I heaved air in and out of my lungs and sweat poured off me. My imaginary battlefield ran red with the blood of my enemies.

I guessed that I had a thirst for blood that I'd never realized before.

Mentally, I felt better but it sucked not having a partner to spar with. Working with Coop had been glorious and made me realize what I was missing. Killing Drake and Blade, even if it was only in my imagination, took second place.

I walked to the planter where Drake's imaginary limb plopped and sank the sword into the soil. Like it did in the garden, it vibrated with energy and the power traveled throughout my body but this time I was ready for it.

Why was I here? The question continued tickling my brain.

I couldn't trust anything the vampires told me. I'd liked Dr. Macos but I could not believe him. My father had ingrained secrecy into me from my first memories. Was I safe? Drake mentioned that someone betrayed him. It had to be a vampire so I answered my own question. I was not.

I groaned aloud. I was feeling sorry for myself. I hadn't felt this way since the months following my father's death. A few plants leaned in but I didn't want their comfort right now.

Another shower was in order. I took a clean pair of jeans from the closet and an olive-green tank top that resembled military colors. This sent my thoughts swirling again. Did the general set this up? He was a disgusting rat who gave rats a bad name. I may not have carried a rank, but I was part of his team and deserved protection.

Was Captain Dickson in on it too? That saddened me. Who knew what I would have done if they had sat me down and told me the truth. I think in the end I would have gone to the vampires if it was asked of me.

The shower was quick and when I came out fully dressed, I heard a knock. I left the bedroom as Hax was walking in. He held some type of long bag.

"Blade has requested you attend dinner. This is your dress. The shoes are at the bottom of the bag."

"When is dinner?" I asked.

"One hour."

"Thank you," I said kindly and received his overly used grunt.

I took the bag from his claws. He left as quickly as he had appeared. I carried the bag into the bedroom, placed it on the bed, and unzipped it. A glittery silver dress met my eyes. There were equally glittery shoes at the bottom of the bag. I removed the hanger and turned the dress so I could see the back. There wasn't one. The material would show the top of my ass. How dare Blade dictate what I wear. I would face the head vamp-man on my own terms. And besides, silver was not my color.

Rumor said vampires hated garlic and unfortunately, I didn't have any handy. The only thing I did in the vamp's favor was use the provided toothbrush from the bathroom. As much as I wanted to, I wouldn't repel him with bad breath. I had combed my wet hair after the shower but I didn't bother doing it again. Blade could eat dirt. I put the sheath on my back and slid the sword home. My knives went in my boots. I allowed my anger to build. When I entered the main room, the plants swayed away from me.

Hax knocked and entered a moment later. His toothy jaw tightened a fraction but he didn't comment on my attire. With more bravado than I felt, I followed him from the room, making sure my boots clomped as loudly as possible. We went deeper into the cavernous underground and I was thoroughly lost. Clomp, clomp, clomp. The twists and turns through the corridors allowed my anger to steadily grow. Hax turned around and stared purposefully at my boots. When he started walking, I made the sounds even louder. He didn't turn again but I became winded after too many twists and turns intermixed with long corridors and the effort it took to lift and stomp my feet downward.

When I decided I must be trapped and forever lost in the never-ending dungeons of hell, a large hall opened. The Victorian room had ornate lighting on the sidewalls that made the ceiling glow. Hax strode to a set of double doors and extended his hand so I would walk through first. I made it three feet before I stopped in my tracks.

The mystery man from my dreams looked back at me.

The large bed with red and gold popped into my mind. This man's sexy body; naked, hot, and strong, lowered over me. My head spun and I bit back a moan.

My dream man was far more exquisite than Drake. I met his eyes and the world stopped spinning while my brain continued doing cartwheels.

His gaze froze me in place. Was I drooling? The possibility mortified me and I tore my eyes from his hold. Air filled my lungs and my feet touched the ground again.

His dark-gray suit was impeccable and fit him perfectly, giving the allure of a muscular body while showing nothing. How could this man who filled so many of my nights with ecstasy be standing in front of me? I tore my gaze from his to save my sanity.

A long table filled the center of the room. Men and women, all gorgeously attired in eveningwear, sat frozen. Their eyes conveyed that I was a disgusting bug not worthy of their regard. But not my dream man. My gaze was forced back to his and a buzz of awareness sizzled throughout my insides. Equal parts sensuous and equal parts wild, it roamed to nerve endings that had never been awakened, even in my dreams.

"Blade," Drake said from his place at the table. "I fear The Promised did not get the dress code memo."

Nervous laughter from the other guests filled the room.

I shook my head slightly and some of the cobwebs receded enough for me to think. The thoughts were not good because I knew I was in trouble. Desire continued stabbing me. It was unlike the caress I experienced when I looked at Drake. My dream man gave me an intimate hammer of lust that went straight to the juncture of my thighs. My panties were in danger of hanging from one of the lampshades and I would be the one tossing them.

My dreams had given me the feel of his fingers running over my body. He'd made me moan and squirm beneath his exquisite touch. The imaginary images invoked unquenchable need and made my knees weak. Pure sexual power dripped off him with every move he made.

My eyes snapped open and I read the truth in his gaze.

Fuck. He had the same dreams.

He was another step closer without me realizing it. My hand tingled, then lifted. How the hell had that happened? He took my fingers, turned them over so my palm was facing up, and kissed my wrist. I felt it from the point of his touch directly to my inner thighs.

This was a deadly game and I didn't know the rules.

Chapter 17

His eyes closed for a moment. When they opened, I saw ravenous need that made my heart skip a beat. He didn't look any happier about it than I did. The look disappeared and a lazy *I don't give a damn* expression took over.

"You smell divine." His voice did more wicked things to me and matched perfectly to my dream man. Smooth as silk, deep, and delicious, it vibrated inside me. "Tara"—my name on his lips was warm velvet—"knew exactly what she was doing." He didn't look at anyone but me while he spoke.

He guided me to the opposite side of the table and I didn't resist. Was I in shock? Had he cast some vampire spell over me?

He turned his attention to the men and women seated at the table.

"Ladies and gentlemen, this is The Promised, the wielder we've been waiting for. She will be staying with us for the foreseeable future."

The words slowly drifted through my head. They were wrong. He was wrong. I bit my tongue until I tasted blood.

Damn. That was the wrong thing to do. Multiple vampire eyes grew hungry. Blade's lips tilted upward at the sides of his mouth.

"Control yourself." His gaze swept the room and then came back to me.

"I…" I tried again after digging my fingernails into my palm. "I am not your guest; I am your prisoner. I will not be here for the foreseeable future. I wish to leave."

His energy pulsed around me, looking for a way inside. "No," I thought silently. "You cannot hold me with your vampire powers no matter what you do to me in my dreams."

Fury flashed in his eyes. It was so quick I almost missed it. I had a feeling he was unaccustomed to someone resisting him. He seated me, then released my hand and took his chair. His magic continued hitting the walls mine produced. The small amount of blood from my sore tongue kept me from falling beneath his spell again. My fingers still tingled where he'd touched me but that was fading too.

He smiled with a flash of fang and there was nothing nice about it.

The fog completely cleared my head and somehow I had to keep it that way. Blade, the king of vampires, was a sexual god and a very dangerous man. I looked away from him and the chandelier above the table began swaying. Crap, was he doing it?

When I glanced back at him, his eyes told me he was. He enjoyed scaring me. He wasn't just a vampire; he was a monster.

Even though I didn't know what I was doing, I pulled on my magic and slowed my racing heart.

"Interesting," he whispered.

"No, deadly," I challenged.

Every vamp at the table heard me. I wasn't sure what I expected, but it damn sure wasn't what happened next.

Blade threw back his head and laughed.

The sensuous sound threaded inside me to a pulsing beat of need. I bit my tongue again and damn, it hurt. I had to stay in control. Something inside me said it was important.

"Blade," the woman sitting directly across from me said in a husky voice that conveyed shared intimacy. She was dressed in a bloodred gown that appeared to be made of rubies. She was far more exquisite than the gown. Even if I had worn the silver dress, she would outshine me like Blade outshone Drake.

Her skin was seemingly made of porcelain without a single flaw. From her high cheekbones to her sensuous mouth, she was perfection.

Instant dislike hissed inside me. I had no idea why. She placed her hand on Blade's arm and batted her eyes. I wanted to decapitate her with my sword. I would place her head on a pike for all to see what happened when you touched my... what? A man I'd dreamt about. A damn vampire. I was quickly losing it but she didn't help matters with her entreaty.

"Must we dine with someone who, ah—what is the more delicate term?" She paused so she had everyone's attention. "Is so unrefined."

Nervous laughter filled the room. Six vampires held seats on the other side of the table and five on mine. Drake sat at the opposite end from Blade. I glanced toward him and he wasn't laughing. His eyes were fixed on Blade. Slowly, I shifted my gaze from the woman and looked at him.

His eyes dropped to the woman's hand and she froze. Fear rose in the room and it came from her. She had crossed some line and she knew it. I didn't understand how my senses were picking up on everything, but they seemed to be in overdrive. The woman's fingers slid from the material of Blade's suit. She placed her hands in her lap and looked down at the table.

I watched as her chair, seemingly of its own volition, slid back from the table.

"No," she cried out and stood. "Please, Blade, I am sorry."

"You have been warned and your repeated claims of remorse are at an end, Kenia. You have overstayed your welcome. Hax will see you out."

The guttybrew was at her side instantly. I had no idea he could move that quickly.

Kenia lifted her eyes and they zeroed in on me. She wanted to jump across the table and rip my head off. I wanted to do the same to her for daring to lay a hand on Blade. If she'd touched his skin, I may have done it. Pure disdain entered my gaze, and I made a shooing motion in her direction with my hand.

I didn't know what brought on my behavior and there was no time to examine it.

Blade caught her mid attack. It had happened so fast; I had no time to react. She wanted me dead.

Note to self: Do not antagonize vampires.

I doubted the note would work. Magnanimous wasn't my middle name. The vampires might be deadlier than the rangers, but the military men were still dangerous and if you didn't stand up for yourself, you might as well roll over and lick their toes.

Blade placed a struggling Kenia on her feet, his face inches from hers. He showed his fangs and she shrank back though his hold kept her from moving far enough away to escape danger.

"You forget yourself for the last time."

"Blade, I am sorry. I will behave."

He stepped back and she tried to move toward him, but something stopped her. She cried out.

"No, my liege, please," she shrieked. "Mercy, I beg for mercy."

The heat in Blade's eyes exploded and Kenia screamed so loud it hurt my ears. Her skin shriveled and blackened. It took minutes that felt like hours as her cries turned to low moans then whimpers. I was so shocked, I didn't move. From one blink to the next, her body turned to dust and floated to the floor.

Blade straightened his suit jacket and took his seat. He didn't look at me, but his eyes met every vampire in the room and their gazes dropped to the table.

"If harm befalls The Promised, the person responsible will die and unlike Kenia, it will be a slow death. You will not be warned again."

"Yes, Liege," they said as one.

After they answered, Blade's gaze found mine. His eyes held fire that was nothing like Drake's.

"My apologies," he said with a nod of his head.

I didn't reply. What could I say? I'd just watched him kill a woman with his gaze. Vampires had violent natures. It had been drilled into me since I was a child. Blade ruled a feudal system that only recognized the strongest among them. Wolves were no different. I no longer needed to bite my tongue. Blade's display had scared me enough to forget his sexual allure.

The flame in his eyes banked and slowly returned to midnight black. I glanced to the end of the table and wished I were sitting with Drake and not Blade.

A small amount of energy sizzled in my fingertips and Blade's gaze went to my hand, then he lifted his eyes.

"Interesting," he whispered, his voice once more purring across my skin.

I didn't know what he meant and it shocked me that he could see the energy. I refused to place my hands in my lap and simply stared.

"I believe I will enjoy this game," he said in the same soft tone.

Chapter 18

"D inner, my liege?" Hax said over Blade's shoulder.

"Yes." Power continued to radiate off him, the waves pulsing around me, trying to find a way in. I wasn't sure if he was doing this on purpose or if it was a natural state of being for him.

What would happen if I pulled my sword? I wanted to. I felt threatened but worse, his seeing my energy turned me on. What did that say about me?

Hax set a new wineglass in front of me and filled it with deep-burgundy liquid. The vampires' wineglasses were filled too.

Was it blood? It had to be.

"Yours is wine," Blade assured me after I stared at the liquid in my glass a moment too long.

I lifted it to my lips and drank half. It wasn't a polite gesture but I needed liquid courage.

Blade grinned and his eyes sparked with subdued flames. Vampire entertainment was not what I was going for when I came to dinner. Blade obviously found me amusing and I didn't like it.

He glanced to the side and gave Hax a small nod. A moment later, the doors opened and three guttybrew entered, two females and one male. The male walked directly to me, holding a plate. Steaming green vegetables and small white potatoes with butter and a sprinkle of fresh herbs left me salivating. The women handed out steaming bowls of what looked like soup to the vampires. A side glance at the vamp to my other side turned my stomach. It was blood. Hot, icky blood.

I fought back the need to escape.

I glanced around the table. The male vampire who was next to Kenia's empty chair was staring when I looked at him. He quickly turned away.

"Please enjoy your meal," Blade said. "I'm aware the food supply is limited at your camp."

He said it with a touch of anger which made no sense. I was beginning to think he didn't like me. Or maybe it was the thought of rice, beans, and sometimes freeze-dried potatoes in place of warm blood. My stomach growled and Blade's lips turned up slightly. His grin was as fake as mine.

I picked up my fork and took a bite of the fresh mixed vegetables. Everything on my plate looked and smelled delicious. As I swallowed, I closed my eyes. When they opened, Blade stared at my lips with such an intent look, I gulped. He took the first spoonful of soup which gave the others permission to eat. Unfortunately, the rules of dinner engagement with a room of vampires were not something I understood. Did I even want to? No, I wanted to go back to Mika and Coop's home. Blade was the vampire who could get me there. I had to stop antagonizing him and stick to entertainment. But most of all, I had to forget about the dreams.

I finished the vegetables and moved on to the potatoes. An orgasmic experience almost ensued and I ate them all.

"My apologies," I said. "I didn't realize how hungry I was and most likely ate like an animal."

Blade simply nodded to the guttybrew waiting slightly behind me and my plate was removed immediately. My gaze returned to Blade. He was so unnerving. One minute I was turned on, then terrified, and the next confused. For the first time since leaving the military post, I missed my friends.

It didn't help that the other vampires at the table watched every move I made. Blade turned away from me and looked at the other vampires. Drake watched Blade. It was an interesting dynamic.

The sensual allure Blade exuded was thankfully gone now. It gave me breathing room.

My attention was caught by the female guttybrew. She brought in the night's pièce de résistance. It was a three-layered chocolate cake with fresh strawberries decorating the top. It was a work of beauty. I hadn't had chocolate in years.

A large piece was placed in front of me and I couldn't hide my sorrowful expression.

"I can't," I said glumly to my dinner host. "I don't wish to offend, but I've eaten more than my stomach can handle."

"Is the cake something you would normally enjoy?" he asked.

I looked at the cake with longing, then turned my eyes to his.

"Normally, I would kill for chocolate cake. I'm simply too full."

"Have it wrapped and delivered to Tara's room," he told the female guttybrew.

She was as strange looking as the males. I hated to use the word ugly because to other guttybrew she was most likely beautiful. Their faces reminded me of a warthog's and walking on two feet was just weird. Then there were the dexterous claws where fingers should be. They'd clicked softly as dinner was put before us. Again, strange and I wouldn't be here long enough to grow accustomed to them.

The cake was whipped away and I turned to Blade.

"Thank you," I said sincerely. I could play nicely and the thought of chocolate cake for breakfast helped.

Blade held up his hand to stop the wineglass holding more blood from being placed in front of him. The other vampires looked at him in question.

"Enjoy your dessert," he told them. Then his hot eyes zeroed in on me.

I forced myself to breathe.

He stood and moved behind my chair. His whisper in my ear placed goose bumps on my neck.

"Would you like to walk off your meal?" he asked silkily.

This was a very bad idea, but how do you say no to the vampire king? I had to speak to him privately and this could be my only chance.

"Your guests?" I asked, delaying the inevitable.

"Are dinner guests by my invitation which is an honor. They will enjoy their sweet blood while we become acquainted." He placed his hand out, and with his other, he moved my chair back as I rose.

"Drake will see to your pleasure," he announced to the room.

He walked me out without giving them a glance. My hand had moved onto his forearm, though I didn't remember placing it there. Blade's body temperature was slightly lower than mine but not cold. I learned from Drake that they had a heartbeat and semi-warm skin.

We climbed two different flights of stairs and made more twisting turns through the building. He steered me through a door and I froze. Twinkling lights filled the area, making it a wonderland of sensory overload.

We were outside, in a garden with flowers and herbs. Some of the herbs I was familiar with—sage, lemon balm, rosemary—but others were a mystery I wanted to solve with my taste buds. Power vibrated through me. I needed a moment to adjust to the remarkable sensation. This was a jungle of energy, alive and pulsing with waves of magic that called to me. I gazed at garden paths that wove through a forest of plants. At the center was a square pool with a fountain in the middle. The entire area of plants and trees was the size of a football field. Walls from the compound surrounded it. I had no idea the building was so large and this was only what was aboveground.

"Do you like it?" Blade asked softly, sending a sensual thread of energy down my spine again.

Did the plants have the same effect on him? Were vamps also part of their wonderous circle?

"It's amazing," I said to answer his question and not appear rude.

He led me down a path to the right and we walked beneath a grape arbor, stopping at a stone bench. I removed my hand from Blade's arm when we sat down. His touch made me uncomfortable. I liked it entirely too much.

"Why am I here?" I asked bluntly.

He started to reply, but I rudely cut him off.

"If you can't tell me the truth, then please remain silent."

"I doubt the truth will comfort you," he said softly.

Why did he speak that way? I deemed it his sensual voice.

"I demand you return me to my friend's home," I said stiffly, trying to keep from panicking.

His eyes flashed burning fire exactly as they had done when he incinerated the female vampire.

"No."

Chapter 19

The word was said so abruptly, I leaned away. The flames in Blade's eyes didn't help. Should I go for my sword? I had a feeling it would do no good.

My anger boiled. If he didn't like me, why did he bring me here?

"I want to leave," I said succinctly, failing to hide my anger.

"It is not safe."

"I've been on my own for six years," I practically shouted. "I do not need your protection."

"You were never on your own," he said bluntly.

"How can you say that?" I demanded. It wasn't just anger rising inside me; power tingled from my fingers to my toes. The grapevines swayed closer and even without their touch, I could feel energy flowing from the vines to me. They were feeding me power.

"You were flown to the outskirts of the city by helicopter. Three gang members accosted you on motorbikes. They were to bring you to me. You killed them and stole one of the bikes. You saved me the trouble of killing them myself because they were to intercept you within minutes of the helicopter leaving and cause you no harm."

"How do you know this?" I demanded.

"As I said before. You have never been alone. I always knew where you were and that you were protected in the military camp."

It terrified me that there was no deception in his words. Had my entire adult life been a lie? What about Mika and Coop? Had they lied to me? Had my father? I felt sick and my head began to ache. A grapevine touched my hand and the faint throb subsided.

"Okay," I said when I gained enough control to speak. "If what you are saying is true, then I need to know it all. Drake seemed surprised that my father had not explained things to me. I'm tired of being in the dark. I have a right to know."

More fire shot through his eyes. I didn't look away or back down. I was angry and hurt that my life was not what it had seemed.

"You and I are part of something beyond our control," he said bitterly. "My life is as regulated as much as yours. Neither of us needs to like it and now that we've met, I doubt either of us will."

No, that didn't sound insulting in the least. I remembered my father's letter. He'd wanted me to have a childhood without knowing I was part of the prophecy. Was that where Blade's anger came from? It didn't matter. I wanted to leave.

"You want me to remain in the dark while being your prisoner until you're ready to explain some great mystery at some unspecific point?" I demanded in disbelief.

"There is one thing I can tell you."

"Don't make me hold my breath," I said before he continued. "I might pass out, and then your words would fall on deaf ears." Snarky, that was me.

"I am waiting for your full power," he said. "Until it arrives, you are my guest."

"I'm tired of hearing about my full power," I said.

"That means your father told you something?"

"From the time I was a small child, he told me to hide my limited power. In recent weeks, it's been nearly impossible." My voice had risen and I would have stood if he hadn't placed his hand on my wrist to keep me seated.

"You no longer need to hide. Allow your power to take over. When it happens, I will explain more."

I met his gaze and saw him looking at my mouth. I licked my lips, and a soft growl came from deep in his chest. He released me and suddenly stood.

"Please consider yourself my highly esteemed guest," he said without the low whisper.

"I am your prisoner no matter what you want to call it. You expect me to sit still and remain your prisoner? I promise that will not happen."

The hardness traveled across his face again and settled in his burning eyes.

"You would not like the consequences if I had to look for you outside these walls," he said.

"Is that a threat?"

"Not to you," he replied. "But whoever helps you, will pay with their lives. I do not go back on my word and I'm giving it to you now."

"You are despicable," I said with all the disgust I could manage in three words.

He shrugged in a very unvampire-like manner.

"I have been called worse."

I was too angry to speak. My hand inched to pull my sword and separate his head from his neck. I was unsure what he would do if I tried. The vampires went to a lot of trouble to get me here and I knew how deadly they were. Blade held his position because he was the most dangerous.

"I wish to return to my room," I said.

"The gardens were designed for you. I thought you would enjoy more time here."

A vine wrapped around my wrist. It didn't want me to go.

"I don't wish to be anywhere around you. I'd rather go to my room."

His eyes flashed again.

"Something we agree on." His gaze remained on mine. "Drake, please accompany The Promised around the gardens. She will be confined to her rooms tomorrow and will regret it if she does not spend time out here tonight." His threat was clear. I had to do what he said or else.

Drake stepped out of the darkness and gave a small bow. He was better company than Blade, even though I didn't like either man. The arrogant king disappeared into the same blackness Drake had walked from.

"I wish to practice with my sword," I told Drake. If I didn't get rid of some of this anger, I would go nuts. "If I were you, I would stand back. I might accidently slice off your head."

Drake laughed and the sound vibrated through me. Damn vampires. The vine released me and I walked away from the maddening vamp and found a large enough area to work in. I warmed up my arms in the dance I'd done since my father taught it to me when I was young. As it progressed, I picked up speed and allowed energy to flow steadily throughout my body. It was stronger than I'd ever felt it.

I drew my sword and repeated the steps. Drake moved closer. I spun around, aiming my slice at his throat. I pulled it at the last second.

"Don't tempt me," I said. "I am not in the mood."

With lightning speed, his hand went behind him and he drew a sword from the sheath on his back I hadn't noticed. He held it in front of him, his stance perfect.

"You don't want to fight me," I said, feeling the anger rise again.

"Oh, but I do."

He attacked.

I blocked, my sword sliding off his. He adjusted his reach to mine. It would be his first mistake. My entire body sizzled with energy as we parried. I spun, went low, and should have sliced his thigh, but he jumped back at the last moment. I sidestepped his next strike, then pulled a strike a centimeter from his heart. His sword pulled one from my gut. We both smiled.

"You're good," he said.

"You're not bad."

He struck harder, and I sped up my parries.

We were fluid in the dance. He was better than Coop. I fought the desire to fire my sword. I wasn't sure why. I performed a classic figure eight but stopped at the sixth point because he thought he knew what I would do. I spun out and clipped him on the back of the legs, bringing him down with the flat of my sword. The point was at his throat when he landed on his back and my foot stomped on his sword hand.

"Death strike," I said with deadly seriousness.

"Who taught you?" Drake asked.

"My father."

"I never met him or fought against him, but I wanted to," he said.

"You would have died."

"Just as well. Blade forbade it."

I changed the subject.

"You tricked me last night. I will not forget that." Undeniable anger rose in my tone. I hoped he knew I was holding back my emotions as much as possible. Fury ran through me and it was hard not to skewer him.

"Are we having this conversation with your sword at my throat?" he asked.

"Was the werewolf attack set up?" I insisted because yes, I was having this conversation with my sword at his throat.

"I can't believe this," he muttered. "If I harm you, Blade will kill me."

"Don't lie to me; that's all I ask." I put a bit more pressure on the sword. It nicked his skin and a thin trail of blood flowed from the cut.

Fire entered his eyes.

Chapter 20

It happened much too fast. My sword went flying. At the same time, my legs flew out from under me and I landed in his former position. Drake didn't bother threatening me with his sword, but his smug expression was infuriatingly worse.

"Someone I have yet to discover," he said. "Leaked information to the wolves that you would be at Murdock's place." His smile turned devilish and I stopped breathing. "Our plan was to entice you to our home. From the smell of your arousal when we met, it may have worked. Our goal wasn't to force you. Our only priority was keeping you safe."

I would give anything to remove his smirk. I was mortified that he could smell my arousal at our meeting. This meant Blade could too. Damn vampires.

Drake placed his hand out. To slap it away would be the sign of a poor loser. I took it and his energy sizzled against mine. There was a small spark not unlike a static electricity zap, but this was much more powerful. He swore and instantly yanked his power back. In my childhood, I could do this too. It was too strong now and I had no control.

"May I pick up my sword?" A bite of belligerence marked the question as I dusted off my clothes.

"Do you wish to continue sparring?"

"If I have any hope of killing Blade, I need the practice," I said glaringly.

His head went back and he laughed. I didn't think it would end. Tears ran down his face by the time he stopped.

"You are exactly what the dark lord needs; he just doesn't know it."

Dark lord fit. Sex on a stick worked too.

"Is that what I should call him?" I asked; the dark lord name, not the stick one.

"Only if you wish a slow death." He winked.

"I noticed he has a thing for slow death."

Drake grew serious. "Don't forget..." his dark eyes burned. "Blade never makes idle threats."

A cold chill passed through me but I shrugged it off. I had a goal and dwelling on the frustrating vampire wouldn't achieve it.

"Will you help me learn to fight vampires?" I asked in place of commenting on Blade.

The smirk returned. "Can we make a deal that my head remains attached to my body?"

"I guess I can live with that. If things change, you'll be the first to know," I told him and fought a smile because he didn't deserve one.

"Your bloodthirsty nature will be the most entertainment I've had in ages. And just so you know, I no longer smell your arousal. I must work on my technique."

I tried to widen his smile with my sword, but he blocked it.

By the time we finished sparring, my arm was shaking with fatigue.

Neither of us spoke while Drake walked me back to my room. It was better that way because my thoughts grew more distant the closer we got to my prison. He left me at the door with a question on his face. I didn't want his pity and entered quickly, shutting the door firmly behind me.

I decided to try a hot bath to relieve some of my muscle aches. The holes in the tub blew water out in strategic places that eased the pain.

When I was done, I dried myself and put on another T-shirt. I walked into the living area and discovered the dessert I'd declined at dinner. If chocolate didn't relieve the melancholy, nothing would.

The first bite was pure bliss and made me think of my father. He enjoyed bringing home rare treats. I smiled over the memory of my attempt to make a chocolate cake with the ingredients he'd purchased for my tenth birthday. The cake sank in the middle and didn't taste very good but we ate it. The following year, he took me to Mika's for the most delicious cake I'd ever eaten. Before I went to bed that night, my father told me my cake the year before was better.

I placed the plate on the table in front of me, pulled up my legs, and rested my head on my knees. I gave in to self-pity for about ten minutes.

I needed books. I would go crazy with nothing to do during the day.

I leaned back against a couch pillow and gazed up at the ceiling. I stared at the vines trailing across a shelf above my head. Several drifted downward as I watched. A branch tickled my throat. Its energy was soothing. I decided to see what happened if I welcomed their touch. I lay still. Slowly, they moved toward me. For the most part, they gently ran over my skin, leaving a feather of energy in their wake. A few slid around my limbs but I didn't feel threatened. When I was ready to be left alone, they immediately slid away.

"Thank you," I said softly.

I was tired and was having trouble keeping my eyes open so I moved into the bedroom. The sword went under the bed, one knife under the pillow, and the other beneath the mattress. I felt safe in the room but I wasn't stupid. This was a house of vampires. It seemed an eternity before I fell asleep. When the darkness closed in, Blade took over my dreams.

We were in the dining hall from earlier. My back was flat against the table, my spread legs hanging over the end. I wore the green tank top with indecent panties that left nothing to the imagination. Blade stood between my thighs and ran his fingers over the barely there lace. He was shirtless; his corded chest muscles were hard lines seemingly drawn by an artist. I reveled in the need to caress each hill and valley.

His eyes had changed from the obsidian of my dreams, to black with flashes of gold fire that inspired insatiable need. My fingernails dug into the table while my eyes pleaded for him to touch me.

"You will beg," he said, his voice as hard as steel.

This wasn't how the dream should go.

***

It was a good thing that Hax's grunt woke me before I could beg because in the real world, begging Blade for sex would never happen. I disregarded the fact that an angry Blade turned me on more than a sensual one.

I didn't jump out of bed with my knife this time.

"There had better be coffee," I said and rolled with the pillow over my head.

"And food," Hax said.

"What time is it?" I asked with a muffled voice.

"One in the afternoon."

I opened my eyes. One was good.

"When will I be able to leave this room?"

"You have a private dinner with Blade this evening." He didn't answer my question.

"If I say no?"

"You will not." He said it like it was fact.

The problem was I would go crazy if I had to stay in the room around the clock. I also needed to ask about books.

"Is he requesting I wear a ridiculous gown?"

"No."

"Okay, I'll go."

He grunted and left.

I rolled over and removed the pillow from my head. My eyes caught sight of my broken fingernails. They weren't like this when I went to bed. I remembered the dream and digging my fingers into the wood. No. It had not happened. Somehow, the cotton sheets did this.

Who was I fooling? I looked at my nails again, then marched into the bathroom and found a file I'd seen in my explorations. I fixed the broken edges and tossed the file back in the drawer. I then checked the front door to see if it was locked. It wouldn't turn in my hand so I had my answer. I took a very quick shower and dressed before I had coffee and food.

I ate the meal without really tasting it while I thought about my predicament. When no answers mysteriously popped into my head, I walked over and stood in the corner with the largest collection of plants. Their branches and vines surrounded me quickly. I accepted their energy. When I was supercharged, I fetched my sword and allowed the blue flame to ignite the steel. My power was growing. I pointed the tip at the door and let loose a small amount of energy. The door shook.

Interesting.

My right arm was sore from sparring with Drake so I worked left-handed for over an hour. I did a full workout and took another shower when I finished. Dressed in only a T-shirt, I explored the room again. Time dragged by and I fought off boredom. In desperation, I tried on the leather clothing. The soft and supple feel surprised me and they had more give than the jeans. They also fit like a glove. I looked in the mirror and felt my badass side come to life. I chose black leather pants, a black tank, and a black leather jacket to cover the sword sheath. After the dream, I needed badass. I brushed my hair to a high shine and left it loose.

Basically, I prepared for dinner with Blade. I needed concessions from him and I was determined to get my way. To do that I couldn't press his buttons. Leather was much sexier than military fatigues or jeans. Not that I wanted to be sexy for Blade.

"Liar," I mumbled. I would not beg though. If anyone did, it would be him.

Hax arrived at the door before I started screaming in boredom. I walked grudgingly to my fate, second-guessing the leather. Drake had proved I wasn't badass when it came to vampires so who was I kidding?

Hax led me to a different room than the one the evening before. Much smaller, and dare I say intimate? Was Blade playing a similar game to mine? Did he need something from me? I think he did.

"Sex and blood," a little voice whispered through my mind.

Chapter 21

Two women in one of the hallways moved aside with malicious glares when Hax grunted. Their faces were pale and I wondered if they were vampires. We passed another woman who had been at the dinner the night before. Energy rolled off her in waves. It made me realize the two glaring ladies were human because they carried no power that I could feel.

Blood donors?

The vampire nodded but didn't speak.

"I'm Tara," I said and placed my hand out.

She looked over my shoulder at Hax, then, at me. She seemed surprised.

"Ambrosia," she said softly and took my hand.

Ambrosia was a small delicate woman with a pixy chin and nose that enhanced her overall beauty. Her dark thick hair fanned around her shoulders and tumbled down her back almost to her waist. She wore a long yellow dress with intricate white embroidery. I wouldn't be caught dead in it but on her it was perfect.

Her thumb slid over my fingers and her grip tightened.

I tried to pull away but she squeezed harder and turned my hand so her eyes settled on the pulse at my wrist. Her fangs peeked out.

Hax snarled and Ambrosia's eyes jumped to his.

"My apologies," she said, her voice trembling. She dropped my hand and looked down at the floor.

Would Blade kill her for this? I couldn't allow that.

"I'm unsure of your customs," I told her. "It is I who should ask your pardon."

"No," she shook her head. "You smell so good and I lost control. It will not happen again."

"My blood smells good?" I asked to clarify her meaning.

"Yes, your blood. It is hard to resist."

"Try," Hax grumbled.

I smiled.

"If you promise not to drink my blood, I promise not to decapitate you," I told her. Her shoulders relaxed so I continued, "I gather I should not shake hands with other vampires?"

"It is difficult for us," she said earnestly.

"I will remember that. The two women I passed before you. They were human?"

"Yes, our sheep," she said.

"Do they wish to be your sheep?"

"Yes," she nodded. "They have free will and can leave anytime they wish."

Unlike me.

"Mistress, we must not keep our liege waiting," Hax said with a touch of exasperation in the words.

"I must go," Ambrosia said and scurried away.

"That was rude," I told the guttybrew.

He ignored me and continued weaving through the corridors.

When I gave up hope of ever learning my way around, we reached our destination.

"Tara," Blade said in a low voice, his back to me when I entered.

He looked forbidding in a dark suit. He faced a small blazing fire. When he turned, ruffles from his white shirt spilled from the open suit jacket. I wouldn't think the style appealing but on him it was mouthwatering. Damn, I should have worn the silver gown I'd placed in the closet. The night before I hadn't felt out of place with all the overdressed vamps but with just Blade, I did.

He held a wineglass with dark-burgundy liquid. I didn't need to ask what it was. It should have disgusted me, but it only made my attraction to him more focused.

My mouth watered and my heart rate accelerated.

His hair fell in waves against his shoulders. His long eyelashes swept down over eyes so dark they held an onyx glow.

His gaze swept my body, but I couldn't tell if he admired me in the leather or not. He was much better at this game because his eyes made me catch my breath as desire pooled inside me.

"Would you like wine?" he asked, knocking me from thoughts I shouldn't be having.

"Yes, please." I was proud my voice didn't quiver.

He crossed to a side table and poured the wine himself.

"Hax, you may deliver Tara's dinner in twenty minutes."

The guttybrew nodded.

"She met Ambrosia on our way here. Ambrosia did not behave properly."

"No," I said and glared at Hax. "She was fine and explained to me that my blood makes it difficult for her. Please do not kill her. She did not harm me." I would beg if I needed to.

"Ambrosia is a young vampire unlike Kenia. She showed restraint and will not be punished," Blade said with a smile playing on his lips.

Hax grunted and stepped from the room. He closed the door behind him.

I took the wineglass from Blade's fingers with special care so we didn't touch.

More amusement lit his expression and gentle flames leaped in his eyes, then quickly died. The somber look returned. He waved at two chairs facing the fire.

"Shall we?" he asked.

I sat in the chair on the left and swirled the wine in my glass before taking a sip. Wine was not my thing, but this was good.

"I'm surprised you wanted to have dinner with me," I said to start a conversation.

"If I gave you the impression that I didn't desire your company, I apologize." He didn't sound sincere.

I waited but he didn't add anything further. He seemed to be suffering the same melancholy that had afflicted me all day.

"I noticed the vampires had warm and cold blood at dinner. Do you normally drink it that way?"

He studied me, his eyes returning to black pools of nothingness.

"This"—he made a small motion with his wineglass—"is cow's blood mixed with wine. The soup was broth mixed with the same blood and heated. It gives us the illusion of enjoying food."

"Is human blood better?" I thought about the blood donor businesses that sprang up in the city.

"It's divine," Blade said. "Would you like to offer up a sample?" he asked seriously, his gaze going to the pulse of my throat. Flames lit his eyes.

"No." My hand lifted to where his gaze rested.

He surprisingly laughed, though he cut it off as quickly as it started.

"I do not take anyone against their will. Sharing blood with a vampire is a gift," he said.

I'd heard many rumors and none of them were good. The rangers gossiped worse than women. They hated vampires and had no trouble talking down about them. When I questioned them about the wolves, they grumbled and changed the subject so I wasn't sure about their werewolf feelings. But vamps were their nemesis.

"I would rather not share that gift, thank you very much," I snapped because for the craziest reason, I wanted to feel the bite of his fangs.

"How was your day?" he asked, instead of furthering the discussion of blood.

"You mean my second day of captivity?"

"If that is how you wish to see it."

"It's exactly what it is." I took a breath to calm myself before continuing. "Boring, if you must know. There is only so much staring at walls one can do without thinking about slitting one's wrists."

The look he gave me was very similar to Leo's when I was particularly irritating. I wasn't sure why, but I didn't want him thinking of me as a kid sister.

He tilted his wineglass at me and another slice of flames settled in the depth of his eyes. I had the strangest feeling that I should leave. "Never run from a predator," ran through my head.

"Do you have any idea how long my forced captivity will last?" I asked.

He tipped his glass to his lips. I watched the action and another wave of desire trembled inside me. I was thankful for the coolness of the glass in my hand.

"I need books to pass the time," I said in a slightly choked voice when he didn't answer. "I stayed up as late as I could and slept until after the noon hour, but I still had too much time on my hands."

He placed his glass on the fireplace mantle and stepped toward me. He removed the glass from my hand and leaned in until he was entirely too close to my throat. I didn't move. He inhaled deeply.

"Books can be arranged," he said against my skin.

"My friend will expect regular messages from me. Can that also be arranged?" I asked nervously.

"Yes. Hax will see they are delivered." He leaned back. The fire in his eyes was so hot it should burn.

"How do you do this to me?" he asked.

"Do what?" I asked huskily.

"I want to hate you."

"Why?" Dammit, I sounded as breathless as I was feeling.

"You think I destroyed your life, but it is quite the opposite."

"What does that mean?"

"We are both the products of events that cannot be changed," he said. "Have you ever lain with a man?"

The change of subject was so fast, I thought I misheard him. The intensity in his gaze told me I hadn't.

"That is none of your business," I said angrily.

"It is absolutely my business. If you have, we can end this charade."

"You are talking in circles. Of course I have slept with men. Many of them."

The flames flared brighter. Not just in his eyes but also in the fireplace.

"You lie." Energy emanated from him and filled the room.

Heat traveled to my neck and warmed my cheeks.

"Why does it matter?" I asked, refusing to admit that I had, in fact, lied. Twenty-four-year-old virgins didn't exist. Well, they did but I had to be the only one.

"You are The Promised," he said with fury. "I cannot wish that fact away no matter how hard I try."

"Why won't you explain what you are talking about? I am not a child. This is about me, but I seem to be the only person who doesn't understand."

His hand grasped the back of my hair and tilted my face up. He kissed me, which was something he had never done in my dreams. At least not on the mouth. It should have been many things. A first kiss. A bad kiss. A wonderful kiss. A stand on my toes kiss.

This kiss was earth-shattering.

I felt it throughout my body. His energy combined with mine and I would swear we were no longer standing on the floor. We were floating in power.

His lips released me and I came down to earth slowly. Our eyes met.

"I have no idea what to do with you," he said, clearly frustrated, the kiss meaning nothing.

Cold water pouring over me would have been kinder.

"Let me return to my home." He had to. I could not win this game. One kiss and I belonged to him.

I truly hated Blade at that moment.

Chapter 22

"Where is this home you speak of?" Blade asked, ignoring my anger.

Everything that had happened since the general called me to his tent brought me up short. Andrews had all but cast me from the only home I'd known for six years. Coop and Mika would allow me to stay with them, but it was their home and would never be mine.

I didn't have anywhere to call my own.

I looked down at the wood floor and Blade's warm fingers tilted my chin so our eyes met.

"Make this your home," he said sincerely, his frustration gone.

The offer pissed me off more.

"You said a moment ago that I had destroyed your life. You don't want me here. You don't even like me."

Fire roared in his eyes, but it wasn't anger. I might be a virgin, but I knew lust when I saw it.

"I like you too much," he said. "I thought I could simply take what the prophecy offered and be done with it, but I cannot."

"You're talking in circles again."

He stepped back. "You are not ready."

My ire rose even higher. I pictured my hands grabbing my sword and bringing it down in an overhanded strike. I wouldn't sever his stubborn head; I would split it in two.

Hax entered and saved Blade's life or so I told myself. He held a tray and took it to a small intimate table on the other side of the room. The tray held another glass of blood wine for Blade.

The vampire took my hand and I wrenched it away. A small smile played on his lips at my defiance. I marched to the table where a huge plate of vegetables waited.

"How do you know I dislike meat?" I asked sharply.

"Do you want meat?" The small grin remained.

My stomach rolled.

"No, but I should."

"Eat and I will explain."

My anger receded a notch. I needed all the knowledge I could get.

He waved Hax from the room.

"There are four elements of matter," Blade said after I took a few bites. "Our power, or magic as it is also known, comes from these elements. During the last few centuries, all power has weakened. The prophecy will see that we are realigned. Vampires control fire and our energy will grow. A werewolf's power comes from air. They too are waiting." He paused and watched me until I started eating again. "Wielders gain energy from the earth. There are certain rules for each gift. Your power is magnifying as you come into it. Earth magic desires what the earth produces. Fire wants blood, and air wants meat. We feed our power to keep it elevated."

"Is this why I gain energy from plants?"

Blade nodded approvingly before he answered.

"Yes, and blood provides a vampire with power. We are controlled by this energy and must have it if we wish to survive. We each feel the deficit but that is almost over."

"A werewolf gets their power from dead animals?" I asked.

"Yes, they are pure carnivore."

"You haven't told me what creature uses water." I stabbed a piece of cooked carrot. Everything on my plate tasted delicious.

"Water is the lesser magic. Humans are the element of water."

It all made sense in a weird way.

"How will I know when my power comes in?"

"It's not just you who will know. Most of the US will be aware that something monumental happened."

"That doesn't sound good."

"Once you have your full power, you will be safer than you are right now. One of my jobs is to keep you from harm. The wolves want you." He let that settle for a moment. "If you leave here, they will find you. Your friends are safer if you stay away from them."

My eyes narrowed. "What do you know of my friends?"

"Not as much as you think but that is simply because they are human. After you killed the gang members and took the bike, you were followed."

I wanted to ask how he knew this because I was out in the desert and it seemed impossible.

"We have no intention of hurting your friends," he assured me. "The wolves will do anything to control you and that includes going through them to get to you. Your friends would not survive."

"But you won't harm them?" I asked snidely. I had no idea where my animosity came from, or maybe I did. He mentioned Mika and Coop and they were the only family I had. I didn't trust him. I couldn't.

"I give my word they will not be harmed. If you wish it, I will have them brought here."

"At gunpoint?"

"If that is what it took."

"No, thank you. Please leave them in peace."

He gave me the regal nod that was becoming familiar.

"Why do the wolves want me?"

"You have gathered too much intelligence this evening. I must have some secrets. Eat your food."

"I'm not a child."

"Then do not act like one."

It was a step too far on his part. I drew back my foot and connected my boot with his shin.

He didn't even flinch but he laughed and I wanted him to kiss me again, dammit.

He took a sip of his blood wine. Funny that I had tasted the wine but not the blood when he kissed me. This evening might have improved if I'd vomited in his mouth.

"Why are you smiling?" he asked.

I shook my head. "A woman must have secrets."

He laughed and desire sparked inside me again.

I went back to eating. "I'm surprised I'm this hungry."

"Calories feed the magic." He paused. "Did your father tell you anything about your power?"

"He told me it was important that it stayed hidden."

"I agree. I'm surprised he didn't explain where it came from," he said with just a touch of ire.

I looked up and drilled him with my eyes.

"I'm wearing my sword," I said in a soft, deadly voice. "If you bad-mouth my father, I will use it."

"My apologies," he said. His ire turned into an infuriating grin.

I was unsure why it seemed he seldom smiled.

"So, what is vampire life like?" I asked offhandedly.

The grin stayed in place.

"You know..." He waved nonchalantly, the lace of his sleeve giving the move a worldly flavor. "We sacrifice a few virgins. If that isn't enough, we slay some puppies but nothing too taxing."

He had a sense of humor. I would never have guessed. It was something else I doubted many people saw. I had to ask myself why I was one of the few. Was it all a lie? Vampires could not be trusted, I reminded myself. I went with the theme though.

"That's all? You don't run over a grandmother or two for good measure?"

"How remiss of me not to mention the grannies. I thought it might be one step too far."

We looked at each other. I saw need in his eyes. It wasn't sexual, or at least I didn't think it was. Normalcy, maybe?

"Allow me to leave," I said softly. "If you want my promise that I will return after I come into my power, I will give it."

His mouth turned into a hard line. Fire burned in his eyes and I was beginning to notice the different nuances between humor, lust, and the anger I saw now.

"No, and there will be no negotiation."

"What are you worried about?" I pushed.

"Eat your food," he said infuriatingly.

I wanted to shove my plate away, but I was still hungry. That wasn't quite right. I was starving. I dug into the food and finished the meal in silence. He poured me a second glass of wine, but when he tried for a third, I placed my hand over the glass.

"I would like to spar later if you allow it, of course. Drake is very sexy. Will he be available?"

Chapter 23

I expected anger or maybe rage. I got neither.

"I believe he's looking forward to it," Blade assured me with little expression. There wasn't even the smallest touch of jealousy in his words.

"Do you spar?" I asked to get rid of the ridiculous angst I felt.

He took a long pull from his wineglass and smiled slightly so I saw fangs.

"Only in bedroom pursuits. If you're ever up for that type of sparring, I will make myself available."

I wanted to throw my wine in his face, but I'd learned from the best. The rangers were rough soldiers. They played with insults the way toddlers played with blocks.

"Is Drake's bed available? I find you boorish." I waved my hand offhandedly.

I didn't see Blade move. My hand was caught in his and he squeezed almost to the point of pain. Had my stab about Drake finally gotten to him?

"You are trying to anger me," he said, his voice pure velvet. "It won't happen by using Drake. He is loyal and he would die for me. Maybe go after Hax."

I couldn't hide my expression. The thought of the guttybrew that way was far from appealing.

Blade laughed and kissed the backs of my fingers. He lowered my hand and turned it so the veins of my wrist were pointing upward. I couldn't see the blood flowing but I swear Blade could. He lifted his head and I wanted him to kiss me again. His sweltering gaze pierced mine but he didn't do as I expected. He stood.

"Would you like to visit the gardens?"

I pulled my hand from his. I'd wanted that kiss too badly. If I continued touching him, the need I felt would grow.

"Lead the way," I said gruffly.

He walked from the room. The turns, long hallways, and endless doorways were still confusing. I didn't think I'd taken the same route twice. We walked into the garden through a door I hadn't noticed the night before.

I breathed in the fresh air. It was truly beautiful and though the sun was no longer shining, the twinkling lights established their own night beauty.

"Does it bother you not to see the sun?" I asked curiously, forgetting my ire when surrounded by plants.

"The moon is a reflection of the sun and it satisfies us," he said. "Moonlight helps feed the energy we need along with blood."

"Could you survive off moon energy with no blood?"

"You are inquisitive for one so young," he answered.

"And you are stodgy for one so old," I quipped. "I'm blind in your world and I want to understand."

"Moon energy alone, no. We must have blood. Our current struggles have forced us to take more blood than usual. We cannot afford diminished strength right now."

I had the strangest notion the struggles he spoke about had something to do with me.

The plants reached out as we walked. I was becoming accustomed to the energy they provided. They stayed away from Blade. We'd only gone about a hundred feet when Blade stopped abruptly.

"Drake has finished his dinner and is available to spar. I have work that must be done. Good evening," he said, his lips in a tight line.

Drake stepped in front of me and Blade faded into the shadows. I wasn't sure if I should feel hurt at his sudden departure or relieved. He turned my emotions upside down.

Drake pulled his arm from behind his back. He held two swords.

"The edges are blunted and I thought we could spar a little harder tonight. You have a long way to go before you take on Blade." His eyes held a question I didn't understand. Maybe he was checking on my mood. Being such good friends with Blade should give him a clue about how frustrating the vampire was.

I took the sword and checked the balance. It was perfect. I ran my finger down what should have been the sharp side of the blade. It was dull but would still hurt.

"Ready when you are," I said with a grin.

The clash of our swords was loud but Drake took it easy on me while I warmed up. Having someone better than me to practice with was just what I needed. After an hour I was sweating and winded.

"Was this garden really made for me?" I asked when we took a break. Vines and branches immediately wove in and out around me, feeding needed energy after the vigorous exercise.

"Yes. They were designed by the guttybrew because of their affinity for plants."

"Are guttybrew and wielders related?" There was no physical resemblance, but my curiosity got the better of me and I needed to ask.

The question made him chuckle.

"No. Most of their existence is spent underground. They are creatures of the earth. They worship the Roman God Vulcan," he continued. "For centuries they made their homes in tree roots. The roots nourished them. When cities of the twentieth century grew, it decimated their people and they came to the vampires for help. An agreement was reached and now they serve Blade."

He more than answered my question.

"I have a question for you," he said.

"I don't feel I'm very interesting but ask," I told him.

"The Promised, uninteresting? I think not."

"Honestly, you have the wrong person. I'll admit my father had power as did my mother, but not to the degree you are looking for. Now, ask your question before I change my mind." I wouldn't but it made me uncomfortable to talk about the prophecy.

"Why did you choose to hide within your US military?"

"That's a simple answer," I told him. "I was blind with grief over my father's death and stumbled into the camp by mistake. I'm unsure why I was allowed to stay and I would have gone to a smaller human town if I were asked to leave. It worked out in my favor so I remained."

He nodded.

"Are you willing to be defeated again or are you still resting?" he asked with a wicked grin.

"One day I will make you eat those words but it probably won't be tonight."

We stood at the same time and I attacked. We fought until my arm was trembling. No amount of plant energy would help by that point. I needed rest. It made me realize how little the hour workout in my tent each night had helped with endurance.

"I will walk you to your room," he told me.

"Good because I wouldn't be able to find it without you."

He laughed and didn't bother denying it.

I tried counting doors and turns, but Drake had taken me through a different door than I entered and different from the night before. He heard me counting and thought it hilarious. Funny how I didn't hold it against Drake. Blade, on the other hand, would look good skewered on my sword.

I stopped counting halfway and concentrated on Drake. His beauty no longer affected me in a sexual way. Thoughts of Blade made my knees weak. It was infuriating.

Chapter 24

I was awake the following morning when Hax came into the bedroom. I had questions and he wasn't getting away without answering.

"Sit down and share coffee with me. I insist," I said it with a touch of command.

"I do not drink coffee," he told me gruffly.

"Do you drink tea?" I asked.

"Herbal. Your garden provides the leaves." His tone held belligerence now.

I smiled, refusing to give in to his perpetually sour mood.

"Please have some delivered and you can drink tea while I have coffee." He gave me a hard stare, but I wasn't dissuaded or intimidated. "I have questions," I told him. "I'll go crazy if I'm not entertained."

"I delivered two boxes of books. They are in the back corner." He nodded toward the other room.

"It's a start but I also wish for stimulating company. Someone who can answer my questions."

"I am not at liberty to answer them." His tone was tight. He wasn't happy to be put on the spot.

I ignored what he said because he didn't know what the questions were.

"When was the outside garden built?" I asked.

He stared at me for a long moment. He didn't roll his eyes but maybe that was because he couldn't. I knew nothing about guttybrew but I planned to learn.

"Six years ago," he finally said.

This aligned with what Blade told me.

"You said the first night I was here that the plants were greeting me. Can you communicate with them?"

He only grunted but I left the question open and waited.

"They communicate in their own way. You would know what they thought if you stopped your jabbering and listened."

I rolled my eyes for both of us.

"Can vampires read the minds of others like you do with plants?"

His large eyes bugged out to the point I wondered if it was painful. Maybe to a female guttybrew he was attractive, but to me he looked like a troll from fairy tales. His disposition reflected the same.

"You think you can trick me." His eyes bugged out a bit farther and he shook his claws in the air. "You are wrong." He turned and stomped from the room.

I couldn't help my grin. It didn't bother me that I upset him. He was rude and I didn't need to like him. I went into the other room to eat and the boxes drew my eyes. I walked over and opened the first one. It held a selection of fiction and nonfiction. I found a book about Roman mythology and another called *On War* by Carl von Clausewitz. The fiction was all over the place from romance to thrillers. The second box held similar titles. There were fifty-two books total; I knew because I counted them. I arranged them on a shelf after moving a few plants. I asked their permission before changing their location. I didn't receive an answer, but I had a general feeling of well-being and decided if they didn't want to be moved, they would somehow make it known.

Before I ate, I wrote a letter to Coop. It was short like the other one had been. I mentioned a guest who had stayed at their establishment when I was young so they knew it was me.

After the meal, I picked up *On War* and started reading. It was an English translation and I had to reread passages so they made sense. It gave me interesting things to think about. After three chapters, I switched to a murder mystery and became engrossed. It was on the light side and exactly what I needed.

I eventually got up and showered and dressed for dinner. I was determined Blade would not have the advantage. I wouldn't allow him to kiss me or take my hand for that matter. If he didn't touch me, I could control the attraction I felt. Hopefully after tonight, I would see him as I saw Drake. Pretty to look at but no desire involved. The dream popped into my head but I squelched the memory.

I dressed in more leather. The pants were dark brown, and I added a red tank top. There was a leather vest that matched the pants. As an adult, I'd never had a wardrobe outside military attire and surprisingly, I enjoyed the selection.

To mentally prepare for dinner with Blade, I sat on the couch and asked the plants to join me. They weren't tentative in the least. Their energy flowed through me and I closed my eyes and simply enjoyed the amazing feeling.

I had no idea how much time had passed when the door opened and Hax entered. He carried a tray and placed it on the table in front of me.

"What is this?" I asked.

"Your dinner."

"I'm not having dinner with Blade?" I didn't bother hiding my shock.

"He is unavailable."

"What about sparring with Drake?" was my next question. It was said with desperation that I couldn't hide.

"He is also unavailable."

"They expect me to sit here all night?"

"I'm sure you will survive."

He left.

I had to take a deep breath to calm myself. I'd wanted to throw my dinner at the door so Hax would see how unhappy I was.

I ate anyway and saved half for a late-night snack. I read until the food settled in my stomach. I removed the jacket and vest to begin a round of warmups. I followed with a hundred push-ups and sit-ups. I went through my nightly tent routine, growing angrier when it should have relaxed me. I was a prisoner and forced to live below ground when I craved sunlight because an asshole vampire held me captive.

When I finished the exercises, I picked up my sword and mentally eviscerated Blade several times and I still wasn't happy. The picture of his bloody entrails in my mind were not nearly satisfying enough.

I longed for my friends. It didn't matter that I had no intention of returning to the military; I missed them and their good cheer. I even missed their teasing.

I was tired of my questions going unanswered and being treated like a child who couldn't handle the truth. It was bullshit.

With a mighty swing that removed a few leaves from a vine that was in the line of attack, I severed Blade's imaginary head. I put my sword down and ate the dessert because if I didn't do something positive, I would cry.

I went into the bedroom, undressed, and took a shower before crawling into bed. Sleep came slowly.

***

The only thing that saved me from insanity the following day was a visit from Doctor Macos. He took out a chessboard and pieces from a cabinet in my living area. I had never played but the doctor persevered.

"I need sunlight," I bemoaned. "I can't live this way."

The doctor stared at me for a long time and must have seen something that didn't sit well with him.

"Talk to Blade. I will speak to him too. He's been preparing for you for years, but he didn't consider that you would need fresh air during the day."

I sulked and halfheartedly moved my pieces even though it was nice to have someone to talk to.

"What would keep Blade away?" I finally asked.

The doctor's gaze was intense.

"Vampire politics," he said carefully.

"I thought Blade was the grand pooh-bah."

That got a smile from him, but then the smile turned serious.

"There are challenging situations I cannot speak of."

"Are you talking about the werewolves?"

"I cannot say."

"Is it something I should be concerned about?" I asked, refusing to let it go.

"No. Blade will give his life for yours. He is keeping you safer than anyone else could."

There was more involved but I could see his stubbornness. I moved my knight, and Macos promptly removed it with a rook and chided me for my lack of finesse.

He trounced me three games in a row.

Chapter 25

The son of a rotten fish head didn't return for five days and the doctor didn't visit again. During Blade's absence, Hax refused to answer a single question even when I screamed about releasing me from hell and threw a boot at him. He calmly picked it up and placed it against the wall making me feel like a raving lunatic which I was quickly becoming.

I also didn't have nightly dreams. Not that I wanted dreams of Blade but I tried to conjure my second dream man and that had been a very frustrating bust. Blade's naked body kept filling my mind and chasing thoughts of dream man two away. I finally groaned in surrender and fell asleep. Each. Damn. Night.

The only things that saved me were the books, my sword, and a bloodthirsty imagination about what I would do to Blade when he returned. When Hax told me to dress for dinner and I would be joining Blade, I almost refused. The thought of fresh air and the opportunity to use my sword on Blade's throat changed my mind.

I refused to wear the leather garments from the closet though they may have been useful at repelling blood. I wore jeans and a large baggie T-shirt that I'd asked Hax to procure for me so I had something loose to sleep in. The shirt swamped me and looked ridiculous as actual clothing.

Hax didn't blink over my slovenly attire. He led me through the twists and turns to the same room where I'd had the private dinner with Blade before he left. I swear we went an entirely different route which drove my anger up another notch.

My plan for this unhappy reunion was set in my mind.

Blade greeted me with a nod of his head. He wore an impeccable dark suit, but his skin was deathly pale and he appeared thinner. It stopped me in my tracks for a moment, but then I decided it was my imagination. He didn't appear to be in a good mood if the furrow between his brows and the hard line of his jaw were anything to go by.

Good. I wasn't in a good mood either.

He walked over to the side table and poured wine for me. He came closer and held it out. I drank the entire glass in one chug and wiped my mouth with the back of my hand when finished. Tequila was preferable, but I did get a slight rush. I held it out and he refilled it.

"Hax told me you are unhappy." His voice was stiff, his face giving away nothing.

Unhappy was an understatement.

"I'm here in the hope I may walk around the garden tonight after being left in the underground rooms for five days." I stared into his eyes. I knew mine were burning with fury, but his seemed cloudy, unlike the eyes I remembered. "Not," I said with heat, "for the company."

"I see," he said with that blasted regal nod of his. He glanced briefly at the door and turned back to me. "Hax will bring in your dinner. I will have Drake take you to the garden when you have finished your meal."

Fire entered his eyes and his voice held something I wasn't sure of. It could have been anger or even pity. I turned my back and walked over to the table and sat while I waited for dinner. I didn't look at him again. The door softly opened and closed. A few minutes later, Hax entered with my meal.

I'd wondered off and on if Hax liked me or not. With his large teeth and overly big jaws, I hadn't been able to tell. Now I could. His grunt was gone and short growls escaped his mouth as he set the tray on the table. Without a word, he walked out, slammed the door, and I was alone.

Drake told me Blade was the only person Hax liked which meant my plan to be a jerk to Blade worked. Unfortunately, I felt guilty which only made me angrier.

Half my food was gone when Drake entered.

He wore jeans like mine, though his shirt fit his muscled chest snugly. He was good eye candy, but I wasn't in the mood.

"I'm impressed," he said. "You've managed to anger Blade." His smile was missing. Drake was as mad as Hax that the great and powerful Blade was in a snit.

"Anger doesn't cover the level of loathing I feel for him at the moment," I told Drake with a snarl I had trouble holding in. "You are not on my good list either. I'm putting up with you because I want to visit the garden." I took a bite of food and promptly ignored him.

Drake paced. He didn't do it like a normal person. He was deadly quiet. If I hadn't seen his legs in my side vision, I wouldn't know he was moving. I'd noticed the vampire stealth ability in the garden.

After eating, I wondered if Drake would answer questions about vampires in general. I knew about the sun, but little else. Maybe tomorrow I would broach the subject. Tonight, I was keeping my anger pulled tightly around me because when it came down to it, I was a prisoner without options. That more than anything infuriated me.

I finished the remainder of my meal and stood.

"I'm ready whenever you are," I told Drake.

He stopped the silent pacing and turned toward the door, his irritation written clearly in his expression. He stomped in angry strides and I followed. He and Blade were not responding the way I had envisioned. I expected them to apologize repeatedly while I refused to speak to them with self-righteous indignation. One night and I'd be over it. I had never been one to hold on to my temper for long. My father had left me alone when he angered me. I always forgave him.

Walking into the greenery immediately calmed my temper. I took a few deep breaths and allowed the plant energy to surround me. Vines moved onto the path where I stood and began winding up my legs; their soft touch another soothing influence.

"Neither I nor Blade expected to be gone more than a day," Drake said softly from behind me. "Blade arranged Macos's visit because he worried about you. Macos was needed with us and that is the reason he didn't return to spend time with you after the first night."

I continued breathing and it seemed as if my harsh feelings were absorbed into the plants that touched and comforted me. I slowly turned and faced Drake.

"Why was Macos needed?" I asked.

"That is something you will need to ask Blade."

I threw up my hands and the vines immediately released me. I marched away from Drake, muttering under my breath.

"Blade was injured," he said from behind me.

My heart dropped into my stomach and my insides twisted.

"What happened?"

"You should discuss this with him."

"You've given me this much information, please continue." Why was my heart beating faster? I also had an overwhelming need to see Blade. Anger was the last thing I was thinking about.

"We discovered who betrayed us the night I met with you. There was more than one traitor and we were attacked. Blade was struck through the chest with a wooden spear. He couldn't be moved for two days."

"But he was walking this evening," I said in disbelief.

"Macos told him he needed a few more days of rest so he could fully heal, but he insisted on having dinner with you."

"Of all the ridiculous notions. Why would I matter enough when he is injured?"

"You are The Promised. You matter more than anything."

I wanted to scream. I couldn't stand not knowing what the heck that meant and I knew he wouldn't tell me.

"I wish to see Blade," I stated firmly.

"No. You need to be outside and he understands. It will only make him feel worse if you miss your garden time because of him." He shook his head. 'He's also having control issues right now."

"What does that mean?" I demanded. "Do not give me some bullshit that you can't tell me."

"Animal blood and moonlight do not provide enough energy for healing. We must feed from humans for that. He will not. I cannot discuss why Blade has refused. Even before the spear strike, he wasn't nourishing himself properly or it wouldn't have happened." He seemed to contemplate what he'd just said and added, "Blade is slower than usual."

"How long has he refrained from human blood?" I asked.

Drake's eyes sparked with the fire I'd been waiting for.

"Since you came here," he said sternly. "He's refused to feed from a single human."

"And this is my fault, though no one will explain how it's my fault."

He relented slightly and gave a frustrated sigh.

"No, it is not your fault. It rests strictly on Blade's shoulders. He won't listen to me but that is the normal way of things."

Did I hear resentment in his words? If so, it was very slight. I couldn't help wondering what Drake and Blade's connection was. Besides the obvious vampire one.

"Do you think there is something I could do to change his mind?"

He gave a brief smile. "Come into your powers and share blood with him."

Chapter 26

D rake was insane.

I would never share my blood with a vampire. I couldn't see that the prophecy would expect me to. As far as my powers went, no one would give me enough information.

The thought that Blade was gravely injured and wouldn't drink human blood bothered me. The thought of him hurt and alone tonight completely dissolved my remaining anger. I would explain to Blade that my temper passed quickly and I was over it. After that was accomplished, I would convince him to drink human blood.

The thought of Blade sucking on some woman's neck made me twitch to use my sword, but that was a ridiculous thought. To stay healthy Blade needed human blood that I was unwilling to provide. I did not want him ill because of me even though he was a vampire.

"I need to spar," I told Drake.

"I thought you would never ask." His smile was less than friendly.

He'd brought the blunted swords and he went harder on me than he had before. It felt good, though the strikes that landed would leave bruises. Drake was relentless and came at me again as soon as I recovered from each round which was a step away from methodical torture. I could barely stay upright when he called a halt to our swordplay. Marching back to my room was nearly impossible, but I made it without whining or asking my snarly teacher for help. Drake gave me an exasperated look before he left me alone in the suite.

I half fell against the door to keep myself upright. It took a few minutes before I decided I could make it to the shower. The bed had never looked so good when I was finally able to crawl beneath the covers.

***

I was sore the next morning but it was a bearable pain. Hax brought my food and was turning to leave when I spoke.

"Please inform Blade that I would like to join him for dinner this evening if he is available."

Hax grunted.

"Also explain that my disposition has improved."

He left and I realized I forgot to ask if there had been a reply from Mika and Coop.

After my food settled, I stretched for an hour to relieve the last of the muscle pain caused by the punishment Drake had delivered. I took another shower and then tried to occupy myself and not give into melancholy from my isolation. I didn't know if Blade had accepted my invitation and it worked on my nerves. When it grew late in the day, I prepared for the dinner I was unsure would take place.

Hax entered the suite after the sun went down. He looked closely at what I was wearing. My pants and jacket were black leather with a purple tank top beneath.

Hax opened the door and waited for me to follow. We climbed the stairs, which was not the usual way to our dinners. A few minutes later, I recognized the courtyard I'd first entered when I came to the house. Blade was standing beside a black Humvee. I peered through the vehicle's window and Drake sat in the driver's seat. We were traveling to some unknown destination. My heart rate doubled.

Blade was dressed in his normal formal wear. His eyes shone with fire when he looked at me and gave a nod. I was relieved to see he appeared healthier. He opened the back door.

"Will I be returning?" I asked.

"Yes. I thought you could use a night out."

If this was his apology, I would take it. I slid into the seat, feeling the discomfort of my sword under my jacket.

"What about my sword?" I asked.

"Keep it. Hopefully you won't need it."

I couldn't decide if that sounded good or bad. The thought of fighting gave me a quick thrill until Blade slid in beside me. The thrill turned into full on bliss. His scent filled the interior and swamped my senses. Blade's skin had more color and I couldn't help wondering if he'd given in and fed on human blood. A spark of energy ran through me which proceeded the stab of jealousy. I slammed it down. How ridiculous could I be?

Blade took my hand and our energy combined. It was similar to what the plants did for me. He looked down at our hands and gripped mine a bit tighter.

"Dare I ask where we are going?"

"I wouldn't if I were you," Drake said from the front seat. "Better to see it and make up your mind."

That didn't sound promising. I sat back, my hand locked in Blade's, and watched lights fly by as Drake picked up speed. Cars were rare in the human sector of the city. It was easier to get around on horseback or by motorcycle.

I'm unsure how far we traveled when the sparce lights in the night changed to a blinking choreography of bright color. I had never seen the like. Mule, I think it was, told me about the city of Las Vegas that was destroyed in the war. This area reminded me of his description, though on a much smaller scale. People walked freely up and down the sidewalk. They looked human and they appeared to be having a good time.

Drake pulled up in front of a dazzling huge building, the largest in the area. A man opened our door.

"My liege," he said with a slight bow.

Blade stepped from the Humvee and placed his hand inside the vehicle for me. He kept my hand after I stood and led me through the double doors that parted for us. I craned my neck because the women dancing behind the glass out front was something I'd never seen. They were scantily clad and each danced within a box.

Music played inside and people were everywhere. Did the military know about this? They had to. It would be hard to keep it a secret.

People filled the dance floor to my right, their bodies grinding to the music. Large comfortable booths held more people on the left. A hundred feet to the front was a large bar. More scantily clad women walked around with drink trays. Blade continued walking and directed me to a staircase. I noticed people dipping their heads in acknowledgment as he passed. I felt a slight tug on my hair and glanced over my shoulder. Drake gave me a large grin, fangs and all.

I also noticed men and women with collars on their throats. Vampires were everywhere because I saw flashes of fire in their eyes as they admired those with the collars. Humans?

We went up the stairs to a dark area where the music was muted. Two guttybrew stood on either side of the staircase. They wore armor and had huge axes affixed to their belts. They gave no sign that they saw Blade as he led me past them to a large seating area that overlooked the entire inner building. The leather couch and chairs were on a raised platform with a glass floor in the center.

Blade ushered me across the glass and placed his hand out, so I sat on the couch which had a small glass table in front of it. Drake took a chair and Blade sat beside me. The corners of the room were too dark to see into them but it didn't take away from the opulence.

"What is this place?" I asked after peering around.

"My nightclub," Blade said. "Before the war it was used to attract humans. Now they come freely."

I watched down below as a tall man caressed a woman's arm and she smiled. She wore a collar; he did not.

"Do the humans all wear collars?" I asked curiously.

"Only if they are available for feeding," he said with a small grin playing on his lips.

"They have a choice?"

"Yes."

A tray was placed on a low table. It held two wineglasses and a shot glass beside a bottle of tequila. Blade poured from the bottle and handed the shot glass to me. He lifted his blood wine and smiled. Drake lifted his and we drank. I finished mine in one swallow.

The military's tequila had nothing on this stuff. Blade poured me another.

"Are you trying to get me drunk?" I asked cheekily, happy that I was out of my darned suite.

"Only if you wish to be. You'll be the one to pay for the aftereffects in the morning."

"Can vampires get drunk?"

He gave me a careful look before he answered.

"If a human is inebriated, it has a similar effect on a vampire when blood is shared."

Interesting. I swallowed the liquid in my glass, enjoying the slight buzz that slid through me.

There was a scuffling noise from the back of the room that was shadowed. I turned sharply to see what it was. Men were escorting two people in our direction. They both struggled within their grasps. I heard a grunt and then another. They stepped into the light cast from the floor below.

"Tara?" Mika said.

Chapter 27

Coop was being dragged next to Mika, vampires gripping both their arms. I jumped from my seat and all but vaulted over the low table. They were released. Mika elbowed one of her captors for good measure, gave him a dirty look then threw her arms around me after I reached her.

"You're okay," she said and kissed me on both cheeks when I pulled back slightly. "They said you were but we didn't believe them." She gave the guards a side eye full of wrath even though they ignored her.

I turned my attention to Coop. He was still angry but I also noticed his relief when he looked at me. I stepped away from Mika and circled my arms around his neck, went on my toes, and kissed his cheek.

He held onto me for a few extra seconds.

"They came for us last night," he whispered into my hair. "We've been kept in a room in the back until now."

I turned and glared at Blade who had approached us.

"I told Drake to keep them in comfort," he said to me. "Turn your angry eyes on him."

"What about the animals?" I turned back to my friends.

"Two men stayed behind to care for them. They said they would sleep in the barn until we returned. I'm unsure if they were human or vampire." He said the word vampire like it tasted nasty on his tongue. His angry eyes snapped to Blade then back to me.

"Where's your sword?" I asked Coop. I'd never known him to be without it.

"The vampire." He glared at Drake this time. "He took it from me when I tried to decapitate him."

I looked at Drake and placed a good amount of force in my words.

"Coop must have his sword," I said.

"For your sake and your sake only, I didn't want to hurt him," Drake said. "He can have the sword back if he plays nice. One of our men is missing a hand. I prefer to keep mine."

Coop's glare didn't waver.

Mika grabbed his forearm.

"Tara is okay. They didn't lie and they didn't harm us, though we gave them reason to."

His eyes flashed to her, then me.

"I won't kill anyone who doesn't need killing," Coop ground out, his fists balled at his sides ready to fly.

Blade threw his head back and laughed. When he stopped, I made introductions.

Coop looked like he wanted to kill again.

"The werewolves attacked me at the meeting with the gang. I have been Blade's guest since that night." I'd decided not to tell them that I was held against my will. I had to keep Mika and Coop out of danger. "Drake was the one who saved me from the wolves." I allowed that to settle in and then smiled. "I didn't tell you this in my notes because I didn't want you to worry."

Blade placed his hand out. After a few seconds, Coop took it.

"You are my guests," Blade said. "Dinner will be delivered in a few minutes." He gave me a quick glance, then turned back to Coop. "My men will see you home when you are ready to return. I promise your house and animals are in good hands."

He was letting me know that Coop and Mika would not be kept prisoners. I released the air from my lungs. I didn't want them caught up in the prophecy. I worried enough about them.

I decided to enjoy the evening and make sure Mika and Coop knew I was okay.

Dinner arrived and we ate while Drake and Blade sipped blood wine. I could tell Coop remained angry, but he also did his best not to show it. I caught Mika and Drake talking a few times and she appeared to enjoy his company. It all seemed so strange and I couldn't help wondering if this would have been our world if humans had accepted vampires and werewolves from the beginning.

My eyes wandered to the dance floor several times. The people were having fun. There was a darkened section with a door beyond the dancing area. When a vampire escorted a human there, the human walked out without their collar a short while later.

The humans didn't appear to be afraid. I wondered if it had been this way six years ago and if my father had ever seen this side of the new world. He was always worried about the vampires and werewolves finding me. I had to promise to stay away from them if anything happened to him. The rangers never mentioned that a place like this existed.

Everything confused me. I wished my father were still around so I could talk to him.

"Would you like to dance?" Blade whispered in my ear, causing me to jump.

I hadn't seen him stand. Coop gave Blade a hard glare which the vampire ignored.

I shook my head and glanced back at the area filled with people writhing to the music. The most fun I'd had in my life was at the canteen when I drank my memories away.

"I've never danced," I said. I wasn't embarrassed; dancing was not part of the military life. Even music was rare.

He reached for my hand.

"I will show you. You dance beautifully when you fight with a sword; this will be easy."

He'd watched me fight against Drake. That surprised me.

"Go," said Mika. "He's right. You move beautifully with your sword. Have some fun. No one cares if they can dance or not."

Coop glared at her but Mika ignored him. Even with Coop on my side, I was outnumbered because Drake had a small smile playing on his lips and I wouldn't receive help from him.

"If I land on my face and embarrass you, it's your fault," I told Blade and took his hand. The warm buzz of energy flowed between us. Was it stronger? Maybe the spike was because I was nervous about the dance floor.

He guided me down the stairs and once we hit the crowded main floor, people parted for him. The music stopped. He walked me to the center of the dancing area and I felt extremely uncomfortable. Everyone watched with varying degrees of condemnation and some even in shock. Blade nodded to someone and a slow, sultry beat commenced.

He lifted my hand and pulled my body close as he began to move. I was stiff in his arms and felt uncomfortable because no one else was dancing.

"I've watched you spar with Drake," he whispered gruffly. "Your friend is right; you move beautifully. Close your eyes and think of all the terrible things you want to do to me with your sword while you feel the rhythm of the music."

"You watch us fight?"

"I watch."

There was so much inflection in the two simple words. He had to have heard me tell Drake I wanted to kill him, but he didn't comment on it. I blocked out the people standing around us and simply absorbed the feeling of Blade's arms around me and our feet moving in unison. It was like sword fighting and Blade led me flawlessly during the battle.

I noticed movement to my right and saw Coop and Mika dancing. I didn't know either of them could. My father kept me sheltered, and then the military did the same. I couldn't imagine Leo, Shep, or Mule on a dance floor.

With the addition of Coop and Mika, others joined. I leaned in a little closer and Blade caressed my back as we moved. I hadn't been sure I liked him bringing my friends into the mess I'd found myself in but now I was glad. As long as he kept his word and took them home, what could it hurt?

Blade did not move like he was injured and I was relieved. The thought of him feeding from a human and the jealousy it caused were ridiculous and I had no right to feel that way. I didn't want him suffering even though he was a vampire.

The music stopped and a faster song started up. Blade turned me toward Drake who gave me a small bow and took over. He grabbed my hips and moved me to the beat. Blade disappeared. Would I ever understand him? For some unknown reason, we were forced together and he didn't like it but he hadn't treated me badly besides refusing my desire to leave. I was sure there were far worse ways to be held captive.

"Stop thinking of him and enjoy the dance," Drake said. His intimate hold on my hips should bother me but it didn't. His smile was devilish. I gave in to the beat and allowed the vampire to guide me into the sensual rhythm.

When the song ended, Drake led me up the stairs where Blade waited. Mika and Coop came with us.

"Is there a ladies' room?" asked Mika.

"I will escort you," said Drake.

"No, Tara can come with me if you will point the direction." Her voice left no room for argument.

The area we were in had a bathroom at the back in the darkest corner, though the bathroom itself had bright lighting.

"Are you okay?" Mika asked and grabbed my hand as soon as the door closed behind us.

Everyone knew she was checking on me.

"I am," I reassured her. "Have you and Coop been safe?"

She searched my eyes and saw the truth in them. She released me and seemed to relax.

"Someone has been watching us and following Coop when he goes out on jobs," she said. "Was it at Blade's command?"

"He hasn't mentioned it, but I would say yes. He knows how important you are to me." It was strange because I could see Blade doing this even though I said not to.

"We've been very worried about you," Mika said. "It would have been worse if we'd known you were with the vampires. Seeing you here changes everything."

"I had no idea this existed." I waved a hand at our surroundings. Questions burned in my mind. "Did you?"

Chapter 28

"I rarely leave the house," Mika said. "Coop mentioned changes and the opening of establishments that cater to humans and vampires. He avoids vampire territory whenever he can and works strictly for humans."

"How long has it been this way?"

"It began after your father's death," she said. "Your father refused to interact with the vampires or werewolves while he was alive. He blamed them for the death of your mother. That's where Coop got his stubbornness. He admired your father greatly. It bothered me to think of vampires feeding off humans, but I've watched them tonight and it's not how I thought it was."

"I've watched them too. This wasn't what I was led to believe even in the military. Things would have been better if humans had simply accepted instead of destroying."

"That is a guaranteed affirmative," she answered. "I'm unsure how the smaller communities work outside the city but our problems were more than cut in half when they pushed the military out."

"You've had no run-ins with the wolves?"

"Not that Coop has talked about. They keep to themselves. I've heard they're extremely violent, but I heard the same about the vampires."

"I met Drake at the gang compound and he was cordial. Then the wolves attacked us. They didn't want to hurt me, just kidnap me. I feel like my entire life has been a lie."

She brought me in close for a short hug.

"No." she said, dropping her arms. "Your father wanted to keep you safe. When you were a baby, things were very different and extremely violent. That I do know. I do not blame him for keeping you away from the werewolves and vampires. Many humans were killed in the beginning of the war. They've had to adapt and they've become more brutal." She gave me a gentle smile. "Trust what your father told you but trust your heart too. Things are changing for the better."

I took a slow deep breath and felt calmer. I loved my father but I'd had so many conflicting thoughts.

"We need to return," she told me. "I know I didn't fool anyone, but Coop must have your assurance that you are okay. He won't leave without it. We will return home in the morning, but we will accept the invitation to return if it is extended."

"I love you," I said. "Assure Coop that I am well and learning about my powers." It was almost the truth. I was a supernatural and I was realizing that my place might never be among humans. It didn't mean Coop and Mika weren't my family.

We went back to the table and Blade poured me another shot of tequila. I was feeling no pain when it was time to go. I hugged my friends tightly and whispered in Coop's ear.

"If Blade says your home is safe, you can trust him."

He made a gruff noise that didn't tell me if he believed me or not.

Blade led me outside to the waiting vehicle. Parting with my friends caused deep emotion and I was fighting back tears.

"Thank you," I said when I was sure I could talk without a quiver in my voice.

His eyes met mine and I saw sincerity when he spoke.

"I had planned to only leave for one night and did not consider that you would be kept to your rooms and how hard it would be." He smiled. "Drake made it known it was unfair to you."

"Drake made it known you were injured and leaving for so long was not your fault."

"Traitor," Drake said from the driver's seat but there was humor in his voice.

Blade gave a slight growl but I didn't think the other vampire was in trouble.

"I hated being stuck in my rooms," I said honestly. "You should have told me to expect your absence." He owed me nothing but I wanted him to talk to me. I wouldn't like being left alone again but having the information would help me cope.

There was a heavy thump on the roof of the car. I looked up, then was blinded by the lights of a vehicle heading straight for us.

Drake swerved but it didn't stop the heavy jolt when the vehicles collided. It happened so fast, I was confused. The fire in Blade's eyes said he knew exactly what was happening.

"Use your sword if they attack," he said. The door flew open and he jumped out. "Stay with her," Blade ordered.

Another vehicle rammed us from behind, making it impossible for the Humvee to move. Drake cussed up a storm.

"The wolves have good hearing so be careful with what you say," he told me.

A man jumped from the roof of the Humvee, twisted in midflight, and landed facing the Humvee's headlights. There was no shirt covering his large muscular chest. He wore jeans on his lower half and his feet were bare. His straight brown hair stopped at his shoulders.

Oh damn. This was my other dream man.

Where Blade's jaw carried perfection in every classical curve, dream man two's face was powerful angles of steel. The only real way to describe him was savage. Shivers of awareness ran down my spine. His entire body screamed power. I was caught in its current.

Blade stepped between him and the Humvee. Thankfully the trance that held me captive dissipated and I could breathe again.

"Your sword should be in your hand," Drake whispered so softly I almost missed it.

I quickly removed my jacket and pulled the sword in the small confines of the vehicle that had seemed roomy a few minutes ago but was too tight a space to wield a sword.

I could just see the wolf in front of me. His eyes glowed amber, very different from the fire I knew was in Blade's. I noticed Drake's burning gaze when he turned quickly to check on me.

Blade and the man spoke but I could barely hear them. I rolled the window down an inch even though I received a killing glance from Drake.

"I am taking her with me," said the wolf.

"No, Rollin," Blade ground out. "That was not our bargain. She has not come into her power. You are in my territory and I will kill you if you do not leave now."

"You will try." There was so much threat in the words.

Huge man-wolves crept from the darkened area of the night and surrounded us.

Blade laughed. "You should have brought a bigger army," he said.

I felt a powerful burst of magic and dream man number two turned into a monster. He launched himself at Blade as did several other wolves.

"We need to get outside," said Drake.

This was a very similar situation to the night I'd met him. I counted four wolves staring into the Humvee. One kept his human form and I recognized him as Alaric who had attacked the first night. He smiled at me with gleaming white teeth.

"How do we fight them?" I asked. This was life or death, and it didn't matter that I doubted we would win; it was time for battle and I wouldn't shy from it.

"Back-to-back," he said. "Climb up here and I will get out first. To kill them you must sever their heads. Half-severed will slow them and they must shift to heal which can take hours if the wound is deep. Watch out for claws but especially teeth."

I tossed my sword into the front seat and awkwardly scrambled after it. Drake had his sword out. I also had my knives but after the claws and teeth warning, I knew it would be impossible to avoid injury with the shorter blades.

"They won't want to hurt you so use it to your advantage," Drake said.

There was no time to ask him questions about his statement because he threw open the door and jumped out with me right behind him. I turned my back to his and a wolf rounded the vehicle. The odds were not in our favor but I wouldn't go down without a fight. Drake engaged a wolf in front of him. The one I faced came in slowly. I swung my sword and he jumped back. Drake moved away from the vehicle and I did the same. If one wolf could jump on it, one or more of them could come at us from above.

We stepped in tandem, our hours of night sparring paying off. We gradually moved to the side until we were far enough away from the Humvee. Snarls and growls filled the air. One of the wolves Blade fought, shrieked. It was so loud, it hurt my ears. What was Blade fighting them with? I wondered.

Two wolves were now facing me. The other three had to be attacking Drake. I advanced on my two and Drake stayed at my back with a foot separating us. I could feel his energy.

A claw almost sliced my face. Power shot down my arms and my blade lit up.

"You lie," Rollin yelled at Blade. "She has come into her power." He'd seen me fire my sword.

I ignored him.

My blade sliced into the chest of one wolf and he jumped back. I swung with all my might and the blade passed through the neck of the other one. It happened so fast; I hadn't noticed the first one regain his feet. He launched himself at me and I fell against Drake. He was busy defending on his side and stepped forward as I went to the ground. The large wolf was on me before I could bring up my sword. Huge jaws bit into my shoulder and his head gave a frenzied shake.

I screamed.

Chapter 29

A scorching burn traveled through my upper body, originating where the teeth clamped on my shoulder. The pain intensified and cut off my scream. His eyes, inches from mine, held death.

The wolf on top of me went flying. I thought it was Drake or Blade but I was wrong. Rollin stood over me. Like Alaric had done, he turned and attacked the wolf he'd saved me from. Blade lifted me in his arms while Drake guarded us.

"You would kill her," Blade snarled after Rollin had beheaded the other wolf with his bare hands. "This stops now. You will only cause more damage. Her power is growing but it has not fully come in. Return to your territory or I will kill you."

The look on Rollin's face was ferocious. His eyes turned downward and met mine. His expression held something I hadn't expected.

Possessiveness.

"Mine," he said in a gruff voice that sounded more animal than human.

I blacked out. When I opened my eyes, the Humvee was traveling at breakneck speed. Metal clanged against the asphalt. My head was on Blade's lap.

"Hold still," he said. "The wound is deep and the wolf's saliva is toxic. Macos will help you."

"Is it healing?" asked Drake from the driver's seat.

"Slowly. She's losing too much blood."

"If they don't want to harm me, why do they keep attacking?" I asked groggily. My shirt was wet and I smelled blood. It had to be mine. Was that why I passed out?

"The damn wolves lose control too easily. Now quiet. Conserve your energy for healing. We'll be home in fifteen minutes."

Home. It had a nice ring. I craved the plants in the garden. The Humvee came to a stop and Blade lifted me from the car. I noticed the back corner of the vehicle was half hanging off and that accounted for the scraping noise that followed us during the trip. Blade quickly carried me through the front door.

"The garden," I managed to whisper.

"She's right," said Macos. He stood in the entryway. "Get her to the garden and hurry."

Like Drake had done when carrying me, Blade ran so fast the walls were a blur. I closed my eyes because it made me dizzier than I already was. When he stopped, I smelled the plants and felt their energy reaching toward me.

"Put her here," Macos said.

My back hit soft grass, but I couldn't help the groan that came from my throat. I managed to open my eyes. Blade was covered in blood.

"Are you hurt?" I whispered.

"No," he said harshly, though I knew his anger wasn't at me. "She's lost too much blood," he told Macos.

Vines circled my legs and wrists, moving up my arms. Energy swelled inside me. It made the pain worse.

"Drink this," said Macos. It was cool water and tasted so good.

Black edges filled the outskirts of my vision. The pain lessened.

"She's lost too much blood," Blade repeated.

"You know what must be done." It sounded like Drake. "I will do it."

A roar which reminded me of one of the wolves filled the night. I cried out. Then my body moved. I opened my eyes and Blade was above me again. I'd never seen the flames in his eyes like this. I would swear if I reached my hand up, my flesh would burn. I smiled at him as the black edges of my vision grew.

"Do it," said Macos. "She hasn't much time."

"Open your lips," Blade said with power behind the words, making it impossible to deny him.

I parted my lips and something ran into my mouth. It was so strange. It tasted wild with a jolting intensity that was unnerving. It held more power than the plants. Energy traveled through my body. I reached up and grabbed warm flesh bringing it to my mouth.

"The wound is closing," said Blade. "Cut the other one."

That too was strange. It didn't feel as if my wound was closing. The warm skin was pulled from my grasp, but it was replaced by faster flowing liquid. I lapped and sucked at it.

"Bite," said Blade. "Take as much as you can."

Then it registered. I was drinking Blade's blood. I tried to push him away but he didn't budge. His blood was impossible to resist. The plants hadn't released me and their energy flowed with greater power.

"No more," I finally said and turned my head aside.

"Allow the plants to heal her from here," said Macos.

Blade laid me back against the grass. The vines twisted and started covering every part of me. They didn't squeeze and I could easily breathe. My mind filled with their scent, clean and pure. My vision blurred and the sounds around me became muted.

"What else can we do?"

I knew it was Blade but I could no longer see him.

"We wait."

I lost my sense of time. A steady current of energy flowed inside me. My shoulder stopped burning and became numb. The plants pulsed and my heart synced with their rhythm. I couldn't remember ever feeling such peace.

***

I woke in my bed, sunlight streaming into the room. Hax sat in a chair a few feet from me. When he saw I was awake, he strode from the room and returned with a tray. It held a glass of water that I downed quickly. Next, he handed me a cup of coffee which felt good in my cold hands.

"How are Drake and Blade?" I asked. "Were they hurt?"

He stared at me in his growly way and I didn't think he would answer.

"Blade is recovering. He should have allowed Drake to heal you."

"Thank you," I said without adding how hard being civil must have been for him.

I took the first sip of the coffee and leaned back against the pillows. I had no pain but I remembered the scorching burn from the attack.

"Will I be able to use my arm again?"

"It has healed."

I circled the joint and it felt as it normally did.

"I drank vampire blood, didn't I?" The thought turned my stomach slightly.

"It healed you. Be thankful Blade was willing to share. As soon as the sun goes down, the doctor will check on you."

"Will I be having dinner with Blade?"

"I will tell him you have requested it," he said with a nod.

I hadn't made a request but I did want to have dinner with Blade so I let it go.

"What time is it?" I asked.

"Four. You have been in bed for two days."

"What?" I all but shrieked.

The guttybrew's smile included a large display of teeth but I knew it for what it was.

"How could I have slept for two days?" I threw the covers back. I was naked and snatched them close to me again.

"Where are my clothes?" I demanded.

I received another smile and possibly a snicker. What happened to the Hax who hated me? This guttybrew had to be an imposter.

"I will leave you to gather them yourself. Food will be delivered to the outer room in thirty minutes. Take a shower first; I believe it is needed."

Great. He was telling me I smelled. He left the room and I jumped up, gathered my clothing, and headed for the bathroom. My shoulder didn't have a single mark nor did it hurt.

I entered the shower and washed my hair, then my body. Energy pulsed from my fingers which seemed strange. It was more than usual. Maybe the plants were responsible or the vampire blood. I wasn't quite sure how I felt about the blood. I had so many small pieces of information but couldn't seem to put it all together. Being in the dark was getting old.

I finished quickly, mainly due to hunger, dressed in jeans and a T-shirt, and went into the main room. Hax entered with a tray piled high with an assortment of raw and cooked vegetables. My stomach rumbled.

"I'll need a light dinner after this meal," I said before I shoveled the first bite into my mouth followed by another and another. "It's good."

Hax gave his usual grunt so I knew whoever stole his body had returned it. I looked up after clearing half the plate and he was gone. After finishing the rest of the meal, I leaned back into the couch cushions and gave my body time to absorb the food. A few minutes later, I uncovered a small dish that had a hefty slice of chocolate cake. I ate it. By the time I finished, I was completely stuffed.

I'd become accustomed to the energy tingles in my hands. Most of the time I barely noticed. Something was different when the tingles started in my fingers and traveled up my arms.

Something was wrong.

Chapter 30

I had just recovered from the bite of a werewolf. This burn was completely different. It wasn't pleasant but I wouldn't call it painful. I sucked in a sharp breath and tried to stand. My legs wabbled, gave out, and my butt hit the cushion.

Strangely enough, the feeling was mixed with desire. My breasts yearned for touch. Between my thighs I felt a burning need. I wanted Blade here. I wanted him feeding these feelings with his hands and his body. I wanted!

Had his blood done this to me?

The room glowed around me and I glanced at my arms. The bright yellow and gold was coming from my skin. It reminded me of the fire in Blade's eyes. This fire was everywhere, eating me from the inside out, making me want the vampire I'd dreamed about for so long.

The plants attacked me. This time their hold wasn't loose; they were tight to the point of cutting off my circulation. The need for Blade died and a craving for sunlight replaced it. The vines took me to the floor. I tried to disentangle myself but I couldn't. The energy flowing through my body wasn't subtle; it was as powerful as a tsunami. The entire room glowed from the energy pouring out of me.

I groaned. It felt as if the plants were trying to kill me. An arc of energy slammed into my head and pulsed into my eyes. I cried out.

What color were my eyes right now? My thoughts were all over the place and almost incoherent. A vine wrapped around my throat and I choked for a moment before it loosened. It weaved beneath my shirt, touching my skin, leaving a cool trail of power.

There was no sunlight in the room, but I felt it. It warmed my skin where the vines cooled it. A vivid rainbow of colors appeared before my eyes. They swirled around the room and contained a fine mist that dampened my skin. The colors changed and purple replaced blue, turquoise replaced green. It was beautiful. I was dazed by everything happening but also afraid of what was building inside me.

The door burst open and I turned my head. It wasn't just Hax; there were more guttybrew than I could count. I didn't want them to see me this way. Hax bent down next to me and reached out his clawed hand. He didn't touch me; he touched one of the vines. The other guttybrew moved around me and found vines to hold on to.

Their power mixed with the plants and with mine. It was too much and I screamed, my voice now hoarse. The guttybrew began to sing a melody in an unknown language.

How many of them were there?

I closed my eyes against a burst of power that lifted my body partially from the floor. Was I floating? No, Hax had my head and upper body situated on his lap when I opened my eyes.

"Do not be frightened," he whispered.

The energy began centering in my chest. My heart was going to burst. My pulse was throbbing inside my head.

"Tara," Blade yelled.

"Stay back," said Hax. "You cannot touch her. She must contain the power."

"What happens if she can't contain the fucking power?" Blade yelled at him.

"Then she is not The Promised."

"Step back, Blade." It was Drake.

I heard a scuffle and tried to open my eyes but it was impossible. The pressure built and I didn't think I would survive.

"The sunlight will harm you both," yelled Hax. "Get out of here."

Was I outside? I tried to breathe in the scents but I couldn't get my lungs to work. I didn't think I was breathing any longer. I would be dead soon and that was okay. I couldn't handle what was happening. I was not The Promised and I'd always known it.

The song grew in volume. The light was so bright I could see it even with my eyes closed. I'd been in the gang's hangout when the explosion happened but this was different. When I burst, my body was torn into a million particles. I was no longer in the room; I could see the garden surrounding me. I could feel the sunlight on my skin and smell the sweet flowers and pungent herbs. I was a part of the plants and they were a part of me. The incredible song of the guttybrew filled my ears. Slowly, it calmed me.

The light was not something I expected in death. I'd always thought the long sleep would be darkness, but I was being rocked on a wave of color.

"Tara?"

I heard my name but I didn't want to answer. I wanted to float on the tide of death and see my father and the mother I never knew.

"Tara."

It was stronger, pulling me back to earth.

"Go away," I whispered. My throat was parched; I needed water. Why would I need water if I were dead? I suddenly realized vines were still wrapped around me but they were slowly detaching themselves. "I am dead. Leave me alone," I insisted.

"You are not dead. Open your eyes."

I recognized the laughter in the voice. I managed to peel my eyelids apart. I wasn't outside. I was lying beside the couch. I was in Blade's lap and I was unsure if Hax holding me happened or if it was a dream. Then I saw Hax's face over Blade's shoulder. And the other guttybrew. They were still here.

"It's daytime; you cannot be out." My body weighed a ton. I couldn't lift my hand to touch Blade's beautiful face.

"It's after midnight. Here, drink this."

I smelled the crisp cool water before I let it pass my lips. It was amazing and tasted like the elixir of the Gods.

"Slowly," Blade cautioned.

I couldn't drink slowly; I needed as much as I could get. Some spilled on the front of my shirt and I didn't care. Blade's laugh rang in my ears and I managed a smile after the last of the water was on or in me.

"Can you sit up?" he asked.

The room was no longer spinning. The colors were gone which was a shame. They had been extraordinary. I didn't answer but Blade helped me to the couch, keeping one arm around my back and then resting my body against his.

"My lady?" This came from Hax. Someone stole him again and replaced him with the nicer Hax.

I looked at him as he went to one knee.

"Hax," I said uncomfortably and placed out my hand to stop him.

It had the opposite effect. He took my hand and leaned his large mouth with all his big teeth forward. His hard lips touched the backs of my fingers. I tried to snatch my hand away, but he kept ahold of it.

"I swear my allegiance to you, Tara Lott, The Promised, the wielder, the bringer of peace. My breath, my blood, my life."

He dropped my hand, stood, and stepped back. Another guttybrew took his place. I didn't know what to say or what to do, but Blade held me in place with gentle pressure around my back.

"This is important," he whispered in my ear.

The sexual need for him returned and I had to fight it back. What would the guttybrew think if I asked Blade to take me on the couch?

I lost count of the number of guttybrew who took my hand and gave their oath even though I had no idea what it meant. The need for Blade stayed in the background but it never left. The one thing I knew for fact was my power had materialized. It was part of me. All of me. I had one burning question.

What could I do with it?

Chapter 31

When the guttybrew finished their ceremony, they left the room with lingering glances. Hax remained with Drake and Blade.

Before I could ask a question, Macos walked in. He gave Blade a look I didn't understand but Blade seemed to.

"I will be back shortly," Blade said.

He pulled his arms away from me and stood. The energy inside me swelled. Was he stabilizing the power? Whatever he did was also working on my sexual needs because without him, it came roaring back. I moaned.

Blade looked at me over his shoulder and the flames in his eyes visually sparked.

"How do you feel?" the doctor asked.

"Strange," I replied truthfully. I wasn't telling anyone about my need to tear Blade's clothes off and throw myself at him.

"The guttybrew know more about what you've been through and how your magic works. Trust Hax," Macos said.

Trust Hax. I saw a new light in Hax's eyes that hadn't been there before. He looked at me differently. I'd always felt his resentment but it was gone now. I looked at Drake who stood in the background, staying out of the doctor's way.

"I wish to go to the garden. Is it possible?" I asked the doctor.

"The garden will be good for you," he said.

"I will escort you," Drake said with a gentle smile.

"Will Blade know where I am?"

This time Drake's smile held a flash of fang.

"He will find you."

"Okay." I stood up and wobbled unsteadily. I waved Drake and the doctor away when they tried to help. "Just a little dizzy. It's passing."

I glanced around the room. The plants looked as if they'd grown. A lot. I didn't say anything. I couldn't stop the need to be in the garden. It grew so strong it put the scorching desire for Blade in the background.

"Should I carry her?" Drake asked the doctor.

"I would follow her direction."

Was he giving Drake a warning?

"If I need help, I will ask," I said grouchily. Their conversation was about me but not directed at me and they needed to understand that I had a say. No scratch that, I had the only say.

"Take it slow," the doctor suggested.

My feet acted like they were several inches off the floor and it was hard to keep my balance. Energy radiated inside of me at the same time it spread out too. After about ten steps to the door, my equilibrium returned. The energy remained, but I could walk without falling.

"Are you coming?" I asked the doctor.

"No, I have another patient to check on."

Drake made a sound half between a laugh and a groan. I glanced at him, but he wouldn't meet my eyes.

I led the way, and he followed. I didn't need to be told how to get to the garden; I could feel it. I climbed several flights of stairs without help. The plants called me to them. Their yearning matched my own.

I made the last turn. Drake stepped in front of me and pushed on the door. I burst into my world.

The entire garden, not just the plants in my room, had grown. I was standing in a jungle of trees, shrubs, and smaller plants, but they were twice, no, three times as large as they were the last time I came here. The trees now had fruit.

"Wow," said Drake.

It was an understatement.

"When did it happen?" I whispered.

Drake huffed out a low sound. "You happened. They responded to your power. The guttybrew planted and tended this garden for years just like the plants in your room. Their patience won after I would have given up."

"The guttybrew built the garden?"

"On Blade's command," Drake said.

I reached my arms out and everything growing moved toward me. A powerful rush traveled from my toes to my fingers. I moved my hands and the plants and trees swayed with the movement.

"I need to be alone," I told Drake.

"That is not possible," he replied.

"Then turn your back because I am removing my clothing." I don't know why I had the sudden urge, but I had to do it. I pulled the T-shirt over my head and quickly shucked the jeans. I undid the bra and pulled down the panties until they fell around my ankles. I glanced over my shoulder. Drake's back was turned. I walked further into the garden.

The plants reached out and slowly surrounded me, traveling over bare skin in soft tickling caresses. Their physical hold was nothing like how they connected with my psyche on an entirely new level. I understood their limited thoughts and laughed as they formed a wall between me and Drake.

"Tara?" he asked, his back still turned.

"I'm here and the plants are protecting me from your eyes. Look," I told him.

"I can't see you," he said a moment later.

I laughed and breathed in the beautiful scent of greenery. The plants were alive and responding to me. I sensed them and understood they would protect me. I'm unsure why I did what happened next, but I couldn't help myself.

"Hold Drake," I whispered so softly I couldn't hear the command in my own ears.

"What the bloody hell," the vampire yelled a few moments later.

I couldn't stop another laugh. They wrapped around the vampire and held him in place. I took a step in his direction and the plants moved with me.

"Stop fighting them."

"They are trying to strangle me," he growled.

"Will strangulation kill a vampire?"

He didn't answer the question.

"You're causing this, aren't you?" he accused and tried to extract his arms from several sturdy vines.

"Turn his back to me," I told the plants, but this time it was done with only my mind.

They turned him and I moved closer.

"I have questions and I want answers."

"Wait for Blade," he said and struggled harder to get away.

"Do not release him," I said aloud. "Drake, I want you to answer my questions. I have some for Blade too, but you can start first."

"Bloody hell," he said again and stopped fighting the vines that circled him. "Go ahead," he said sullenly.

"Question one, who is The Promised?"

"You could have worked up to that one," he said. "You've made it clear that it's definitely you."

"That's not what I mean and you know it." I tightened my hand into a fist and the plants tightened on Drake.

"If this continues, I will tear these vines apart," he threatened.

"And I will be very angry if you do." I sent a burst of power into the vines holding me. The energy now had a color and I watched it travel along the vines to the ones holding Drake.

"Damn, that feels good," he said, his voice husky.

"Who and what is The Promised," I demanded.

"The guttybrew started it with their whining. When we didn't heed what they said, we were bombarded by dreams and still we didn't trust them." He struggled against the vines but they wouldn't let go. In frustration, he continued, "Then Blade started dreaming of you and he finally believed."

My skin heated. Had Blade's dreams matched mine? Worse, had he seen the dreams I'd had of Rollin?

"What is the purpose of The Promised?"

Drake groaned. Some of the plants may have been a little too tight. When he groaned again, I knew it was something else.

"The Promised will end the war between the vampires and the were-wolves," he said with exasperation. "The Promised will bring peace through her power. Your power." His voice turned breathy again and I realized he was absorbing the energy that I was pulsing through the vines.

"How is The Promised connected to Blade besides the dreams?"

"Dammit, don't make me answer that."

"Tell me," I demanded.

"I think you've had enough fun," said Blade as he stepped from the shadow of a tree.

I jumped. The vampire king was staring at me as the vines slowly dropped away from my naked body.

Chapter 32

"Leave us," Blade told Drake.

"I would have left ten minutes ago if I could have," the vampire grumbled.

The vines fell away from Drake but I didn't command them. When Drake was gone, Blade stared at my nakedness. Flames roared in his eyes. It wasn't like the fire I'd seen before. This was ignited by desire and need. For a moment, he frightened me.

"You are The Promised and yes, I dreamed of you as you dreamed of me." He sounded angry and my fear was replaced with irritation.

He didn't mention my dreams of the werewolf and I'd be damned if I did.

Blade walked closer and brushed his fingers along my throat to the top of my breast. My heart rate accelerated and desire replaced irritation. The fire wasn't in my eyes, it was burning inside my body. It heated my breasts. I yearned for Blade's touch at the juncture of my thighs. His fingers and his mouth, I wanted to feel everything he was capable of doing to me. Just like the dreams, but I wanted more. I needed him inside me. Deep inside until our bodies were one.

My breathing was harsh as I stared at him.

"I want you too," he whispered. "Your call is so strong it's impossible to resist."

"Then why resist?" I asked huskily. I wanted him and I was past embarrassment.

"You need a day," he said like it was a forgone conclusion that I would sleep with him. And dammit, he was right. "Your power is stabilizing and it is dangerous until it settles. Everyone can feel it. The guttybrew are struggling to stay away from you because the magic cries out to them. Macos is with them and trying to help."

"I don't want time; I want you." I couldn't believe I said it.

We were inches apart and his groan was filled with need. It made mine even harder to fight.

"Put your clothes on and I will answer your questions." His voice was sweet velvet to my ears while his fingers trailed more fire along my flesh.

"And if I refuse?" I leaned into his touch, using my body to entice. The magic had turned me into a vixen and all I could think of was Blade taking me here in the grass. Hell, I was ready to take him.

Would the plants hold Blade like they had Drake? Another burst of energy traveled through me and I fought a whimper. I was too far gone to figure out who's energy was controlling me. I didn't actually care.

"I will leave and send Hax to the garden." Blade's voice was still filled with need but he was serious.

His words were like cold water pouring over me. I did not want Hax to see me this way.

"Drake could have broken the hold if he wanted to," Blade said. "He was enjoying the power burst too much."

"How did you know what I was thinking?" I asked carefully, my desire dissolving quickly. What would I do if he could read my thoughts?

"Bits and pieces are coming through. There's a lack of context which is frustrating. I've had these glimpses into your life since the day you were born." He pulled his hand away and picked up my clothes, handing them to me. "It was even more frustrating because the glimpses did not tell me who or where you were. I could only feel the burn of your energy."

"You can read my mind," I accused.

He shrugged. "Not as much as I would like."

I pulled the clothes on, giving myself time to consider that my thoughts were not solely my own. When I stood upright to face him, he took my hand. A strong burst of sexual desire almost sent me to my knees.

"I feel it too," he said with what sounded like pain.

The grass beneath my bare feet tickled with fine threads of energy as we walked.

Blade's hand tightened on mine.

"I can feel your bond with the plants," he said. "It wasn't there before."

I no longer felt resentment from Blade. His bitterness was gone and something else had taken its place.

"Do the guttybrew have this strong a bond with plants?" I asked.

"Not as heightened as yours is now. Think past your connection with the plants and you should feel the guttybrew."

I did as he said while having no idea exactly how to do it. I thought the words and suddenly the energy from Hax and his people was there. I stumbled a bit because their power was stronger than I expected.

Blade placed his other hand beneath my elbow and righted me. We continued our walk while the guttybrew's power simmered beneath the surface of my mind.

"Why did Hax dislike me when I arrived?"

Blade laughed gruffly and the sound traveled over my nerve endings, settling between my thighs. I tried not to think about it. I didn't want Blade picking up on my sexual need again.

"Hax is old and set in his ways. He has served me for many years, waiting for you to come. I think he'd given up hope and when you arrived, he didn't believe you were The Promised. He knows exactly who you are now."

"Are there others like me or am I truly the last one?" I asked.

"It's possible, but doubtful. My awareness of you began on the day you were born. Wielders hid their children when it looked like they would be annihilated. The children were given to human families but they were found and murdered."

Horror filled my voice. "The children were killed?"

He stopped and faced me, his eyes still burning with flames.

"Wielders became too dangerous. Sometimes the werewolves killed entire families."

"Werewolves, not vampires, were responsible for ending the wielders?" I needed clarity to understand.

He stared at me and I didn't think he would answer.

"It wasn't all werewolves. Vampires did not like the power wielder blood held over them and treated them abominably." He paused and tightened his fingers on mine. "When your kind decided they no longer wanted to be ruled by vampires, we helped the werewolves."

"You personally killed wielders?"

"No, but I didn't have enough power back then to stop it."

"You believe every wielder but me is dead?"

"None has been discovered since your father died."

"If there are more, will you kill them?"

"Only if they need killing. I will allow no harm to come to you. There is a delicate balance between the vampires and werewolves. You might call it a truce. Additional wielders could disrupt what we have built. I hope you have control over any wielders who survived and our three species can be at peace again."

"But the werewolves attacked us," I said sternly. "A werewolf bit me and I could have died."

"It may also be what ignited your power. We don't know enough about it. There was a time that our three species relied on each other. Wolf packs and vampire families all had wielders within their ranks. It is said wielders control other's magic."

"Do you believe it?"

"Your power woke me from the sunlight sleep which is not common. All my vampires woke up."

"What about the guttybrew? How do they fit into this?"

He smiled. "They are cantankerous creatures. They lived underground for centuries. I had them watch you when you exited the helicopter. Hax said you dispatched the men who were sent to escort you with ease."

I heard his anger over what the men had done. I changed the subject to the burning question I'd asked Drake.

"Why are you and I connected?"

He closed his eyes for a moment, his long sweeping lashes incredibly sensual. When they opened, flames danced and sent a burst of need through me. The tangy copper taste of his blood after the attack filled my senses. It no longer repelled me. I wanted more. I needed to share my blood with him.

"I'm unsure if you want to know the answer," he finally said.

"I must know."

His other hand covered the one he held.

"You, Tara the wielder, The Promised, the bringer of peace and the fire of change." The fire in his eyes consumed me. "Are my chosen."

Chapter 33

Chosen. The word hung in the air.

What did it mean? Was he ordered to choose me? Was it against his will? He'd all but told me it was. I shook off his hands, not wanting him touching me for the rest of this conversation.

"Do you want me as your chosen?" I asked carefully.

His eyes closed again and when they opened, they were onyx without a hint of flame and I wasn't sure how he felt.

"Our joining is foretold. We can't fight it."

He hadn't answered the question which I guessed, in its own way, was an answer.

"If I choose to leave here, will you allow it now that I have my power?"

"I ask that you give us both time. I've been resentful for years and fought the prophecy. I no longer what to fight it, but I want to explore this as equals."

"How can we be equals if I am your prisoner?"

"The werewolves want you. You need my protection." He hesitated. "I will make a pact with you. If you swear on your honor that you will remain for three months, I will not hold you prisoner."

I huffed a laugh.

"My honor will hold me prisoner. What happens at the end of three months?"

"Renegotiation," he said with a soft smile.

I was about to find out if I could trust a vampire.

A wave of tiredness engulfed me. My body ached and the bursts of energy changed from electrifying to draining.

"The plants will help," Blade said. "Hax has moved some into your bedroom while we've been out here."

"It bothers me that you can read my mind," I told him.

"You can also read mine if you try. I will teach you to block your thoughts. I have this connection to my vampires. Learning will tire you and you're not ready. Food and sleep in that order are what you require. I will escort you back to your room."

I was suddenly too exhausted to argue. He took my hand again which was a good thing because I stumbled after walking a few feet.

"It will go away," he said.

"Who will teach me about my power?" I asked.

"Hax has shared little of his wielder knowledge, but he's sworn to you now. Once your magic settles, ask him for help."

"I want to learn about vampires too." Before he spoke, I continued. "You are not what I was led to believe. I want to understand."

His expression changed and I didn't like what I saw.

"We are everything you've heard," he whispered harshly. I pictured him killing Kenia and I shivered. "Never forget it."

His voice, besides being harsh, sounded odd. I had the strangest feeling he didn't like vampires which meant he didn't like himself. I'd been told they were monsters, but then again, I was told anything supernatural was a monster.

I turned when we reached my door and I went to my tiptoes. Leaning in, I gave Blade a soft kiss.

The flames in his eyes had dulled but they came back to life. With a soft growl, he pulled me closer and his mouth took mine in a brutal kiss. The kiss consumed me and power burst throughout my body. Somehow, and it should have bothered me but didn't, I knew he was feeding from my power.

He wrenched his lips away and stepped back. I almost fell but he didn't place his hands out to steady me. He didn't look at me when he spoke.

"You need time. Food is waiting for you. Nourishment and sleep are vital. I will see you tomorrow."

He moved away so fast I didn't see it happen. He hadn't even moved like this when he fought the werewolves. He *had* fed from my power. If he was energized so much from a kiss, what would my blood be like for him?

I had no idea why I'd had that thought. I also didn't understand why it turned me on so much. I opened the door and went inside where food waited. The plants swayed toward me but I stopped their touch with a thought.

Hax was no longer in the room, but I could sense his energy and knew he had just left. A tray waited for me on the low table.

I sat down on the couch and attacked the food like someone who hadn't eaten in weeks. I didn't bother saving the dessert for later and ate it as fast as the main course.

Water called to me and I spent an hour under the shower's stinging spray. Power coursed through me the entire time. After drying off and placing a T-shirt over my head, I crawled into bed. Vines touched me and helped soothe the erratic bursts of energy. I fell asleep thinking of Blade.

***

The dream seemed so real. Hard, powerful hands ran over my naked body. I opened my eyes, expecting to see Blade, but it was Rollin in the darkened room.

"I taste your power," he whispered.

His hand cupped between my thighs and I moaned.

"I am sorry my werewolf hurt you," he said with a groan. "I swear I'll protect you."

His lips kissed along my inner thighs and I moaned. When he pulled away, I opened my eyes. I was alone in the room, my fingers between my legs.

"Damn." I rolled and moaned into my pillow, energy threading across my skin. I was falling in love with Blade so why did I dream about Rollin?

The thought stopped me. Was it really love? Could it happen this fast. I had thought of Blade as my enemy. He'd done nothing to hurt me. The werewolves had attacked. As far as I knew, Blade had not lied to me. Rollin was a dream and any desire I had for him would remain unfulfilled.

I decided to change love to lust. I'd never been tempted to have sex with anyone. Oh, I thought about the rangers and how sexy they were but really, they didn't temp me.

I leaned into the pillows. The sun wasn't quite up. I strangely knew this as fact. Vines reached closer and I wondered why they'd moved away. A musky odor filled my nostrils and I looked into the darker corners of the room but there was no one there.

"Sleep," Blade's voice whispered from the shadows.

Was I still dreaming?

When I opened my eyes again, I felt full sunlight outside. This had to be part of my new power.

"I am coming with your coffee and breakfast," Hax said.

His voice was like a small explosion in my mind and it startled me because the guttybrew was not in the suite.

"Thank you," I responded silently and had no idea if he heard me.

The thought of Hax reading my mind was too much. I considered taking a shower but I heard the door open in the main room. I put on the robe and walked out. I had too many questions for Hax to pass up this opportunity.

"My lady," he said with a deep nod.

"I have questions," I said sharply. "I demand you sit in that chair"—I pointed to the chair beside the couch—"and answer them."

"Yes, my lady."

"And stop that. Act like yourself; you are weirding me out."

He looked stricken.

I reached up my hands, dug my fingers into my hair, and pulled. I was shaken up by the damn dream. I inhaled deeply and started over.

"I apologize. Things are happening that I don't understand and I need help. I don't even know where to begin."

"Your powers are settling," he said carefully. His short legs barely reached the ground. It didn't take away from his fierceness but it relaxed me for want of a better word.

"What does that mean?" I asked, my tone friendlier.

"You are holding too much magic and your body is adjusting. The plants will help. If you need to expel magic, they will take it. If you need to gain power, they will give it."

I turned and reached my arm out. A vine trailed toward me and I relaxed even more with its touch. I was jumping into the fire with the next question but I had to know.

"Blade kissed me last night. Did he feed from my energy?"

"Yes."

"Is that a good or bad thing?"

He frowned and his jaw hardened.

"He has been denying himself human blood," Hax said. "It was good for him but not for you. Your magic must stabilize before he fulfills the prophecy."

Now we were getting somewhere. "Tell me of the prophecy."

"We, the guttybrew, are born knowing instinctually of the prophecy. I informed Blade of who he was and gave him fealty until The Promised made herself known. That was two centuries ago."

"As in two hundred years," I asked to be sure I'd heard him correctly.

"Yes, my lady."

I let the "my lady" pass. "Can you read my mind?"

He sat back in the chair, relaxing a bit.

"No. I felt when you woke up. It is the first time—" He thought about it for a moment. "No, the second," he said. "I knew you had woken up earlier. I felt your energy."

Oh crap, did he know about the dream? Heat suffused my cheeks. If he couldn't read my mind, he most likely didn't. I changed the subject.

"Blade said you didn't believe I was The Promised. Why is that?"

"We thought we would feel your birth and we did not. We were still waiting. Blade said he felt it, but we couldn't be sure. It is possible your mother and father hid the power created when you were born. They held very strong magic."

"You knew of them?"

"No, but I know they were powerful. They had to be."

"What can you tell me about my powers? And," I continued, "can you teach me to use them?"

"That is our purpose, my lady. The guttybrew are yours to command. We will guard you with our lives. You live in a dangerous time."

"I need to learn. Can we start this morning?"

"Yes, but you must eat first. You need to understand that your power can be unsafe to those around you if you don't know how to use it. Until you have full control, you must have a full meal before practicing."

I looked at the covered platter and my stomach grumbled. Hax stood and poured coffee.

"Please bring your tea and join me tomorrow. Your breakfast too if you would like. I have a feeling we will be spending a lot of time together."

Yes, I knew for certain, a guttybrew could smile.

Chapter 34

Hax waited for me to eat and change clothes. I came from the bedroom in jeans and a tank top. I carried my sword but placed it on the couch.

Hax went to the center of the room and sat cross-legged on the floor. With his short arms and legs, I was surprised he made it look so easy. I sat across from him.

"You must breathe deeply to gather your energy," he said. "Close your eyes and try to see the colors. It will become easier with time."

"Do you have this energy?" I asked. "Is that why you know what I need to do?"

"I hold a very small part of your magic. I was born knowing how to teach you."

"Do all the guttybrew know this?"

"No. Like Blade, I was given a place in the prophecy. Because of it, my power is slightly stronger than other guttybrew but nothing like yours."

I closed my eyes and breathed deeply as he requested. The colors began spiraling behind my eyelids. I opened them and saw the colors in the room.

"That is your power," Hax said. "You must pull it into you. Think of it like strings you can draw inward. Wrap them inside until you no longer see them and only feel."

This was harder than I expected. It took an hour before I managed to rope them in. The word "string" didn't work in my head, but rope did.

"Can you see the colors?" I asked before I had gathered the last ones.

"Yes, but they are almost gone from my sight. Do you feel them?"

"Yes. I'm unsure if it's a good feeling."

"You will grow accustomed to it soon and be bereft without this energy."

It took ten more minutes before I had all the colors wrapped inside me. I took a deep breath.

"What now?" I asked.

"You have choices. We won't work on it today but you hold within you a very powerful weapon. You must have better control before you use it. Focus on the empty dishes in front of you and lift them with your mind. Imagine a single thread moving outward and taking hold of the dish."

I remembered doing this as a child, though I'd never seen the mental connection. My father punished me when I moved items. By the time I was ten or so, I'd lost the ability. Lost might be the keyword. I had a feeling I'd forgotten how to do it, but I could have if I remembered.

I allowed one rope to slip from my hold, but I bypassed the empty dish. My power wanted something more. I wrapped it around the table legs and lifted it.

Hax jerked back. And then, very slowly, I heard a guttybrew laugh.

For an hour, I worked on moving objects to different locations and bringing them to me. They were all objects in my line of sight.

"Try something from the other room," Hax told me.

My sword. I pictured where it was and lifted it with another rope of magic. The sword reacted to my power. It didn't float like the other items; it appeared in my hand and instantly glowed.

"Your sword is magic," said Hax with a surprised look on his face.

"It was a gift."

"A powerful gift."

My father had empowered the sword. I felt his energy. It was my turn to smile, and then I laughed. The sword vibrated with my magic and its own. An idea sparked inside me. I sent a rope out, through the streets, a path I wasn't familiar with, but the rope was drawn to the picture of the box in my mind. It found Mika and Coop's home, traveled inside and up to the room I had chosen. It touched the block of wood. It appeared in my hand exactly as the sword had.

Hax jumped while staring intently at the wood.

"I feel a different magic," he said slowly, his eyes never leaving my hand.

"This belonged to my father and it was kept for me by my friends." I wouldn't tell Hax that it took a drop of blood to activate it so it became a box.

I suddenly knew whose magic the box contained. My mother's. It shook me and I hugged the wood to my chest.

"Your lesson for today is over," Hax said. "You are more powerful than I imagined and your control is very good." He held up a claw. "Not that it doesn't need work."

"There's so much I don't know and I still need your help," I told him solemnly.

"Of course, my lady." His eyes held a touch of fear.

Was my power that surprising? I leaned over and took his clawed hand.

"Thank you. Would you answer questions about vampires for me?"

He looked down at my fingers but didn't move his away. I felt the power he exuded. It was tamer than mine.

"Yes," he said still looking at our joined hands.

I watched him fight not to pull away.

"We can do it tomorrow if you would rather?" I didn't want to scare him or anyone else.

He pulled himself together with a shaky inhale. Making the wood appear had distressed him and I wasn't sure why.

"Please allow the plants to soothe you while we speak about vampires," he told me.

I released him and with my mind, I called on the vines. They didn't soothe me at first; they recharged my energy. I would keep that to myself. Using the power calmed me. I was born of magic and had been denied it for far too long.

"Can vampires have children?" I asked him and settled against the cushion while the vines feathered my skin.

"Not in the way you mean. They cannot produce babies, but they make other vampires and consider them their children."

"How are they made?" I asked.

"That is knowledge only the vampires have. For as long as I have been with Blade, I have not discovered how it is done."

"Could Blade turn me into a vampire?"

Horror filled Hax's expression and he growled.

"I do not know, my lady, but if he ever tries, you must stop him. I have heard it must be done with free will. I do not know if that is true, but I believe it is. You must never allow it."

"How do you kill a vampire?"

Hax's smile returned which surprised me.

"Very carefully. Take the head and burn the body."

"What about a wooden stake?"

He laughed. It was a low guttural sound and I liked it.

"No, that is fiction."

"What about werewolves?"

"The same. Head and burning the body is the only way to be sure."

"Have you ever killed a werewolf?" I was simply curious.

"I have killed both wolves and vampires. Both were our enemies. I protected my people. I have not killed a vampire since I began serving Blade."

The next question had been running through my mind.

"Do you still serve Blade?"

"No. If you asked me to kill him, I would try."

Chapter 35

Startled wasn't quite the word for what I felt with Hax's declaration. It led to another question.

"Is there reason to kill Blade so I am safe?" I held my breath, waiting for his answer.

"No, my lady. He plays a major part in the prophecy. He doesn't wish you harm, but he is a vampire."

I exhaled and thought about Kenia.

"Was Kenia a danger to me?"

"Yes, but all the vampires are dangerous. Before you arrived, Blade told them you were off-limits and if any touched or threatened you, he would kill them. Blade does not go back on his word and the vampires know this."

"She was jealous of me," I said because Kenia had made that obvious. I wasn't sure if I truly wanted to know the answer to the next question but I went ahead and asked. "Were they intimate?"

Hax looked uncertain. I needed the information on Kenia to under-stand the vulnerabilities and dangers I faced while navigating vampires. I was just about to tell him this when he answered.

"They had sexual relations," he finally said. "The emotional end of their entanglement was one sided. Blade put up with her jealousies and manipulations and she provided sex. He had no intention of keeping her around forever and everyone knew it including her. When you were discovered, Blade terminated the relationship immediately. "

"Six years ago?" I asked in disbelief. Kenia's attitude had led me to believe it was an ongoing relationship, not one that had ended years before.

"Yes. Blade's connection to you was absolute after your father died." His tone was apologetic. "We, the guttybrew, were uncertain. He knew the truth and he never wavered that you were The Promised."

"Why was Blade so angry over my arrival?"

Hax gave his weird, full of teeth smile again.

"Blade is the ruler of his domain," he said and I think he even chuckled. "No one controls the liege or so he thought. The prophecy is stronger than all of us."

"He was angry about the prophecy?"

"In a way." The guttybrew thought about it for a moment. "He was angry he couldn't control the prophecy. Blade fought his way to the top. He is stronger and more powerful than ninety percent of the vampires out there. He takes what he wants, but with you, he had to rethink his plans."

That brought me to another problem I had been mulling over.

"The military sent me to the city to discover what happened to a team of rangers. Have you heard anything about that?"

"The rangers are in the werewolves pockets. They go in and out of the city all the time."

This was news to me. I was unaware the rangers could enter the city at all. I knew the general set me up but I thought it was because I was expendable. Maybe he was on the werewolves' payroll. It relieved my mind, though. My being here with the vampires was not endangering the military.

Hax had given me much to think about and I needed time to absorb it all. My sword was calling for a workout. The energy inside me had settled a bit, but there was no mistaking the need to expend what was left.

I stood and Hax did the same.

"Will there be anything more, my lady?" he asked with a slight bow that was new.

"Not for now."

He nodded. "If you have need of me, send the message through the plants and I will come."

I didn't ask how to do it because I somehow knew. It was all so strange but my internal instincts sensed things. The ability to bring my father's box was one of them. Sending messages through the plants was now another.

It was time to see what my sword could do.

A second after the door closed behind Hax, I stood and lifted my sword. I was knocked back two steps. The power was so much greater than it had been. It took a moment to accustom myself and settle the energy. After moving to the cleared part of the room, I warmed my wrist by making small figure eights, gradually growing larger as I worked. I began another drill followed by another.

The plants hummed softly in my mind and I was one with the blade. Besides the sword's added energy, my control was fine-tuned. The sword flowed gently through the air, seemingly held with my power and not my hands. I needed to spar with Drake to understand the full extent of my new abilities. I continued practicing until sweat covered me. My imaginary opponents had died many times when I finally stopped.

I craved water on my skin and took a shower. My hands smoothed over wet soapy flesh while I thought of Blade. I'd made a decision and now I was having trouble holding back the unquenchable need for him. Unfortunately, my hands wouldn't do the trick and I forced myself to stop.

All I could think about was food after the shower. I touched one of the vines in the main room and sent a message to Hax. A small zing entered my fingers when he received it. Communicating with the plants was very different than I expected. They were an extension of my power and connected me to the earth and to the guttybrew. Hax arrived ten minutes later with a full meal.

"I'm starving and couldn't wait for dinner," I told him.

"You will need extra nourishment to feed your power. Eat when you are hungry, bathe when you crave the water, and drink when you thirst."

"Dinner will be with Blade?" I made it a question, though I knew the answer.

"Yes, my lady."

"I need a favor," I told the guttybrew.

"Whatever you wish."

"You don't know what I need," I said with a slight smile.

"Anything," he grunted.

I'd insulted him. He waited for my request.

"When the sun goes down would it be possible to bring me the vampire who belongs to Blade's private guard? Her name is Lizbet."

"Of course my lady," he bowed again and left.

Lizbet always watched me from a distance. The first night I met her, she was unable to hide her jealousy that Drake had brought me to the compound. I hadn't sensed the jealousy again, but I wasn't sure what she thought of me. She was respected by Blade's people and stood second to Drake in the power hierarchy. I admired her. I also needed help and she was the person most likely to answer my questions.

I ate the food and satisfied my hunger. When I leaned back on the couch, the vines touched my bare arms and energy pulsed from them to me. When my power equalized, I found a book and read until there was a knock at my door.

Lizbet stood looking at me, her gorgeous features held a pinched expression most likely due to me having her pulled from whatever she was doing. I placed my hand out to the beautiful vampire. Today her hair was piled on her head with small tendrils curled around her face. It made her look a bit older, but more than that it gave her a regal appearance. Her blood red gown was skintight with sparkles here and there throughout the material. I would never be able to carry it off, but on her, it looked fantastic. I had thought about asking for Ambrosia's advice but she was too timid. Lizbet was exactly who I needed.

"Thank you for coming. Please step inside."

She carefully took my hand, gave it a gentle squeeze, released it and walked tentatively into the suite. She gazed around before her eyes landed back on me. She remained tense.

"I need your help," I said.

"I'm unsure how I could help you," she said questioningly.

"You are in love with Drake," I stated boldly.

"Maybe." The look in her eyes said there was *no* maybe.

"I want to seduce a vampire and I need you to teach me how to go about it."

I thought my words would calm her but she looked angry and took a step away from me. My heart dropped. I had really hoped she would help.

"I'm sorry," I told her. "You may leave." I turned away, not wanting my yearning for Blade to affect her.

"May I ask the name of the vampire you wish to seduce?" she asked tightly.

I spun around.

"Blade. What other vampire would I possibly wish to have sex with?"

Her entire body language changed and a smile grew until the tips of her sharp fangs showed. They looked so blasted perfect on her. Not that I would say it aloud, but I feared I had vampire envy.

"You wish to seduce Blade and you want my help," she muttered. "What makes you think it would be hard?"

Damn it. This was so embarrassing, but I really needed help.

"I'm a virgin."

Chapter 36

After a moment of shock, Lizbet's laughter vibrated through the apartment. My face reddened in embarrassment.

"Let me rephrase my question," she said. "Why do you think you need to seduce Blade?"

"Umm, isn't that how it's done?" My ire was beginning to rise. I shouldn't have asked her here.

She took my hand again and smiled mischievously. This made her appear somewhere around my age. Her eyes belied it, though. I saw shrewd intelligence that reminded me of my father and Coop. She was much older than she appeared and much stronger too. Tendrils of her energy played on my hand where she touched me. As part of Blade's private guard, she would need to be powerful.

"My darling girl," she said, adding years to her age with the phrase. "Blade is already in your pocket. It's one of the reasons we were so worried when you came here."

"We," I asked, "as in the other vampires?"

"Yes." She continued holding my hand. "We knew you could upset the balance that's been established between vampires and weres." She waved her hand around the room. "You were foretold and chances were good that you would take Blade's power. To us, you were an unknown and we were not happy that you came here."

"You thought I would steal Blade's power?" I asked. Was that even possible?

Her smile held but her eyes were deadly.

"Vampires are at the top of the food chain and there is little we fear. To control vampires you must be strong. We require structure to stop our basic instincts and a person to make sure we abide by the established rules. Blade is strong enough to hold us to his rules. We felt your presence would cause instability which would be very dangerous."

"Has it?" I should have spoken to Lisbet before asking anyone else questions. Would they have brought her to my room before my power came in? Most likely not. I was so glad I'd sent for her.

"Blade has always been territorial," Lizbet said. "He does not put up with disobedience but he is fair. His thirst for you, even with you under our roof, has not gotten in the way of his leadership."

"Do the vampires hate me because of what happened to Kenia?" I had worried about this since the first night.

"Kenia was a bitch," Lizbet said. "Due to her connection with Blade, we put up with her many cruelties. There may be a few of her friends that are angry, but for most of us, we're relieved."

I smiled back at her and squeezed her fingers. She turned my wrist and looked down. Fire sparked in her eyes. She dropped my hand and stepped back.

"Your power sings through your blood," she said. "I want a taste even knowing Blade would kill me."

"Should you leave?" I asked. I wasn't worried, but maybe I should have been.

"No, but if you call for me again, have blood wine served."

I sent thoughts to the plants and they sent the message to Hax.

"Hax will deliver your wine shortly," I told her.

She looked around the room before turning back to me and shaking her head slightly.

"I won't ask how you accomplished that. Let's get started making you so appealing to Blade that you don't leave his bed for a week."

I cringed slightly. Was that truly what I wanted?

"I'm not saying you'll stay in bed that long just that it's what you'll both want. You asked for my help." A smile played on her lips. The fire was gone from her eyes and she was ready to assist. "Are you scared?"

She was challenging me and it was exactly what I needed.

"Let's do it," I told her, my voice strong.

"You need a dress," Lisbet said.

"I may have one that will work."

"Show me."

I walked into the bedroom with Lizbet on my heels.

I'd lied to myself about silver not being my color. I'd never worn a dress in my life but for some reason this dress called to me. She lifted it from the closet and laid it on the bed and unwrapped the plastic surrounding it. After picking it up, she held it beside me and her smile grew again.

"This is perfect," she said.

"You think it will work?" I asked suspiciously.

"He will only want to remove it. Isn't that the point?"

I gulped while feeling heat rise in my cheeks which made Lizbet laugh again.

"The shoes that match the dress are in the closet," I told her. "I'm afraid I'll fall off them and break a leg."

My normal boots had a three quarter inch heel. The heels Lizbet wore were higher than anything I'd ever had on. The shoes in the closet were about an inch shorter than hers, but still perilous.

"Put the shoes on and you can practice in them while we prepare you."

"You think the shoes and dress will seduce Blade?"

"No, but you will. The dress and shoes are only the candy's wrapper."

Hax delivered the blood wine and Lizbet got to work after a few sips. The front of my hair was secured on top of my head with wispy tendrils left dangling.

"He needs to see your throat," she said which didn't help unwind the knot in my stomach.

She curled the rest of my hair and allowed it to flow freely down my back. She applied a small amount of makeup from the bathroom drawers but not enough for me to object to. She used it to enhance my features and not cover them up. I watched her technique and knew it would take a lot of practice to do it so easily.

I sat or walked across the room when she told me to. Walking was to work on balance while wearing the heels. Before she was finished, I forgot about them. Sword fighting and balance went hand in hand.

I was naked beneath the robe she'd had me put on and when she said, "strip," I took a step back.

"I don't see how any of this will seduce Blade. I don't know what to say or how to act. I need ideas, suggestions, or flat out orders."

This made her laugh again.

"He's awake at this moment thinking of you," she said.

"You don't know that," I replied.

"I can feel it. All the vampires in the entire area can feel him. Since the day you walked into our compound, the energy he emits changed. We call it blood lust and you are calling him to you."

"I am not," I argued.

"Really?" her eyebrows lifted. "He lusts for you. That's what we feel. I could dress you in a sack and he would still feel your call." She saw my panic. "Trust me," she said. "Go to dinner with him and allow whatever happens to happen. You will not need to do much if anything. Now stop delaying. I want to see you in the dress."

I removed the robe and stood naked, which was not something I was accustomed to either. A bra would show if I wore one. Lizbet barely looked at my nude body before she lifted the material above my head. It slinked over my skin, clinging in all the right places. She made a few adjustments by straightening the material before she turned me toward the mirror.

Wow!

The silver sparkly material looked painted on. The back had multiple thin straps crisscrossing delicately across my skin. It dipped to my waist. The front of the dress was only slightly more modest. It seemed like my breasts held the material up. Both sides of the dress were split to my upper thigh and when I walked across the room at Lizbet's order, I knew the material wouldn't inhibit me from fighting. Not that I would be fighting, at least I hoped not.

Was this me? I asked myself as I looked in the mirror again. I would give anything if my ranger friends could see me now. They would spit out whatever they were drinking. Their kid sister was all grown up. I smiled at myself and then rubbed my fingers together nervously. They were callused from working the kitchen for so many years.

"Let me see those," Lizbet said. She took a closer look at my nails and marched into the bathroom for a file. "No polish. We'll even them up and they'll be fine."

"Can you file off the calluses?" I asked.

"They show you're a strong fighter. Never be embarrassed because you can take care of yourself. It's something the vampires admire about you."

I wasn't sure if I believed her. I decided not to think about my faults. No, that's not true. I decided the calluses were not a fault and went with Lizbet's take on them.

When I was finally ready, she had me turn around slowly.

"Perfection," she whispered, her fangs causing the word to slur the slightest bit. "I must leave you now to quench my thirst. Blood wine will not do it. I've been a good girl for far too long."

I couldn't help myself and wrapped my arms around her.

"Thank you," I said. "I wouldn't have made it through this without you."

She carefully untangled herself from my hold and grinned at me while fire burned in her eyes.

"Blade will fall at your feet. Don't make this easy on him."

She left me with nervous energy that would require sword work to burn off and that wasn't happening. Preparing for Blade's seduction was nerve-racking and enlightening. Now, it was time to wait and not chicken out.

Chapter 37

It had taken us a long time to prepare so it was only thirty-minutes before Hax came to get me. I kept forgetting to check the door and see if I could leave on my own. This time he knocked and didn't enter until I opened the door and my question was answered.

"My lady," Hax said with a slow nod of his head and a gleam in his eyes I'd not seen before.

"Hax," I replied. I had to walk through that door and go to Blade. I was suddenly terrified.

Hax placed his arm out, which shocked me and at the same time gave me the courage to move forward. We stepped together toward the cozy dining room.

Vampires were standing at almost every turn. I nodded and said hello. I hadn't seen this many before. I knew why when I saw Lizbet and three other vampires chatting at the end of a long hallway.

She winked at me and waved me along. She'd told the vampires what I was up to.

I should feel embarrassed but for some reason, her approval had my chin lifting a notch. We continued on our way and finally passed a lone male vampire. He bowed to me. He wasn't as gorgeous as Blade, but he was still incredibly handsome. He was wearing what I'd begun to think of as a uniform. I'd passed several vampires dressed this way in the halls. It consisted of a black silk shirt with a logo where the pocket would be. Eagle or hawk claws in a gold circle. The shirt was tucked into black pants that weren't quite tactical like the military wore because these didn't have all the pockets.

His power feathered across my skin. He'd been one of the vampires at the dinner that now seemed so long ago.

"My lady," he said, his expression neutral.

"Tara, please call me Tara."

"Yes, my lady Tara."

Not what I meant, but I continued, "May I ask your name?"

"Genesis, my lady Tara."

It clicked. Drake had called him by name the night I'd arrived. He'd secured the gate or door or something; the mad rush was a blur.

"Thank you, Genesis," I said. "Have a pleasant night."

"Yes, my lady Tara."

Ugh. I was stuck with "my lady" because I had no idea what to do about it. This wasn't my home and I did not know the finer points of vampire etiquette. The last thing I wanted to do was get Genesis in trouble. I nervously pushed a wisp of hair from my eyes and continued with Hax. I'd only stopped to speak with the vampire to stall the dinner with Blade. With every step closer, I felt more like an imposter playing dress-up. Trying to resemble a lady was a ruse and I was about to fail miserably.

Hax dropped my arm and stepped forward to open the door. I walked through. Blade's back was to me and I stopped when the door closed. I gripped my hands into fists nervously at my sides. I waited for what seemed like an eternity. My nerves were at the breaking point.

He turned. Flames simmered in his eyes.

Heat ran up and down my body. He stared for so long, I began to feel even more uncomfortable. Running away was not an option.

"You are stunning," he said at last, his husky voice dripping with want. "The dress simply accentuates your beauty." His power flared. It was nothing like Lizbet's or Drake's. Blakes energy accented my own similar to what the plants fed me, but then again entirely different. I could feel the undercurrents of his desire. My own ramped up a notch as we stared at each other. I didn't know if I were truly as stunning as he'd said but his eyes told me he thought so. There was also no female vampire in the room to compare me to. His energy continued to warm my flesh and all I could think about was lying naked in his arms.

I was no longer fooling myself because I would absolutely beg on my knees if need be.

There was a polite knock on the door that tore our gazes apart. Hax entered with a tray. He placed it on the table without looking at either of us and walked out. Blade stepped forward and took my hand. The burst of energy between us was overwhelming and I stumbled the slightest bit in the shoes. I looked up and smiled at him.

"I've never worn heels before. If I twist an ankle, you will need to carry me."

"That can be arranged," he said in a deep voice that conveyed that he would like it very much.

He pulled out my chair and I sat down. He poured my wine and the blood wine mixture he enjoyed for himself. He removed the platter's cover and placed the plate in front of me. Steamed vegetables and sautéed red potatoes with fresh spices sent a delicious scent through the air. I was hungry again and started eating.

Blade watched me. His eyes were on my throat.

"You're making me nervous," I finally said.

His smile was slow and deliberate. Fangs flashed and a hot burst of desire settled between my thighs. I recalled my dreams of him when I was at the military camp. I knew the feel of his hands and lips against my skin.

"Finish your meal," he said huskily and took a drink of his wine.

"I'll eat my dessert later," I told him after I finished with what was on the plate and he started to uncover the smaller platter.

"Would you like to walk in the garden?" he asked.

For the oddest reason, he appeared nervous, but that wasn't the Blade I knew and lov—no, I wasn't going there tonight even though I'd already admitted my feelings to myself. I looked into his eyes and placed my heart in the next words.

"I would like to see where a vampire sleeps," I said softly.

Chapter 38

Blade's eyes seared me. I swear I could feel the hot sparks.

He didn't argue or ask why. He stood and took my hand. I walked with him until we reached a deep set of stairs. Moving suddenly, he swooped me into his arms and carried me deeper into his lair. I couldn't help my small nervous laugh as I circled my arms around his neck.

He placed me on my feet when we reached the bottom. Low lights high on the wall lit the way as we continued walking, my hand in his. He opened the door and his rooms were a suite like mine though larger. The furniture and décor looked like they came from a past century, maybe two.

"I only have the wine and blood mixture on hand. Drake and Hax are the only two who come to my rooms and Hax prefers water." His eyes stayed on mine.

"Did Kenia come here?" The question slipped out before I could stop myself.

A flash of pain entered his eyes, but then it was gone.

"No. When we were together, I went to her room," he said honestly.

"Did you love her?" My mouth was going to ruin this but suddenly it seemed important. Maybe he loved her and it was one of the reasons for his resentment of me in the beginning.

"I had a fondness for her. Sadly, she loved me. When I discovered who you were, I cut our ties."

This was what Hax told me.

"I'm sorry you had to kill her."

"I'm not," he said. The truth of his words was in his eyes. "She threatened you long before the night she died. She was part of the group who betrayed me, though I didn't know it when I killed her. Her death was inevitable, along with the other vampires involved."

I reached out and touched his cheek, my fingers trailing over his jaw and down to the collar of his shirt.

"I'm sorry you had to kill her."

He clasped my hand and I flattened it as he moved it over his heart and pressed it into his shirt.

"With your full magic, you are more able to protect yourself. I have feared other vampires in my extended family. Your blood is now a beacon of power and within a few days, it will be as if you have always had it. I hope Hax is helping you and not just carrying tales."

I smiled at the lighter words. We would never discuss Kenia again. He hadn't brought her here and the small bit of jealousy I'd felt when Hax told me they were together years ago melted completely. I looked around.

"This room is amazing but I was hoping to see the bedroom."

I didn't get the response I expected. Blade stepped back, putting a few feet between us.

"You must understand what you are doing," he said. "Vampires share blood when they pair. I have waited years for this night and I don't know if I can control myself."

"Did you share blood with Kenia?" There I went, bringing her up again. Why couldn't I keep my damn mouth shut? If I kicked myself, I had a feeling the heels would leave a scar.

"I must give my blood to my vampires. It keeps them calm. I do not take their blood, nor did I ever drink from Kenia. That is reserved only for a pairing."

"Am I paired with you?"

His smile grew.

"Can't you feel it?"

I closed my eyes for a moment. We were so far underground and there were no plants in his room. The bond with Blade was like the colors of my power. This rope was thicker and I couldn't pull it inside me but it connected us.

I opened my eyes.

"Yes, I can feel it. I want you."

He lifted me again and carried me into his bedroom.

I already knew what it would look like. I had been here too many times to count. He released my legs and lowered me gently until I was standing in front of him. He slipped off the heels and they made a soft sound against the floor where they landed. My legs were shaky, my hands trembling. He turned me around and I looked at the bed. The ornate bedposts were straight out of my dreams.

"I've dreamed of you," I told him.

He captured the material of the dress in his fingers. Shivers ran across my skin.

"I dreamed of you too," he said and then kissed the side of my neck, his lips a hot promise that dreams do come true.

He leaned away and turned me so we faced each other. He lifted the dress until it came over my head. He tossed it to the floor. His eyes blazed as he looked at my nakedness. I read so many things in his gaze. They said Lizbet was right. He would take me even if I came in wearing a sack.

My hands went to his suit jacket and I pushed it past his shoulders. He shrugged out of it and it fell on top of the dress. I started undoing the shirt buttons but he stopped me. With a low growl, he impatiently pulled the shirt apart, the buttons flying and making a small sound as they hit the floor. He lifted me and placed me on his bed.

His stomach rippled with strength, the muscled valley making me lick my lips. His skin was flawless and stretched over the muscles that begged for kisses.

He looked at me and the flames in his eyes danced with desire. He took off his belt and it too hit the floor. He kicked off his shoes, and then I heard the zipper of his pants exactly as I had in one of the dreams.

He stood before me, erect and beautiful. I'd been in a military camp with all men and I'd seen them in various degrees of nakedness, but none were as exquisite as Blade. His muscles flexed as he lowered himself, his hands going to either side of my head, boxing me in. His musky scent surrounded me. My heart felt like it would burst from my chest. Fear and anticipation filled me. I think he could see it. He lowered his head and kissed my lips.

"Mine," he breathed when he pulled back slightly. "My other half," he added when his body lowered and I could feel all of him.

The fear left and he rolled us so I was on top. His lips traveled from my mouth to my throat. He lifted me higher above him and circled a nipple with his tongue. He sucked and I could feel the slightest pinprick from his sharp fangs but it didn't hurt. It was glorious. I moaned as he moved to my other breast.

My hands were on his arms and I squeezed his tight muscles. My power shimmered around us or maybe it was our combined power. He released my nipple and turned us on our sides. His fingers traveled lower and I pushed against them when they found their way between my legs. He circled the slick juice and I flicked his nipple with my tongue. I was breathing hard and made a noise when his finger slid inside me.

"Shh," he whispered and flattened his hand over my mound, adding pressure as I pressed harder against him.

He pushed me onto my back and began kissing his way down my body until he was between my legs. We were atop his comforter and I grabbed it into my fists. His fangs grazed one thigh and I cried out. His husky laugh filled me until his tongue found my center.

"Please," I moaned.

A finger slid inside me and he sucked my clit between his lips. My hips rose from the bed. I needed more. I needed him. He was giving me everything I asked for but I was greedy.

My power centered in my gut and traveled down to where his mouth touched me. A second finger entered and I only managed to stay still because his powerful hands forced me too.

"Let go," he whispered against my flesh.

I had no choice. The room rocked with the rush of power that flowed out of me. Blade groaned but his lips continued torturing me until I couldn't stop the rising tide and I exploded into a million pieces. My dreams hadn't come close to this.

He climbed up my body and his long, thick shaft entered me before I came back to earth. No matter that he was large, I stretched to take him fully. I writhed with need beneath him. My nails dug into his skin as the storm built again.

I was almost there when his fangs pierced my throat. I screamed.

Chapter 39

The power surge detonated out of me and Blade took it along with my blood. I throbbed where we were intimately joined and his strokes grew more rapid. My heels dug into his ass as he took and took and took.

There was no way to describe what was happening. I was completely undone, completely consumed, and completely his. With a final arch of his hips, he came. A groan thundered from his throat to meet my cry. My entire body vibrated beneath his. His skin was cool and mine hot as our breathing settled.

I smoothed my hands over his back and unlocked my legs.

His mouth covered mine again and I tasted blood and my desire. He pulled away and lifted his weight slightly so I could breathe.

I looked into his eyes.

"Mine. My other half." I repeated the words he'd said because it seemed right.

He rolled to the side and took me with him so we lay facing each other.

"Thank you for this gift," he said.

My hand traveled between his legs and I took him in my hand. He was half-erect.

"Mine is a gift that keeps giving and giving," I teased.

He chuckled and kissed me. Within a few minutes, we made love again and the same soul shattering feelings enveloped me.

"I will need more nourishment to do that again," I whispered when we came up for air.

His chest rumbled with laughter.

"Inform Hax that you wish sustenance and he will deliver it." He smiled wryly. "My connection with the ornery man is no longer there so some things you must do on your own."

"I know how to do it with the plants, but you have none in here."

"Use the plants in your rooms or from the garden. They will hear your call."

I reached out and made the connection with vines from the garden and then with Hax. I told him what I needed and where to deliver it.

"Bring the robe from my closet," I said as an afterthought which embarrassed me.

Hax would know what we'd done and would be doing again. I had to accept that it was okay. I wasn't sure what was entailed in pairing, but I knew what we had done felt right. My magic rejoiced. The bond between me and Blade was larger and more secure than it had been before we made love.

"Your skin is warmer," I said as I skimmed my hand over his chest.

He lifted my fingers and kissed them.

"That is the gift of your blood."

I leaned in and gently kissed his chest.

When Hax arrived, he spoke to Blade while I stayed in bed beneath the covers. I didn't know why I was worried about the guttybrew's condemnation, but I was. He left and Blade returned to the room.

He'd brought my robe and I put it on, then sat in Blade's lap and ate the fresh vegetables. His fingers explored inside the robe at every opportunity and I laughed and slapped his hand away. Desire was interfering with food.

"I'm starving," I told him.

"So am I," he said huskily.

Between bites I asked for information.

"Tell me about your connection to the guttybrew."

I could feel his smile against my hair.

"What?" I asked when he didn't answer immediately.

"My past connection. They are loyal to you now. They understood my part in the prophecy and were there when I needed them. I will always be in their debt."

"How did they help?"

He took his time in answering because he'd cupped my breast and was playing with my nipple.

"When we first came out to the humans, our lives were in chaos. I don't know why we didn't expect the backlash that happened. The werewolves were involved in a mishap and people were injured. All hell broke loose. It became fight or die and we had the battle on two fronts. The guttybrew stepped in and made tunnels so we could hide underground and regroup. The military found a group of guttybrew and killed half of them. We managed to save the other half. Their entire colony moved into my territory after that."

"The humans knew about guttybrew?"

He squeezed me a bit tighter, his chin still resting on my head.

"The guttybrew had successfully remained hidden until they helped us. The military knew about vampires and weres years before we came out," he said. "The military used us to do their dirty work. When we finally stood up to them, they extorted us. This was the catalyst to going public."

"Then why did you leave me with the military?" I asked, hurt. "If they had discovered what I was, they would have killed me."

He adjusted my body, pulling me slightly upward so he could see my eyes.

"You were never in danger. If they had found out about what you could do, you would have been used to their benefit. I would have removed you immediately."

I let it go, at least for now. I wasn't sure I liked the fact that I was purposefully left with people who could have harmed me.

"Why are the vampires and werewolves at war?"

He seemed relieved that I'd moved on.

"That goes back centuries and has to do with wielders too. We lived, not quite in harmony, but what you might say was a cohesive agreement. The world didn't know we existed and we wanted to keep it that way. Wielders supercharged vampires with their blood, and their power also helped control werewolf magic. Without it, the weres were wild and unpredictable. Something happened and a pack of wolves killed a large family of wielders who had aligned more with my people than they had with the werewolves. We took revenge and killed them without knowing one of them was their king's brother."

I could see a lot happening in Blade's expression. He was remembering the past.

"Was it Rollin's brother?" I asked.

His eyes instantly burned and he looked away. One of his hands was in my hair and he fisted it to the point of pain. He stopped when he realized what he'd done, but he didn't look at me.

"Yes. It was Rollin's brother."

I decided not to continue down that road. My feelings for Rollin were confusing.

"Do you know how it all started? Vampires, werewolves, wielders, I guess I'm asking about. The very beginning."

He took a breath and I knew he was relieved I'd changed the subject again.

"There is a legend about vampires and werewolves but I'm unsure about wielders and guttybrew."

"Would you tell me?" I asked.

He looked at me and smiled softly.

"There was a man with twin sons. His wife was unable to have more children but he loved her and was unwilling to cast her aside. His sons were his world. They became very ill and he made a deal with a god. If the god spared his sons, he would give his life for theirs. The god agreed. He saved the boys by making one of the twins a vampire and one a werewolf. When the vampire woke, he drank his father's blood and the werewolf ate him."

"That's horrible," I whispered. "Do you believe it?"

"It's the only explanation I've heard."

"What happened to their mother?"

"It's said the god loved her and wanted the husband out of the way. Some think she cheated on her husband and her sons were the byproduct of the god."

He looked at me, his eyes suddenly flaming so bright I caught my breath, and I wasn't sure why.

"I'm hungry," he said.

Good. I was hungry too.

Chapter 40

I wasn't sure why I woke up in my bed. I didn't remember coming here. Blade and I stayed up most of the night. I groggily remembered falling asleep in his bed before the sun came up.

I rolled over and saw a note on the bedside table.

Visit the sun today.

I will find you when it goes down.

I jumped out of bed and hit the shower. Blade's note made me realize how much I needed sunshine. I sent a message to Hax so he would deliver my meal in the garden and to bring tea for himself. I smiled when I felt his grunt.

I dressed in leather pants and a tank top but left off the jacket. I opened the door to my room and quickly walked the twists and turns without thought. I knew where I was going; the energy from the garden was my guide. I opened the last door and walked into my daytime wonderland.

I took a deep breath and relished the heat on my bare arms. When I looked around, I saw Hax in the shadowed part of the garden, waiting patiently.

"My apologies," I said when I was closer. "I didn't think about the sunlight bothering you. Please don't stay out here on my account."

"I brought tea, my lady." He nodded toward the table. "The sunlight will quickly burn my skin, but if I stay in the shadows, it has no effect."

"Good. I have questions."

I laughed when he grunted. For the first time since Drake brought me here, I felt free. The sun told me it was around three in the afternoon. I took a seat at the table and devoured the food. Vines rubbed against my legs but didn't try to touch bare skin. Hax calmly drank his tea. I wasn't sure if he was happy about my night with Blade or not.

"Do you approve of my being with Blade?" I asked after the last bite. I'd decided I didn't want Hax's opinion ruining my meal.

"Your union is in the prophecy. Blade had to wait for your power or it would have happened sooner." His voice was strained.

"That doesn't mean you approve," I said skeptically.

"Blade fought the prophecy for so long, I worried he would cause trouble."

"Hmm." I tried to decipher what he wasn't saying. A thought occurred to me. "You told me about Kenia, but I didn't ask if there was another woman he cared about before or after her."

"No, my lady. There was no one after her. His lovers before her did not last long."

I was still missing a key link to what was happening, but I didn't know the right questions so I peppered Hax with small ones. After an hour, I stood and began warming my arms and wrists after taking my sword from its sheath.

"Do you think it would be possible for Mika and Coop to visit me here? I would love to spar with Coop in the daylight."

"If you ask Blade, I am sure he would grant your wish."

"I'll do that."

I continued asking questions while I went through my drills and killed imaginary fighters. The sun felt glorious. Hax finally went inside and I walked through the garden when I grew tired of sword work. I eventually lay in the grass and absorbed the energy around me. I watched the sun go down and then took another stroll.

A small shriek escaped my throat when Blade closed his arms around me from behind.

"You scared me," I said reproachfully. His energy melded with mine.

He chuckled softly in my ear which sent shivers over my skin. He kissed my neck and pulled me closer.

"I should have showered," I said. "I've been out here since I woke up."

He licked my neck and my body instantly throbbed with need.

"You taste good," he said huskily. "Would you like to eat dinner out here? We can take advantage of the pool after eating."

I turned in his arms and looked into his eyes. At that instant, I knew I loved him with all my being. Maybe it was part of mating, but I didn't think so. I read the same in his eyes. I went to my tiptoes and kissed him. His hand wrapped in my ponytail and when he pulled away from my lips, his mouth traveled to my throat. I felt the slight nick of his fangs but he didn't feed.

"I don't mind," I told him. "My blood is yours."

He growled softly and continued making small biting kisses on my neck.

"When we make love, there is little pain. I can wait," he promised.

"Does it hurt when you feed your pack?"

"Yes, but it makes us stronger."

I took a step back and peered into his fire-filled eyes.

"I burn for you," I groaned.

I didn't see him move. We were suddenly on the soft grass, his fangs buried in my throat. He was right; it hurt but the energy flowing between us helped. As his body took power from mine, he fed it back and the pain floated on waves of energy. It was bearable.

When he lifted his head, he smiled so I could see his fangs. They turned me on and I wanted more.

"I love you," I said softly.

His expression changed and I couldn't read his thoughts, but he pulled me to him and buried his face in my hair, holding me close and caressing my bare skin beneath the tank top. He didn't say the words, but I knew he loved me. We were paired and no one could take that from us.

***

Two weeks later, Blade had Mika and Coop brought to his home for a week. They were given rooms next to mine. When I fell asleep in Blade's arms each night, he carried me to my bed and I woke up without him. I would ask him about it after my friends left.

"I see this has been a true hardship for you," Mika said when she looked around the garden.

I'd brought her and Coop outside in the early afternoon so I could spar with my friend.

"Extremely difficult," I said with a sly grin.

We'd stayed up late the previous evening after their arrival and I'd told them about my relationship with Blade. Mika was happy for me and Coop concerned. I'd expected both responses.

"Are you ready to spar?" I asked Coop. "I'll go easy on you."

I sparred with Drake and I was so much faster now. We usually ended in a draw. I would go easy on Coop. I hadn't explained about my power or the prophecy.

"Don't be so sure of yourself," he said with a smile. "I too have been working on my skills."

After an hour, he lowered his sword.

"Something is different," he said. "I feel heat from your sword, but I can't see the flame."

I'd been working at controlling my power with Drake. If I fired my sword, he couldn't beat me and Coop had no chance.

"I have something to show you," I told him. I trusted Coop and Mika. They might be the last two humans I could trust. I'd debated showing them what I had become because I didn't want them endangered by the knowledge. I also wanted them to reach out to me if there was trouble, and if they worried about harming me, they wouldn't.

I handed my sword to Coop and walked about ten feet away. Mika was lying on a blanket in the grass. I lifted my arms and called the plants. They immediately swayed toward me and the vines traveled from around the garden, growing when they needed to so they could reach me. They circled my feet and traveled up my legs, around my waist, and along my torso. I raised my arms higher and they lifted me and moved me closer to Coop.

Mika gasped as magic spilled from my body, raining down around us. Coop lifted his hand and grabbed sparkles from the air.

"You're glorious," he said, his expression of awe matching the words.

I laughed. "I'm learning new things about my power every day."

I lowered my arms, though the movement wasn't necessary. I could communicate with the plants in my mind. I reached out and my sword appeared in my hand. Coop jumped and Mika laughed, covering her mouth at his expression.

"If you have need of me," I told them. "Whisper it in your garden at home and I will come."

Chapter 41

My fairy-tale relationship with Blade lasted for two months.

I stepped into a room I was unfamiliar with and Rollin was sitting on his throne. He was shirtless and wore black leather pants that conformed to his body. His muscles bunched when he saw me and then rippled when he stood.

The people surrounding him departed and I walked forward until we were a few feet apart. He didn't smile as he had in the past. A rumbling noise sounded from his throat.

"You are mine," he snarled. The words held so much power, I almost went to my knees. It was a different energy than Blade's, wild and completely untamed. It traveled over my skin and I thrilled at the feel, but I told him the truth.

"No," I said. "I belong to Blade."

We were suddenly standing inches apart.

"You are mine," he repeated with a growl, breathing the words against my lips. He kissed me.

Rollin drank my power much as Blade had and I couldn't fight him. I wasn't sure I wanted to. I'd closed my eyes when his lips met mine and when I opened them, we were beneath the trees, him over me. We were both naked and I placed my arms around him.

Power sizzled from my body to his, and when he entered me, I screamed.

That's when I opened my eyes. I was in Blade's bed, the smell of him settling my heartbeat. Blade wasn't in the bedroom. I got up and looked for him, but he was gone. Disturbed by the dream, I went back to my suite.

I didn't see Blade until the following evening. We ate in the garden which had become our favorite place. There was a wicker box that held a blanket and pillows which we used when we made love on the grass.

He hadn't said much when he found me waiting for him. I kissed him, but he stepped away quickly. The dream had shaken me and I'd wanted to talk to him about it but felt this wasn't the time.

"I will be gone for several days," he told me without looking into my eyes. "Maybe a week."

He may not be looking at me, but I could see the angry flames in his gaze.

"Where are you going?" I asked carefully.

"That is not important. Hax will care for you until my return." He stood.

"Blade, what is wrong?" Did he know about the dream? If so, we needed to talk. The fire burning in his eyes reminded me of the night he killed Kenia. It had been months since I was afraid of him, but fear brought a cold sweat to my skin.

He was suddenly beside me, his hand in my hair pulling my neck back, and his fangs entered my throat. It burned worse than it had before. This was something we rarely did without sex because as he's said, it was easier on me and more enjoyable while we made love.

When he released me, he wiped blood from his lip. My blood.

"Why did you do that?" I demanded, now becoming angry even though I was still afraid.

"You," he bit out, "are mine. Do not forget it."

He stepped back and the shadows swallowed him. Part of his words were exactly as Rollin had said. He did know about the dream, quite possibly all the dreams. Why had he never said anything? I was asleep and if he knew of a way to stop them, he could have told me.

My anger rose and energy flared around me, lighting up the dark garden.

"My lady?" Hax asked quietly.

I walked away from him and went to my rooms. Then I did the last thing I wanted to do.

I cried.

***

Blade was gone for a week. He came to my room the night of his return. His skin was gray much like it had been when he'd been injured.

"I need you," he said simply.

I walked forward and gave him my throat.

"No," he whispered against my skin. "Not like this."

He lifted me off my feet and carried me to the bed. He made love to me and he drank my blood, turning his skin healthy. When we were both sated, he rolled me to my side so we were facing each other. This was our talking time and had become a pleasurable habit.

It was then I noticed the jagged cut on his chest. It ran from his collarbone, across his chest, under his arm. It had been deep, though I could see it was healing.

"You should have fed," I told him.

His hand cupped my face. "I feed from you," he said.

"Then you should have taken me with you. I forbid you to leave again without me. I can take care of myself. I'm as dangerous as a vampire."

His expression turned serious.

"I think you are. If I go away again, I will take you."

"Did you kill him?" I asked. He looked at me questioningly. "The man who did this," I clarified as I gently ran my finger around the wound.

"No. But I will."

The fire I'd seen the day he left was back in his eyes. It was my turn to cup his face.

"You scare me when you look this way. I love you and I am yours."

His eyes changed and the angry fire banked to desire. It was hours before I ate dinner, and I was weak when I sent a message to Hax to bring food.

The guttybrew's eyes chastised me but he didn't say anything when he delivered the tray.

After I devoured dinner, we returned to the bedroom. I woke the next day with Blade gone and the plants gripping my body, replenishing the power Blade had taken.

He didn't join me that night or the next. I was caught between anger and fear when he came to me on the third evening. His skin wasn't gray like it had been after his week away, but it wasn't healthy.

I had just finished my meal and without thinking, the plate flew across the room and crashed into his chest. I wasn't sure who was more shocked. His incredulous look made me angrier.

"I am not your whore, Blade. You will not come here simply because you need blood."

He came forward and his lips found mine. He drew energy from the kiss and I didn't stop him. He carried me to the bedroom and took what he needed. Then he left me again.

I screamed my anger and hurt, but only the plants heard me. They wrapped around me in comfort.

***

Blade slipped into my bed several nights later. His mouth worshipped me and I moaned into the dark room, unable to resist him. He flipped us over and I rode his body until we both cried out.

His fangs entered my throat and he took my blood.

If it wasn't for the dark drops on the sheets the next day, I would have thought I'd dreamed it.

My unease grew with a change in Hax and Drake. They both had trouble meeting my gaze. What had I done? They were angry with me but I had no clue why. I tried to talk to them both, but they went silent when I spoke of Blade. I wanted to run away, go back to Mika and Coop, and lick my wounds.

The dreams about Rollin didn't return, but I dreamed of Blade.

I was his blood whore.

Chapter 42

Four weeks after I'd dreamed of Rollin, something changed. I knew it the minute I opened my eyes. Hax entered my bedroom, which was something he'd stopped doing after I had the ability to call him through the plants.

"Blade has asked for you to accompany him this evening. He would like you to pack a bag for a week's stay." He lifted a large case for me to use. "He has requested you wear the gown inside."

Blade was taking me with him. I almost forgave him for how he'd treated me this past month. Almost. I would have time with him and we could talk. The place in my gut that had been wrapped tight, loosened.

Hax's eyes barely met mine. Unfortunately, I was too excited to really notice.

"Eat first, my lady, and I will help you pack."

I shoveled down my food. When I finished, I washed my hands and opened the travel bag to see what was inside. Instead of silver, this gown dripped glittering gold that looked like fine chain mail over shiny gold material. I laid it out on the bed and took out the shoes which were slightly higher than the silver ones. I would practice walking later.

As promised, Hax helped me fill the travel case. I slipped my father's box inside, unwilling to part with it. It held his letter and my mother's necklace and drawing. Hax didn't question me packing a piece of wood.

When we finished, I shooed him out of the suite. He took the case with him. I showered with extra care, washing my body thoroughly and scrubbing as much rough skin as possible from my hands. I wanted to be beautiful for Blade and for some reason, soft hands went along with how good I wanted to look. I used copious amounts of lotion too.

Blade arrived an hour after the sun went down. I'd placed my hair in the same style Lizbet had used for Blade's seduction. It displayed my throat and that's exactly what I wanted.

He looked at me and flames sparked in his eyes.

"You are beautiful," he said huskily.

He wore a black suit and I wanted to strip it away from him and kiss every inch of skin beneath the material. I sensed sadness from him but I ignored it. I was determined to discover what continued to weigh him down. If we needed to discuss Rollin, we would. As far as I was concerned, we could have a knock-down, drag-out fight, but we would fix this.

I hadn't noticed the hand he held behind his back. He pulled it forward. A large velvet box sat on his palm. He opened it.

A diamond necklace rested inside. The top part was a two-strand diamond choker affixed in gold with three additional strands of diamonds hanging down from it. The final strand held a large emerald. The stone would drop almost between my breasts.

"It's exquisite," I told him.

"It will only accentuate your beauty. You are exquisite. May I?"

I turned around and his hand glided over the skin of my throat.

"Blade?" I asked gently.

"Yes, my love."

He'd never said he loved me, and I knew what I would ask next was perfect for this occasion.

"Feed before you place the necklace on me." I said it softly but I knew he heard.

He turned me around and his eyes locked on mine.

"Please," I all but begged.

I'd missed him so much and I didn't care about the pain. I wanted him with a passion I hadn't known existed, but discarding the dress and delaying our departure was not happening.

I didn't get another chance to breathe before he struck. I gloried in the pain and gave him the gift of my blood. I loved him and would never deny him.

He kissed me after his fangs released my flesh. He tasted like my blood and Blade. It was a taste I'd grown accustomed to, and desire hit harder. The kiss ended and he held me in his arms, swaying gently.

Thank you," he said. "Will you wear the necklace now?"

I turned around and he put it on. I took his hand and pulled him into the bathroom so I could see it in the mirror. He stood behind me with a soft smile.

"Another fable that isn't true," I said.

His expression changed to questioning.

"I can see you in the mirror. The books say vampires have no reflection."

He laughed. I placed my hand to my throat.

"I love it," I said.

His fangs flashed and I tightened my thighs to hold back my need. He was so damn sexy. I wanted everything wrong with the two of us to go away.

"I will carry your sword," he told me.

I hadn't seen a way to wear it without taking away from the breathtaking gown, but I wanted it with us. I handed it to him and he took my hand and walked me outside.

Before we reached the front, Ambrosia ran toward me. She seemed panicked. Lizbet came from behind and stopped her. I couldn't hear what she said but Ambrosia turned and ran away. Blade squeezed my hand.

"We must hurry," he said.

I hadn't seen Ambrosia during the past week. When I returned, I would seek her out and discover what was wrong. I left these thoughts behind and went with Blade to the Humvee that was waiting.

I took his hand again once we were situated in the back seat. Drake came out of the house and sat in front as he'd done the first time, though he wasn't driving tonight. There were six dark vehicles accompanying us, two in front and four in back. After our run-in with Rollin the last time, I suspected Blade was taking no chances.

I began to recognize the area before we arrived at the club. Relief passed through me at the destination. Maybe we were staying in town. We pulled in front of the lighted building and the Humvee's door opened. Blade led me inside. The last time we'd come here, he surprised me by bringing Coop and Mika to the club. It was a memorable night made more so by an attack from the werewolf pack and being bitten by one. Rollin had saved me. I tossed the thought into the background. Bad things happened when I thought about Rollin.

Blade had been helping me shield my thoughts, but I was unsure if it worked. I hadn't dreamed about the werewolf again, but I couldn't help feeling my last dream was the cause of all the problems between me and Blade.

We walked up the stairs to the private section that overlooked the club. Like before, people were dancing and arranging wicked meetings in the back area where vampires could drink human blood. Would Blade take me back there? I would ask later. The thought turned me on. I couldn't help wondering if they had sex too.

I was watching the lower floor when Blade's hand gently pushed on my lower back and steered me toward the grouping of chairs.

I stopped when I saw who was waiting.

Rollin.

I glanced up at Blade. His jaw was clenched. He must have felt my gaze because he looked down and our eyes met.

His gaze carried sadness, fury, and possessiveness. I had to trust that he knew what he was doing. His fingers increased the pressure on my back and I stepped forward. Blade pulled back the furthest chair from Rollin and I sat in it. He then took the closer chair to his enemy, protecting me.

"Rollin," said Blade.

"Vampire," said Rollin, his voice a rough semi-growl. He turned and looked at me. His expression was like Blade's but it lacked sadness. What I noticed most was the possessiveness of his gaze. "Tara," he said in his deep velvety tone that was nothing like Blade's but conveyed the same intonation of desire.

I couldn't believe this was happening or that Blade brought me to a meeting with Rollin. That had to be what this was. I had no idea about the politics that were required to keep the peace. Nothing would improve with the vampires and wolves fighting. I was the bridge to peace and it started tonight.

I glanced behind us and saw several of Blade's vampires standing guard. Rollin had werewolves behind him too.

Drake placed a filled wineglass in front of me and I took a sip.

"This will be easier," Blade said, "if you are more relaxed."

I wasn't sure what he meant, but I trusted him and took a heftier swallow. He smiled and I took his hand beneath the table. He squeezed my fingers, then released me. Maybe he wanted both his hands free.

"I didn't think you would show," Rollin said.

Blade's body stiffened and I knew without looking that there was angry fire in his eyes.

"We had an agreement and unlike you, I do not go back on my word," he said.

I took another drink. I reached for the plants in the club and connected with several. They soothed me as they always did. I was hot and I lifted my hand to my warm flushed cheek. It was the tension in the room. I pulled on the energy of the plants to keep me calm.

"Does she know?" asked Rollin.

"No," Blade said angrily.

"Know what?" I demanded, looking back and forth between the two men.

"The longer I stay, the more dangerous this situation is," Rollin said. "We don't need theatrics or long goodbyes."

"You have no idea what you are doing," Blade said softly. His voice didn't qualify as angry, it was enraged. The hot fire in his words sent chills over my skin. I looked up at him and the room tilted.

"Blade," I said urgently. "There is something wrong." Drake pushed another wineglass toward me.

"Drink and you will feel better," Drake said.

I gazed at the wine in horror and my eyes shot to Drake's.

"You put something in the wine."

Chapter 43

Drake looked over my head at Blade, and then he glanced behind us. Two vampires stepped forward and placed their hands on Blade's shoulders. My mate looked at me and I saw more than sadness now. He shook off the arms holding him and grabbed me, pulling me in for a punishing kiss.

Rollin's growls filled my ears, but Blade ignored them.

"I love you," he said, looking into my eyes. "I will always love you."

He was wrenched away and Drake's hand landed on my shoulder.

"You need to get her out of here," Drake told Rollin. "Now. We will have trouble holding him."

I started struggling against Drake. Had he set Blade up? Drake turned my body so I was facing him and we were both standing, though I had no idea when I stood up. He was holding both my shoulders now.

"Blade never goes back on his word. Remember that," he said. "Rollin will not harm you."

"No," I said as the room spun.

My power, I thought. I must use my power. I tried but it wouldn't work. Drake had drugged me and Blade had betrayed me. I had to escape. I tried but I fell against Drake. His hand went into my hair and he hugged me and then let me go. Strong arms lifted me and I looked up.

Rollin stared down at me.

I was carried to a waiting vehicle. My head spun and I fought to keep my eyes open. It was a losing battle.

Chapter 44

I woke up in a small room with a single light. There was nothing on the walls, no windows, and the room held only a bed and a wooden nightstand. I was dizzy and it took a few minutes to remember what had happened. As memories flooded me, I wanted to scream. I somehow held them back.

There were two doors. After contemplating my next move for several minutes, I stood and opened the first one. It was a bathroom. I tried the other door and it was locked. I pounded on it in frustration.

No matter that I remembered what happened, I couldn't believe Drake gave me to the werewolves. No, that wasn't right. Blade did this. He'd said he loved me but that was a lie.

No one answered my insistent pounding and I couldn't hold back the tears. Feeling sorry for myself, I curled up on the bed and cried.

When a long crying jag of self-pity got me nowhere, I stood and entered the bathroom. Using one of the plain white towels, I wet the edge and washed my face. Next, I went to my travel case which was in the corner. My sword was propped next to it against the wall. The sword surprised me. Did Rollin not think I would use it on him?

I grabbed comfortable clothes from the bag and took them into the bathroom. I had to get out of the gown. I removed the necklace first, unwilling to have it on any longer. I changed into jeans and a T-shirt. I had to go back to the bag for socks and shoes. I slipped them on my feet and went back to the bag, dumping the expensive necklace inside.

I found the piece of wood from my father at the bottom. After removing my sword from the sheath, I carried both to the bed. I rested the sword beside me and placed the wood in my lap. The slice to my finger was deeper than I intended but I didn't think about it when I touched my blood to the wood. I looked down at my box and placed the finger into my mouth to stop the bleeding. I needed to read my father's words again.

I opened the lid and stopped breathing. There was another letter in the box.

How?

I carefully unfolded the white paper. The bold script was from Blade's hand. I could smell him on the paper.

Tara,

I know you do not understand. For that, I am sorrier than you could ever know. You trusted me and I betrayed that trust.

You are The Promised and you belong to two men. It hasn't been easy for me to accept this since we paired. I fought against the promises I made but the prophecy refuses to be denied. I thought about taking you away. My dreams told me we would both die. You know the dreams are true just as I do.

No matter how much you hate me right now, I could not allow you to die.

Rollin will care for you. Do not fear him. I only say this because I know it will be hard. I hate him more than you could possibly understand. I hate the thought of him seeing you smile. The are no words to describe how I feel about him touching you.

At some point, I hope you can forgive me. We will see each other again. This is the only thing that keeps me alive.

You are most likely wondering how I got into the box. It is activated with blood and I control blood.

I love you and always will,

Blade

Tears were running down my cheeks. My hands shook as I read the letter again. My heart hurt so much I thought I would die. I reached out with my power and connected with plants that grew nearby. I had no idea where they were, but they were not from my garden. These grew wild and their energy felt different in a good way.

It strengthened me for what was to come.

The door opened and I looked up.

Alaric stepped inside. He had saved me once but he had also been trying to kidnap me so there was that. I didn't fear the werewolf. That would require feelings.

"Tara, I am glad you are awake. I am sure you are hungry. Rollin would like to see you before you eat."

I placed the box on the bed and the letter inside before closing the lid. I lifted the sword and walked over and placed it in the sheath, then put the sheath on my back.

I followed Alaric from the room as he led me outside.

The trees and plants I'd connected to were here. I breathed in their scent. Even the tallest tree swayed toward me. Small rocks bit into my feet and I didn't care.

"Come," said Alaric.

I remained silent but followed him down a narrow path. Log cabins were peppered throughout the area. He led me to the largest. It looked as if it had once been a church.

The door was opened by another werewolf. He nodded as we passed.

I felt the hard marble beneath my feet. It was a large foyer. Two double doors at the far end opened. I walked through and stopped. This room was in my dream and like the dream, Rollin sat on a large chair that doubled as his throne.

It wasn't Rollin who captured my attention though.

Three men stood behind him. Three men whom I knew and had known for years.

Mule, Shep, and Leo stared at me with faces of stone. No welcoming smile, no hello. I gulped, the hurt swelling inside me.

"Tara," Rollin said in his deep voice.

Our eyes met and my hatred ignited. The walls shook with the power that roared out of me. There were stained glass windows on either side of the room. They cracked with a mighty sound. The floor beneath me trembled. The doors behind me were shut but they flew open.

I didn't realize I was screaming but when I did, I continued. Tears fogged my vision and still my power raged.

Hard arms pulled me against an equally hard chest. A rough hand smoothed over my hair that had fallen from its clasp.

I smelled the wild, the untamed. Rollin's scent filled me. My rage turned to deep sorrow and my legs buckled. The werewolf lifted me. I went limp in his arms. I hated him but I was to overcome with emotion to tell him so.

I wanted my vampire.

Chapter 45

PART TWO: THE PROMISE

Lifting the quilted cover, I inspected my fully clothed body. I wasn't sure how I got from point A to point B. The last thing I remembered was screaming on the floor of some throne-looking room like a complete lunatic.

My clothes were on. Check. My shoes were off and, after a quick glance, I found them resting on the floor. Check. My sword and the bag that held the box from my father were in the corner. Check.

I looked around at the slightly larger room than the original one I was brought to. The sheets were soft white cotton. The quilted cover was gorgeous. A door was open across from where I lay, and I could see a private bathroom. There was a window with thin, white-laced curtains pulled to the side, sunlight streaming inside with treetops visible from where I was lying.

Mental pain wrapped around my insides and squeezed. I had never felt as hopeless as I did at that moment. I turned and stared at the wall.

The image of three faces sliced through my memory. I had always believed they were my friends. The betrayal twisted my heart and added to the deep ache in my stomach, and I feared it would never stop.

Shep, Leo, and Mule. It hurt so much. They were not my friends. They were the enemy. Tears threatened, but I held them back. The enemy did not deserve my tears. I had to face a life without Blade, and it was his betrayal that hurt the most. So many lies. He allowed me to fall in love with him, knowing he would discard me when I'd served his purpose.

Hell. Blade sold me to his enemy.

I was also furious that I had barely looked for my father's killer. Blade took vengeance away from me, and I hadn't thought about retribution in months. I had no idea where I was, but I knew I was nowhere near the city.

Hours ticked by, and still, I couldn't grasp the totality of what had happened. Melancholy finally took a back seat to anger and burned its way up my chest. In order to survive, something had to drive me forward. Hatred would do.

My energy changed the air around me to deep angry red with lighter shades of pinks and purples adding contrast. This was what hatred looked like. Blade took the top spot on my list.

I needed the anger to burn so hot that I no longer loved him. His smile flashed in my mind, and I turned the memory to what I could do to him with my sword. Blood. Begging. Leaving him to die with his entrails cascading over the floor while he writhed in pain.

I wanted him to hold me so badly. No, I would not cry. I closed my eyes and decided that pulling the quilt over my head was by far the best way to deal with the insanity that had become my life. They weren't even keeping me high up in some tower that I could throw myself from. Maybe I would be forgotten in this room, and I could die of starvation.

A muffled tapping noise sounded, and I turned my attention to it. The noise came again, and to discover what it was, I would need to take the cover off my head. Dare I? Wallowing in self-pity sounded like a great idea. Curiosity won.

I peeled back the covers and looked in the direction of the sound. Someone scratched on the window. Someone with claws, and I recognized those claws. Hax.

The pent-up anger extinguished, and my heart raced with relief. Hax lifted himself so he could see above the window line. His large eyes stared into mine for a few seconds before he dropped out of sight again.

I had an ally.

Loud voices came from beyond the window. I threw aside the cover and ran toward where Hax had been. Men scrambled around the area shouting and pointing downward. I went to my tiptoes so I could see where they pointed. There was a hole in the ground. Hax had burrowed into enemy territory.

A man ran into the clearing carrying a long spear. He poked it into the hole, driving it deep. My stomach leapt to my throat. They would kill him. The man lifted the spear and shook his head at the other men. I could hear their voices, but I couldn't make out the words.

Hax had gotten away. Blade said the guttybrew watched me when I took out the men on the motorcycles after the helicopter ride. They had been below ground. My joy ramped up another notch. Hax followed me, and he was here.

My thoughts changed rapidly now that someone had my back. I still wore jeans and a T-shirt. I walked to the door and turned the handle. Unlocked. A short hall was directly outside the room. I turned in the direction that I considered the front of the home, passing several more closed doors. Light spilled from a central room, and I followed the brightness. High vaulted ceilings with ten-foot windows greeted me. It was empty. After traversing more turns, I located the sturdy front door and stepped outside. Fresh air. I took a long deep breath and filled my lungs. The trees and plants came to attention, forming tiny sparks inside me. Our energy merged in a way I'd never felt. The beautiful forest pulled on every part of me that connected with the plants. The fauna didn't struggle due to heat or lack of water from the state's desert climate. They thrived here. Their energy traveled through my body, sinking into my soul.

"Home," they whispered in my mind. This was where I belonged, and it was the last place I wanted to be. I couldn't be mad at the trees and plants that offered comfort. Blade betrayed me. The thought of him hurt physically, and the plants felt it and sent me more warm energy. I didn't want them giving more than they should, so I cut Blade from my thoughts.

When I snapped from an almost trance, four burly men in jeans and flannel shirts stared at me. Large muscles and what I estimated as little brain power made them almost identical. When I stared back without moving, they turned their attention to the man with the spear while he continued poking into the hole left by Hax. And they laughed.

It was their first mistake. No, make it their second. Being born would get the first spot.

I raised my hands, and my power built. The feeling was glorious. Energy ran along my fingers clear to my toes. It expanded in my chest, and delicious heat filled me. Fully grown trees swayed and then bent. The men turned as one and stared at the trees.

They were looking in the wrong direction. I was the danger. I was vengeance.

"Are you doing that?" one of the men demanded.

Crack.

The top of a pine tree snapped, and a giant section of it fell. The men scrambled to get away and, unfortunately, succeeded.

"Leave my friend alone," I bit out in a voice I barely recognized as my own.

"Shit," the man with the stick said before he dropped it. The other men looked unsure.

I gave the trees a gentle caress of power. They moved back and forth to the point they might break before swaying to the other side as I fed my will into them. My chin went up a notch, my gaze burning into the men.

"If you hurt or kill my friend with a stick, gun, or claw, I will kill you."

I turned my back to them and returned to the house without waiting to see how they reacted to my declaration. There was a small part of me that hoped they would test it. Destroying everyone within the werewolf territory might be the only thing that would make me happy again.

Chapter 46

I didn't care about the house enough to search it. I also didn't want to see or speak to anyone. Hax would return. I went back to the bedroom and lifted my sheath from the corner where it rested. I removed the sword and carried it to the bed along with a soft piece of cloth I had taken from my bag.

With long, practiced strokes, I polished the sword. The repetition calmed me. I mentally went to a place where happiness, sadness, and anger no longer occupied my mind. The air in my lungs released slowly, and I inhaled just as deliberately.

There were no plants in the room, but that was okay. I could feel the ones outside. The door opened, and Rollin walked in like he owned the place. I guess he did. Suddenly, the room became too small. Dark wavy hair fell on his shoulders in complete disarray. His muscles bulged on his bare chest and arms, with jeans slung low on his slender hips. He was mouthwatering if you liked the look. Oh, he was pretty too, just not my type. Blade had refined muscle; it wasn't over the top like the Neanderthal staring at me.

My eyebrows arched as I waited for him to speak. I didn't stop the movement of my hand. Long strokes up, then down. I may have added a bit more pressure.

"Dinner will be served shortly." The gruff words were minimal and distinct. His weight rested on the balls of his feet, his eyes partially trained on the sword. I turned it over and proceeded to polish the other side. The strokes steady and unhurried.

His dark eyes slowly shifted to amber, their glow exactly as I remembered from the attack on the road when I was with Blade and Drake. This time I had longer to examine his eyes, and I realized what was happening. His eyes didn't glow because he planned to attack me. The stupid werewolf was turned on.

Rollin's tongue ran over his lush lips before his hand went to the front of his jeans, and he rearranged himself. While I watched! A musky odor filled the room. It wasn't unpleasant. I inhaled a bit because it was such an unusual scent. If he'd handled his crotch in front of me at the military camp, my friends would have beaten him within an inch of his life.

The thought brought me up short. Mule, Shep, and Leo were not my friends, and from what I'd seen, their allegiance was to Rollin. They would more than likely hold me down if their king decided he wanted a taste. I exhaled suddenly and stared daggers at half the cause of my current captive situation.

"I am not hungry," I said succinctly.

"You will eat." It was an order. My hand stopped mid-stroke. I gave him the full weight of my anger in my next words.

"Make. Me." It was a challenge. I gathered energy from the trees outside. Tendrils of power ran throughout my body. I wasn't prepared when Rollin launched himself onto the bed. I hadn't expected the move, and I barely had time to bring the sword up. I wielded a dexterous jab that missed because he pushed the sword aside so quickly I almost missed the movement. A fine trail of blood welled where the sword sliced his hand.

Two hundred pounds of half-covered male body landed on me, and I no longer had control of my weapon. Hot amber eyes burned into mine.

"What will you do now, little rabbit?" he asked huskily. That damn pet name. I might gag.

Energy flung out from me. Rollin grunted and bucked slightly. It was enough. I rolled to the left and scrambled off the bed, the sword lifted and ready to take his head. The low chuckle that came from his chest was not what I expected.

"You think you can take me?" he asked when his laughter faded.

"Why don't we test it." He lay back against the pillows, his arms arching up behind his head casually. He crossed his legs and widened his grin so I could see most of his white teeth.

I lifted the sword higher. His laughter filled the room again. Once more shivers traveled across my skin. This scene had never played out in my dreams.

Rollin was between me and the door. With my back to the wall, I had little room to put power behind the strike. I readied the sword anyway.

His eyebrows arched higher, but he didn't move, just waited. This was my chance, and I wanted so badly to bring the sword down. When push came to shove, I couldn't do it. I needed plants in the room. Ones with vines to secure him and make him pay for the fact I was here and not with Blade.

Crap, Blade betrayed me. I didn't want to be with him. Liar.

Rollin rolled on his side and patted the quilt beside him.

"Join me?" he asked. He was tempting me to attack. Without conscious thought, my eyes traveled down his body, and sure enough, he was hard and pushing against the jeans.

"You're bleeding on my bed cover," I said to distract myself. My arms were also tired from holding the sword up, but I refused to drop it.

Very slowly, Rollin ran his finger across the cut and lifted the blood to his mouth, licking it with his tongue. My thighs clenched. No, I didn't want his body, but any hot-blooded woman would be unable to look away. He patted the side of the bed again.

"Why don't we stop with the games and you join me like you want to. I promise, I'm warmer than your vampire."

I saw red again, and with every bit of strength I possessed, I brought the sword down.

Chapter 47

I aimed mid-body. I would cleave him in two. And dammit, he moved too fast. I didn't realize he wasn't there until I saw down feathers floating in the air from the eight-inch slice I put in the quilt.

He grabbed my arms and held them at my sides. I blinked and landed on the bed with Rollin on top of me. I no longer needed to see his erection because I could feel every hard inch. The bastard.

"Is rape your style?" I ground out behind my hair, which completely covered my face. "Do you feel more like an animal if you take me against my will?"

I expected rage and shook my head slightly to get the hair from my eyes. His lips surprisingly quirked.

"Do you want me to take you doggy style?" he jibed and ground his erection into me.

I no longer had the sword. It was somewhere on the floor. I needed to see his blood, and the scratch I gave him earlier wasn't enough. Cold fury filled me, and I did the last thing I should have. Tears leaked from my eyes, and I gulped to hold back the first sob. The pressure against my chest disappeared, and Rollin landed beside me. He lifted me into his arms and rolled us so we were on our sides facing each other. His expression held kindness which made everything worse.

"I don't need you to be kind," I said testily because I was embarrassed.

"Shh. Kindness never hurt anyone." He swiped more hair from my face as his eye color changed to pure beautiful black. Could he see into my soul? He was a lovely man but he wasn't the man I wanted. I sniffed loudly.

"I can't offer a shirt to use as your snot rag, and for that, you have my apology."

Laughter bubbled up from my chest. I chuckled again after another loud sniff.

"Dinner should be ready by now," he said. "I don't want to force you to eat, but I will if it's needed." I stiffened, but he continued, his expression turning formidable. "Your well-being is my priority. Nothing will stop me from keeping you safe, and that means you will eat."

I wanted to argue, but it would have been for the sake of argument and would get me nowhere. He smelled so damn good. The musk of his body was drawing me in along with the dreams that were cemented in my memory. If I bottled the scent to sell at Hell's Market, I would make a fortune.

"You are my mate," Rollin said. "The position holds power within my pack."

"I am not your mate," I said testily. "I'm not under your rule, and I won't rollover and pretend to do your bidding or be in any position over your pack."

He closed his eyes for a moment.

"You are so innocent, little rabbit," he said. "It will get you in trouble."

"Trouble?" I asked, ignoring his insistence on the pet name little rabbit for now.

My power shimmered below the surface. I'd been gathering it since I zapped him earlier. His fingers in my hair tightened, and his lips dipped in my direction.

I let go with everything I had.

It wasn't me flying through the air; it was the arrogant werewolf who thought to threaten me. The sword appeared in my hand when I called it, and I held it to his throat.

His eyes turned amber again, and he growled softly. I wondered if he would shift so we could finish the farce.

I put pressure on the sword, and even then he didn't look afraid. If anything, his arrogance grew.

"I am leaving here," I told him.

"No," he growled, the sound low and menacing.

There was no trace of desire left in his tone. Stepping back, I placed the sword on the bed. It wasn't time to kill him.

Yet.

Chapter 48

I planned to stick to my guns and refuse food. I wasn't even sure why. I think it was the fact I didn't want to be told what to do. I'd cooperated with just about everything in my life until this past year. I was done with doing anything that wasn't in my best interest.

The smell of food drifted beneath the door, and hunger ground in my stomach. Rollin left the room ten minutes before the delicious scent of food enticed me to forget that I wasn't giving in.

Who was I kidding. I was starving. I stepped from the room and heard voices coming from the front of the house. I took a minute to explore so I knew the layout. On this side there were five bedrooms, each a suite with its own bathroom. There was another corridor to another part of the house that I didn't explore because the hallway was dark.

The voices became louder as I approached the front of the house. I turned to the left and entered a large formal dining room. It was nothing like what I'd seen in the vampire compound. This was a home. It was casual with nothing ornate resting on delicate tables. Old Victorian art didn't cover the walls. Instead, artistic metalwork of trees and animal shapes decorated the space. And also unlike the vampires, the people sitting around the table were having a good time.

"Sit," said a woman from behind me. I jumped, and my hand lifted to the pommel of my sword, which was in the back sheath.

She was holding a large platter with about fifty pounds of sizzling steak. My stomach rolled over at the smell, and I dropped my arm. This was not the odor that wafted beneath my door. I glanced back at the table, which had gone silent.

I moved to the only empty seat on Rollin's left. He nodded when I walked toward him. He didn't stand to pull my chair out. I was glad. I didn't want to use my manners. I wanted to be rude and snarly because that's how I felt.

After dropping into the chair, I glanced at everyone seated. All but three stared back in open curiosity. Only the swine Mule, Shep, and Leo kept their heads down, and thankfully, they sat at the opposite end of the table. I turned my attention away from them.

In all, there were eleven male werewolves plus me. Two men smiled. I turned away from them quickly. Along with manners, I didn't want to make friends. As soon as I could, I would be gone. I also wondered why there were no women present for the meal other than the one delivering food. Did they make them eat outside? I wouldn't be surprised.

The woman who carried the platter placed it near the center of the table. She hurriedly walked from the room, and the chatter returned.

"I'm glad you decided to join us," Rollin said softly.

"Did I have a choice?"

"No, but some here would have enjoyed me dragging you in by the hair." His lips quirked, which made him look younger. "You took the fun from their evening."

What was it about him? He looked better than he had when he was in my room earlier, though he hadn't changed clothes or done anything specific that I noticed. He looked more stately or kingly or something. I shouldn't be attracted. No dammit, I wasn't attracted. To him. No, I was not.

"I'm very sorry I ruined their evening with my willing presence." My voice was syrupy sweet.

Another platter was carried in. This one held what appeared to be a mountain of fried chicken legs.

Rollin could not make me eat meat. I would fry him so soundly that smoke would come from his ears. The room went quiet again. The three men I refused to acknowledge were staring at me. Alaric sat on Rollin's other side. His gaze traveled the room. I glanced back at Rollin, who stared too. At me.

The woman who delivered the food placed a medium-sized platter in front of me. It was filled with grilled vegetables. My stomach growled. Rollin smiled and seemed pleased with himself.

Another dish with a mountain of raw vegetables landed next to the grilled veggies. No one moved, and I swung my attention back to Rollin. He reached for one of the platters and placed two large steaks on his plate. He then scooped up about ten chicken legs, sliding them next to the steak. He nodded to the others, and, as if by command, they began filling their plates.

"You may eat," he told me before cutting into his disgusting bloody food.

His nod to the others had been a command. "They can't eat until you nod your approval?" I asked. He put his fork down and gave me his attention. The others rested their utensils on their plates and waited.

"It takes a lot of fuel to shift," he said. "Food is very important to us, and one of the perks of being alpha is taking what I want before the others. He looked dubiously at my plate. "Your food is not something I want, but custom dictates you wait for my permission."

I would have objected, but my stomach growled again, and I wasn't taking a chance that my argument might get me booted from the room. I ate my meal. No one spoke. They used forks and knives, though it still surprised me when they didn't lick their fingers when they were done. A large platter with individual dessert cakes was placed on the table. Rollin smiled at me when I gave him a questioning look.

"Meat and sugar are our favorites. Please choose one."

They looked too good to pass up. For too many years I lived off of military rations. I might not eat like the weres, but I too liked sugar. I placed my hand out and quickly snatched one from the tray. Rollin's grin stayed in place, and he took one, a little slower than I had, then nodded to the others.

Again, no one uttered a word while we ate. When all forks and knives were resting on our dessert plates, Rollin spoke, "Each of you will introduce yourself to my mate," he said.

One by one, they made introductions. I didn't try to remember the names or what they said. Mule, Shep, and Leo were last.

"Don't bother," I told them. "I do not care who you really are. Stay away from me, and I'll stay away from you."

Mule's mouth formed a firm line. Shep shook his head, and Leo growled low in his chest.

"Maybe I'm not making myself clear," I said succinctly. "If you come near me, I will kill you."

I stood and left the room muttering under my breath. I'd just threatened more of Rollin's men. I was so damn angry, but at least I had a full stomach.

Top of Form

Chapter 49

The bedroom they'd assigned to me hadn't changed except to add a new quilt. The walls were still white, the new bedspread—or rather, quilt—a colorful forest scene, and the two pictures on the walls were of wolves. I stepped closer and examined one of the pictures. I knew very little about werewolves. Did they have an actual wolf form or just the ugly, oversized monster that I had seen? There were no answers within the wooden frame.

I paced the floor and regretted speaking out against my ex-friends. I would rather them think I didn't care, but I was finding it hard to hold my feelings inside. Maybe if it were just anger I would be okay. It wasn't. I felt betrayed and hurt to the point of pain. It ground against my insides and threatened to make me spew what food I'd consumed.

There was a lock on the bedroom door. I turned around and made sure it was secured. I paced some more and got nowhere, which I guess was the idea behind pacing. It was possible I needed to get my feelings about Mule, Shep, and Leo into the open and have it out with them. Murder was not the answer. But not now, I was too raw.

I lay on the bed because it was easier to feel sorry for oneself while laying down. Occasionally, a shadow passed the window, and I supposed it was guards. About a minute after I saw a shadow, a familiar scratching came from the window.

It was Hax.

I threw the window open and leaned over so I could see him. "Step back, my lady, and I will jump into the room."

If I had to guess, I would have said the improbability of a four-foot, muscled Guttybrew jumping six inches was fairly low. Jumping four feet through the window of the room, impossible.

I was wrong.

Hax's wide muscular body, short arms and all, flew through the window with little effort. As soon as he righted himself, I leaned over, threw my arms around his neck, and squeezed. "Thank you," I whispered against his rough skin.

"Breathing would be nice," he choked.

I loosened my arms and stepped back. I wiped a tear while Hax stared at me. I had to ask, "Did you know?"

He didn't need to say "know what" because he knew exactly what I was speaking of.

Hax looked uncomfortable, and I was sorry I asked. "I knew Blade had an arrangement with Rollin, but I didn't know all the details," he said.

"Did you suspect what the details were?"

He pranced from one foot to the other, which looked ridiculous. "It goes back to the prophecy," he said stubbornly.

I threw up my hands. "Maybe someone could tell me the entire prophecy, where it came from, and who I need to kill to make it stop ruining my life. No more surprises."

I walked over to one of four large chairs in the room and landed on a cushion with a grunt of frustration. Hax sat in the chair opposite me.

"You will not like what I tell you."

I gave him a look that I hoped would make his breath freeze in his lungs.

"You think I like being here? The man I love sent me to be with another man and betrayed me. I don't like anything that's happening, and I need to understand."

His breath left in a huff. "A vampire cannot make a child, and the prophecy requires your child to fulfill it."

I gave him my evil glare when he didn't immediately keep talking. I held his eyes until he spoke again.

"The prophecy says you will have the love of two great men and bear a child by the wolf. That would be Rollin," he said.

I didn't panic or leap from my chair and grab my sword. I had asked, but maybe I was asking the wrong question. "Why does the prophecy care if I have a child? What does it mean?"

"Your child shall rule for one hundred years."

"Rule what?" I asked while trying to wrap my head around one hundred years. The average lifespan of a human today is around fifty. It was a dangerous time for humans. I wasn't human, though.

"Does it say how long I live?" I asked out of curiosity.

"No, but it does say you will hold your first grandchild."

I sat back and sank further into the cushion. "So Blade gave me to Rollin to impregnate?" Yeah, my voice rose.

"My allegiance is to you, my lady, but I know what Blade did was not easy for him."

"Do not defend him," I snapped with a glacial expression. "Does the prophecy say I return to him with a child in my belly?"

"No. You have your choice of either man. It says two of you will rule together until you retire, but it does not tell us who you choose."

I stood. Seated was not working for me. I walked over and pulled my sword from its sheath. I stayed far enough away from Hax that I wasn't a danger to him. I flicked my wrist and went into one of my drills. I went through it again without it calming me. I would carry Rollin's child, and I didn't see how it was possible unless he raped me. If the man tried, I would end his life, prophecy or no.

Hax remained seated and watched. "I need to learn about werewolves. What do you know?" I went into another drill.

"They run off highly charged emotion, and they smell bad," Hax huffed.

My glare came back, and I took a swipe at him that wouldn't reach, but he got the message. "They are an emotional species," he said. "These emotions tie in with their ability to shift. Much of what I know is rumored. I have not lived with the weres like I did the vampires."

"You still know more than me, so spill everything you have so I'm not tempted to remove your head." It was said without heat. I needed to know enough to survive and escape this place.

"They are loyal, and their alpha means everything to the pack. He protects and guides them. Rollin specifically has been at it for a long time. They have many secrets that we have not discovered. Those secrets have helped them survive."

"He looks like he's in his thirties," I grumbled.

"Looks are deceiving," he said. "He brought the weres into line, and every pack in the country follows him. He's good at business, and he's made them a lot of money. He's violent and unpredictable, but that's a common flaw among the weres. He also lives with his pack and shares their duties." Hax gave me a look I couldn't decipher. "He's drawn to the wild."

"Will he rape me to fulfill the prophecy?"

"It says you must be loved by both men, and you will love them in return."

I laughed. A threesome. After reading one of the romance novels Hax brought me at Blade's compound, I knew what it was. It would never happen.

"Rollin does not love me, and if Blade loved me, he would not have sent me here." That made me think of something. "Exactly where are we?"

"In the northern mountains about three hours from the city."

"You followed me?" I went back to my drills.

"Yes."

I stopped and lowered the sword. "Thank you."

He grunted.

"You did not answer my question," I said. "I don't care if both men love me; I may need to kill Rollin, and if he attempts to rape me, I will."

"He would never cause you harm."

I moved closer to Hax's chair and looked him straight in the eyes. "Bringing me here caused harm, and I hate both men for it. I am nothing but a pawn in a game of monsters. They forget that I am also a monster. Does the prophecy say anything about what would happen if I don't have a child or choose one of them?"

"The world will burn."

"Ha," I said and pointed my sword in his direction. "I've been told the world was burning since I was a child. Everything that has happened in my life was due to a burning world."

His craggy features remained stoic. "Our world will cease to exist," he said with such intent, I shuddered. "The only hope we have is if the vampires and werewolves maintain their extremely tentative peace treaty and stomp out the remaining humans making trouble. You are the key. Your child's birth will fulfill the prophecy."

"You think I want humans stamped out?" Anger built inside me.

He shook his head, his jaws forming into what looked like sorrow. "You were kept unaware of the world around you for far too long," he said. "Humans tried to annihilate the vamps and weres. They almost succeeded. They filled their world with war and violence long before they knew of the supernatural creatures they hate. They have killed their own kind for loving what they find abhorrent. They are the only ones who do not want peace, and they must die so we can have it. You are the key to that."

"Me?" I asked in astonishment.

"You. Humans started the war and the monsters end it with your help."

"How many humans are we talking about?" I asked.

"They have pulled in their forces. I would say combined, they have two hundred and fifty thousand seasoned soldiers who hate us and want every last one of us, including our children, destroyed. They would kill you just for sleeping with Blade."

"But the city," I questioned. "The people in the city seemed to live in unity, humans, vamps and weres. I didn't see fighting. Are the humans in the city enslaved by Blade and Rollin?"

"No. They have chosen to side with the supernaturals. Blade took the city and told them they could leave if they chose. He and Rollin knew of you, and they made a pact. They protect the humans who stayed behind. The city was in complete chaos before Blade took it.

The citizens were mistreated, and much of the food was confiscated and controlled by the military. They allowed many children to starve. The humans who stayed hate our enemy too."

This was a lot to take in. "What about the gangs?" I asked.

"Rollin and Blade control them. Mostly because they are rough, but also because they do what they are told. If they kill someone without provocation, they are eliminated. Their primary function is to be the go-between for the humans who remained."

Maybe I had looked at the city through the eyes I was taught at the military camp. Murdock was a thug, but I didn't actually see him harm anyone. I tried to remember what Coop had said about the gangs. He said they worked with the vamps and weres, and he hadn't said anything against what Hax was telling me.

"I stayed at the military outpost for years and knew none of this," I finally said. "Did you know that the men I thought of as my friends were actually werewolves acting like soldiers?"

"I did not know, but it does not surprise me. I was not apprised of anything regarding the pact other than you would be brought to Blade's lair shortly before your power manifested. I did not think you were The Promised, so I wasn't concerned. That is my fault, and I give you my sincerest apology."

Suddenly, a loud shout came from outside the window, and angry voices were heard.

Hax shrugged. "They found the new tunnel I made."

I had pulled the blind closed after Hax came into the room.

Someone pounded on my door at the same time there were sounds directly outside the window. I walked over and threw the door open. Hax couldn't leave through the window or door. The werewolves would not harm my friend.

I lifted my arm and blocked Alaric from entering more than a step inside.

"I have a visitor, and you are interrupting. Leave." I poured as much venom into the words as I could without using my power.

Alaric was looking over my head, which wasn't hard because he was much taller than me.

"He's a Guttybrew," Alaric said, making the words sound like Hax was some kind of roach.

"Hax is my friend. You will speak respectfully to him and about him," I said with a look in my eyes that should give him pause.

"He, uh, he can't be here," he stuttered.

Something hit the cabin with a heavy thud. Alaric looked upward.

"You should be looking at me," I said sweetly. "I caused damage to your roof. It will need repairing before the next rain." I pushed against the solid wall of his body and got my way simply because he wasn't expecting the shove. I shut the door in his startled face.

I walked over and took the chair across from Hax again.

"Where were we?" I asked.

Chapter 50

"I am here to serve you, my lady. I would like to bring my family here to help you through this time," Hax said.

"You have a family?" he'd never mentioned anyone else.

"All guttybrew are family. Our kind is tied by blood and the oath we took to protect The Promised."

"How many guttybrew are you talking about?"

"Fifty, give or take a few children."

"They would leave Blade and come here?"

His head inclined.

"It is our purpose, my lady."

A heavy fist struck the door and I knew exactly who it was.

Rollin's hand was raised when I threw it open.

"Please come in," I said.

He marched in and Alaric tried to come in behind him.

"Not you," I said and lifted my hand to stop him.

"Wait in the hall," Rollin commanded.

"My alpha, the guttybrew is dangerous. You should not be alone with him."

"You are arguing a direct order." Rollin's voice rose. "Do I need to repeat myself?" It turned into a roar.

Alaric stepped back into the hall and I shut the door.

Rollin took the chair I was sitting in and I took the one beside it.

"Hax will be bringing his family here to be with me. There are approximately fifty of them."

"We cannot accommodate fifty guttybrew," he growled, his eyes not leaving my guest.

Hax sat up straighter.

"We prefer to live underground when we are not working," said the guttybrew. "We will not eat your food or require assistance of any kind."

Rollin tried to stare him down but Hax didn't so much as twitch.

"What type of work are you talking about?" Rollin asked with frustration curling in his voice.

"We take care of the needs of The Promised. We can also make life easier for your people if you let us. Our primary function is caring for Tara, but my family prefers to stay busy. Heavy work like laundry is considered a blessing."

"This will throw my people into chaos," Rollin grumbled but I heard resolution in the words. He turned to me. "I will make this pact under the condition the guttybrew will not help you leave. I want you to give me thirty days to decide about being my mate."

I had to leave. But where would I go? I couldn't return to the military camp now. I had no intention of being Rollin's mate. Although I hated Blade, I still loved him and that was so messed up, I couldn't believe it. The damned prophecy was destroying my life.

I glanced at Hax who was focused on me. He gave a slight nod. I turned back to Rollin.

"Thirty days. Am I free to walk in the forest?"

"Of course. Please take at least four guttybrew and two of my men with you as personal guards."

"That's ridiculous. I need time alone."

"Two Guttybrew and one of my men. That is as low as I will go. We do not know if the humans are aware of you and we cannot take a chance with your safety. The only time you will not have a guard is if you are in the forest with me. I will also require you to accompany me on walks in the evening."

"No," I objected.

He stared with the glaring eye trick again.

"Fine," I gave in ungracefully.

Rollin held out his hand. I looked at it for a few seconds before I lifted mine to his. Our skin touched and a sudden warmth passed through me. I quickly pulled my arm away. Rollin turned to Hax.

"I am Rollin, leader of the US pack. I welcome you to my home. I will place Alaric at your disposal to make your transition easier." He placed his hand out to the guttybrew.

Hax did not have the hesitation I had and he placed his clawed fingers into Rollin's hand, and they shook. Rollin turned his attention back on me.

"I want you safe and I also want you happy. I know this is not easy for you. I ask that you enter the thirty days with an open mind. My people are also adjusting. We have never had a human here before."

"Then you have a perfect record. Neither Hax nor I are human. I will give you thirty days, but I will never love you or want you for a mate."

Rollin smiled, and my breath caught.

He was too damn sexy for his own good.

Chapter 51

It took three days for the guttybrew to move in completely. A bedroom to one side of me was given to two females and the room on the other side to two males, one of which was Hax. They would sleep in the rooms at night and keep track of me during the day. Alaric was the werewolf guard assigned to plaster himself at my side. He now lived across the hallway from my room. Rollin slept in the wing I hadn't explored.

Hax was currently in one of the guttybrew tunnels helping with something I didn't understand that had to do with the integrity of the dirt walls. He told me it was important because it kept the tunnels intact. Before he left, he introduced me to the other three guttybrew guards. They were now situating their belongings while Alaric was in my room trying to persuade me to schedule my days in advance so he knew what was going on.

"Make a list of everything I need to do each day in your community, and I'll write that schedule," I said.

His nagging bothered me no end. I didn't know what I was supposed to be doing. I wanted to train with my sword, and I had to spend time outside with the local fauna. Depression was eating at me, and I couldn't think past dragging myself to those two pursuits.

"A list?" Alaric questioned.

"Yes, you know, you take a writing instrument, access your brain power, and come up with what needs to be done that I can do or help with. I would like one hour per day to train and an hour to spend outside. I've never been here or in any mountains for that matter. What needs to be done?"

My time with the vamps had major spots of inactivity that drove me crazy. Mostly when not training, I read books. Right now, I couldn't sit still long enough to read, and my mind wandered to Blade, which had to stop. I needed hard labor if I was going to get over Blade and depression.

"You are the mate," Alaric said in horror. "I can make no list."

"What does Rollin do all day?" I asked in frustration.

"He is our alpha. He runs the pack."

"Do I run the pack too?"

The horror in his expression turned to astonishment.

"At his side," he replied reluctantly after a moment's hesitation.

"I promised him thirty days. Inform him that I need something to do." I could tell Alaric was thrown off his badass stride. I decided it was a good time to change the subject.

"Are you allowed to answer my questions?" I asked.

"You have asked many questions and I have answered them," he said defensively, his mind obviously on me doing physical labor.

"I have not asked about Rollin. If I do, will you answer?"

"You and Rollin are bound together. You should ask him your questions."

"So you won't answer me," I pointed out.

He sighed then gave me a hard stare, calculating what he should tell me. I could almost see the gears turning inside his brain. Today Alaric was wearing jeans with a dark blue T-shirt that looked like a second skin, enshrining his bulging muscle. This seemed to be the requirement for Rollin's men. Braun yes, brains no, or so I told myself. His dusty hair was held back in a ponytail, and I was sure his harem of women enjoyed running their fingers through it when loose. If it wasn't for the five-inch scar running down the side of his face, I would say in the looks department, he was perfect. I inwardly shrugged. The scar made him more attractive.

This was the major problem with the weres and vampires. The men were gorgeous. Had they ever heard of average? I felt average when beside them. Not that they got close enough to stand beside me. I was watched from a distance, and so far, no one had gone out of their way to speak to me except Alaric. And where the hell were the women? I had only seen the one who served meals.

"How long have you and Rollin been friends?" Maybe this question would be something he would answer, and if I got him talking, I could squeeze in a few more.

"We shared a cradle as babies," Alaric said. "Our mothers are cousins, but Rollin is more like my brother."

"How old are you?" I asked next.

"We do not live as long as vampires, but if we are not killed, we can live for several hundred years."

"Are you going to tell me how old you are?" I asked after the pause in conversation grew too long.

"I have seen my second century."

To live for over two hundred years was amazing. The things he must have seen. I knew from history that he'd hidden what he truly was for most of that time. I must have gaped a little too long.

He smiled for the first time.

"You think me in my dotage?"

I shook my head. "No, it just surprised me. I felt the same about the vampires."

The small spark in Alaric's eyes changed, and amber highlights burned in them.

"You do not like the vampires?" I asked sweetly. His hands fisted, and he couldn't hide his feelings.

"They have been our enemy for more centuries than I have lived," he said. "I see nothing wrong with how things were." Each word was bit out through grinding teeth.

"We have something in common," I said. "We both hate the prophecy," I added when he continued to stare at me.

He grunted.

"I consider Blade my mate," I told him. "I love him." It was said simply, but at the same time, the words stabbed my heart. The person I loved betrayed me.

His jaw unclenched slightly.

"You will be better off with Rollin. His blood runs hot, and the ladies seem to like it."

I blushed. I'd seen and touched every inch of Rollin's body in my dreams. Blade shared my dreams too, and he knew of them as Rollin must. My face grew a shade darker.

"You already want him," Alaric said with laughter in his voice.

"In his dreams," I said, and it was my jaw that was clenched this time.

"Awe yes, the dreams." His smile grew.

I would kill Rollin. He'd shared our intimate dreams with his friend.

"Are you any good with a sword?" I asked because if I didn't do something physical, I might bring vines from outside and strangle this man.

"I am passably good," he replied.

"That will do. I need to be in the great outdoors so I can work off some energy or I'll go crazy." The last thing I would do is tell him about my feelings of melancholy or that I wanted to strangle him.

I grabbed my sword and waited outside Alaric's room while he collected his. The trees and plants greeted me with a gentle flutter when we walked outside. Alaric led me past several medium-sized cabins. There was no one around, and I wondered where they were. The vamps slept during the day, and I'd learned how their world operated. I had to keep an open mind for thirty days, and hopefully somewhere in that time, I could decide where to go next. Mika and Coop were a possibility for the short term.

"Please thirty days, go by swiftly," I muttered under my breath.

Alaric turned and grinned at me. He had very acute hearing, and I needed to remember it.

"Where is everyone?" I asked as we walked.

"There is a challenge for dominance."

"Do you want to watch it?" I asked.

"I know what the outcome will be, but I would like to see the fight."

"So why aren't you there."

He looked at me like I'd asked a very dumb question, made a small, disgruntled noise, and continued walking without answering.

"Because of me?" I asked and pointed at my chest.

We entered a large clearing where the trees and bushes were cut back into a perfect circle. We faced each other.

"I have been assigned to watch over you. Rollin did not feel you would enjoy the violence of the challenge, so here we are."

A few short months ago, I wasn't as bloodthirsty as I was now, but even then, I would have been excited over watching a battle of this type.

"Is it taking place right now?"

He looked up at the sun and judged the sky.

"In about fifteen minutes."

"Take me. We can wield swords afterward."

His eyes stared into mine, studying me.

"Rollin won't like it," he said at last.

I would not smile. I would not smile. I would not smile.

Dammit, I couldn't help myself.

"Your funeral," he said.

"Most likely yours, but I'll rescue you."

He grumbled under his breath and stormed off walking faster than he had earlier. About a half-mile away, I heard hushed voices. At least three dozen men stood around a large approximately fifty-foot circle that was dug out into a pit about six feet deep. I was the only woman.

"The alpha's mate," I heard someone whisper and everyone turned toward me and Alaric.

They parted, and we walked closer to the pit. No one was in it. I peered up and saw Rollin on the other side. He was naked. Yes, this was the amazingly hot man from my dreams. I wiped my chin in case I was drooling. I didn't need to like the guy to appreciate his extraordinary body. Living in a military camp had opened my eyes to male beauty, but I wasn't even sure Blade compared to Rollin. The dreams didn't do Rollin justice. Sweat clung like glitter on his tanned skin. Each muscle was perfection. My gaze followed his flesh downward. Oh my. My eyes jerked to his unhappy expression.

Another man about six feet from him was also naked and about fifty pounds heavier and none of it fat. He and Rollin leapt into the pit and moved to opposite sides. Rollin looked up and glared at Alaric. He wasn't happy that I was here. I'd had no idea it was him who was challenged.

The man across from him shifted to his monster form.

"You didn't tell me Rollin was fighting," I whispered.

"Everyone can hear you," Alaric said. "It won't matter how low you speak."

That shut me up.

A man standing on the other side of the pit rang a large bell, and Rollin went airborne, shifting form as he did it. The two men collided. Giant teeth bit into Rollin's shoulder and he growled. He easily flung the large man away from him and attacked again. They used claws, teeth, and muscle to outmaneuver each other. Rollin was faster and moved better on his feet. It was quickly apparent that he was playing with the other man. Rollin was bleeding from the bite to his arm, and he had a small claw slice to his abdomen, but the other man was quickly bleeding out from multiple sources.

Rollin raked his giant claws across the other man's face, leaving a deep furrow. The man fell, and Rollin leapt on top of him. With a roar, his teeth clamped on the man's throat.

I wanted to slam my eyes shut because I knew what came next.

The man gurgled, then brought his hand down in a heavy slap against the earth beneath him. Rollin released him immediately, threw back his head, blood dripping from his teeth, and roared louder than he had before. I almost covered my ears. He spun in a slow circle, his hands raised, until he found me. The people around the pit were cheering. He turned back to the downed man and placed his hand out. The man took it, and Rollin pulled him up and slapped him on the back.

"Better luck next time."

My mouth hung open, and I snapped it shut.

Rollin leapt from the pit in his monster form, lifted, and pulled me over his shoulder before I realized what he was going to do. He ran away from everyone.

The cheering grew louder.

My sword slipped from the sheath, and Alaric picked it up. Rollin went into a deep part of the forest and didn't stop. Did he think me defenseless?

"Put me down," I yelled at his hairy butt.

He ignored me, and I bit his ass, wolf hair and all.

"Put. Me. Down," I yelled again after he grunted.

Chapter 52

Rollin continued for another hundred yards before dropping me on the pine needle-covered ground. He backed up several feet and watched as I scrambled upright. The forest came alive around me, and I vividly knew the placement of every tree, branch, and vine. I called the vines to me, and they made a small crackling noise as they drew closer. Rollin didn't seem to notice because all his focus was on me.

"I did not want you there," Rollin growled in a lower tone than his usual human voice.

"You think a little blood will put me off?" I asked incredulously. I wanted his attention on me as the plants obeyed my call. He thought I would cower from him in this form and he thought wrong.

"You agreed to thirty days," he insisted.

"Yes, I did. During our thirty days, I have decisions to make. How will I do what's best for me if you insist on only showing me one side of you? I've lived with soldiers. I understand battle. What I don't understand is why you didn't kill that man. I thought he challenged you."

"He did. He is a valued member of my pack. There are too few of us, and we do not fight to the death among ourselves.

"Why didn't you really want me there?" I asked just to keep his attention on me.

"You—," he said as the vines grabbed his feet and pulled them out from under him. They came from every direction, and he fell with a loud umph. The vines tightened while they pulled on his arms and legs.

"You think this will hold me?" he demanded.

"Maybe," I said, really having no idea if they could.

He was massive in this form, and he wasn't a small man when he was human. He was now over seven feet tall. His body relaxed as the vines pulled him spread-eagle. He shifted back to his human form and oh my, oh my, oh my.

His erection looked almost painful, and I gulped at the size of him. Nope, this never happened in my dreams.

"Do you like what you see?" he asked huskily.

"You are so full of yourself," I stated.

His laugh was huskier than his voice.

"Come closer," he said.

"No," was my witty comeback.

His grin widened.

Argh. I allowed the vines to loosen. I was not good at this game, and thoughts of Blade invaded the moment.

"You are thinking of him?" Rollin asked.

"If you mean Blade, then yes. I'm thinking of him. His betrayal hurts, but I haven't stopped loving him."

Rollin got to his feet and looked down at me.

"I've asked for thirty days."

"I'm giving them to you, but you cannot control my thoughts. Love doesn't work that way. I can't stop these feelings even though I want to."

He inhaled slowly before he leaned in and kissed my lips. It was only the slightest touch and then it was gone. He took my hand and wove his fingers through mine.

"Walk with me," he said.

"You're naked."

"Believe me, it's my best quality." His eyes were laughing, and his lips held the slightest tilt.

"If being naked is your best quality, you should never put on clothes."

"For you, I can arrange it."

"Walk, you insufferable beast."

This time he did smile, and we started walking, but I released his hand.

"How does it feel to have your full power?" he asked after a few minutes.

I wanted to remain silent and snarly, but it wouldn't gain me answers.

"Like I've lived my entire life in murky waters that finally cleared." I told him. "Everything clicked into place. I feel whole."

"I could feel you sometimes," he said.

"Feel me how?" I asked and felt myself blush. I should have kept my mouth shut.

"I wasn't speaking of the dreams," he said with a laugh. "Sometimes I knew where you were and what you were doing. Not in detail but a general outline."

"I'm sure those thoughts were brought on by your spies. They told you what I was up to."

Rollin stopped walking, and we faced each other.

"Their job was to watch over you and keep you alive. It was not to spy on you."

"Yeah, right." My jaw clenched, and I tried to hold the anger back.

"They care about you. Their job was also to protect you from me and Blade. They would have fought me to the death if I had tried to take you."

"They would go against their alpha?"

"They separated from our pack in order to keep you safe. The only person they answered to was Dickson."

"Captain Dickson is a werewolf?"

"He's from an eastern pack."

"Did he return home?" I asked.

"Not exactly. The outlying packs in the east are gathering and preparing for the final battle against the humans. They are making a stand with us."

"Do they know about the prophecy?" I asked because I knew nothing about how the werewolves interacted.

"They know. With them, we have more soldiers than the vampires, but it will take all of us to end the war." He shook his head. "It shouldn't have taken a prophecy to make this happen, but I can't change our history, only our future."

We began walking again. There was a glade with tall grass and wildflowers. I released his hand and threw myself among them, rolling and laughing at the same time. Power grew inside me with small tingles under my skin.

Rollin's expression was one of wonder.

"They respond to you," he said.

"I feel them. All the plants for miles create a steady sound much like a heartbeat." I rolled to my back and used my arm to shelter my eyes from the sun. "Could I stay here for a bit?" I asked. The energy around me was too strong to walk away from.

"We're too far from the cabins, so I will stay with you for as long as you want to be here."

He tumbled beside me, and I laughed. Then, sadness filled me. Blade would never have this. Sunlight was his nemesis and sunlight was my lifeblood. Rollin was part of the sunlight. Both men were forced on me by the prophecy. The three of us had no true freedom. I was back at square one with a man who was forced to love me. I found it heart-breaking.

"Have you ever been in love?" I asked.

He didn't answer right away, and I waited.

"I thought I was when I was younger."

"Had you learned of the prophecy yet?"

"Yes. I was angry and wanted to rule my destiny."

I knew that feeling so well.

"What happened?"

He turned to his side so we were facing each other. He pulled dry grass from my hair and played with it in his fingers while he spoke. "She was not as in love as I. She found someone else."

"I'm sorry."

He smiled, and it turned devilish.

"Don't be. She made me realize that lust and love were not the same thing. I got over her quickly."

His eyes were literally twinkling.

"You slept your way through a dozen other women to get over her," I accused.

"Maybe half a dozen." His grin remained in place.

"When did you decide to heed the prophecy?"

His palm cupped my cheek, and I couldn't help the small shiver of awareness.

"The dreams," he whispered.

Heat suffused my cheeks.

Rollin laughed in his husky way, and it only made my embarrassment worse. He released me and rolled to his back, staring up at the sky. The sun had gone behind a cloud, and I also rolled to my back.

We lay there silently, and I knew we were both thinking of the dreams. I didn't have the guts to look at his nakedness and see how they affected him.

Chapter 53

Rollin requested that I eat meals with him and his pack. I requested that Hax join me. It was all good until I told Hax.

"No, my lady. I will not share food with you. I am in your service and it would be unseemly."

"Bull. You are my friend. I would like you to sit with me."

"It is not the guttybrew way," he said solemnly.

"You are leaving me to fend for myself among a group of werewolves who I don't know."

"You will make friends."

"Will the guttybrew make friends?" I demanded.

"We brought our friendships with us."

"You seem to have an answer for everything. I don't want to make friends here."

"If you keep hungry wolfs waiting, your wish will become reality."

Argh. I never won arguments with Hax and it was extremely frustrating.

I sat next to Rollin again and ignored the consumption of meat, though the smells and sounds of chewing didn't help. Food cemented relationships among the weres, and the werewolves had a schedule for sharing meals at Rollin's house so everyone had a turn sitting at his table.

Dressing for dinner was easy here, and I wore jeans and a tee. I removed the sword sheath from my back and hung it from the back of my chair. No one paid attention. His men laughed and spoke about their day.

After dessert, which was chocolate cake, the conversation between Alaric and Rollin turned to what the human military was doing.

"Andrews is staying low but he's up to something," Alaric said.

It clicked in my head.

"Are you talking about General Andrews?"

Rollin grunted, which showed exactly what he thought of the man.

"Yes. He is a thorn in our side," Alaric said. "He should have been taken out when he last visited the camp you were in. Our people failed in their duty."

"Andrews is a dufus," I said. I had never liked the general. He was a blowhard, and as far as I knew, he had little tactical training. I said as much.

"We thought so too, but he has someone guiding him, and we have no idea who it is," Rollin said, his lips in a firm line. "He may not look or act the part, but he's deadly, and many of our people have been killed in ambushes by his troops."

"Do you still have your own people in the human camps?"

"After you left, General Andrews ordered blood tests for all military personnel," Rollin said. "Mule, Shep, and Leo escaped. Two wolves did not, and we haven't heard from them."

"Do you think he had them killed?"

Something passed between Alaric and Rollin.

"No, I don't think they're dead. We're planning to go after them."

"When?"

"Tomorrow."

"I want to come."

Rollin stared at me for several minutes. "Will you follow orders?" he finally asked.

"Yes."

***

We left at first light. Pickup trucks were used to get us out of the mountains. Fifteen of Rollin's top fighters came with us. This number included Mule, Shep, and Leo. I hadn't considered that they would be part of our group. It took a few deep breaths to control my anger.

Alaric stayed at the camp. I left a note in my room for Hax. I hadn't seen him before we left, and he wouldn't be happy.

A set of military camouflage fatigues was delivered to my room after our dinner the evening before. They were comfortable and would help us blend.

Two hours into our trek, the dense forest changed to shorter pine trees and less dense underbrush. After another hour, the temperature climbed, and the landscape changed even more. We were now in high desert. The trees had shallower roots, and the water wasn't absorbed into the soil like it was at the higher elevation. It still held its beauty. In the distance, you could read the passage of time with the different layers of color in the low hills.

We ditched the trucks in a valley. Rollin drifted to the back of the line to speak with some of the men.

"The tires kick up sand, and it can be seen for miles," said one of the men closest to me. "Are you up for jogging?"

I was in good shape, but I wasn't sure if I could keep up with Rollin and his men.

"I'll do my best," I told him.

"If you can't, Rollin will carry you."

"Am I too heavy for you?" I asked jokingly.

"No, I just don't wish to die before the fight."

I looked up, and Rollin was watching us closely.

"Do not be deceived," the man said quietly after nodding his head at Rollin. "Jealousy runs in our blood. We do not like other men around our mates. Rollin is showing great restraint. I would like to keep it that way."

I kept my mouth shut even though I wanted to argue. I was only Rollin's mate if I said I was, and it wouldn't happen. I also wondered if this was the reason for the lack of women. "We are jealous monsters who cannot possibly trust a female," I huffed completely under my breath.

We hiked for over two hours. Rollin paid little attention to me, and I wondered why he allowed me to come. I guessed it was my own fault. I'd told him I needed to see all sides of him. I just hadn't been truthful and told him that, in the end, it wouldn't matter.

Mule, Shep, and Leo stayed as far from me as they could. I couldn't feel their watchful eyes, and for that, I was thankful.

When we were near our target, we split up. Half the men would circle around to the other side. I stayed with Rollin. The encampment held over one hundred tents and even more men. Our group stayed in place, ate cold food that we carried, and drank water.

I'd managed to keep up with Rollin's men even though I suspected they were kept at a slower pace than usual. I had a problem, though, and I wasn't sure what to do. My dilemma finally reared its ugly head, and I could no longer hold my bladder.

"I need to use the bathroom," I told Rollin.

"I'll take you. We're only going no more than fifty feet from here," he warned.

Thankfully, I'd lived most of my adult life in a military camp.

Once I located a spot, Rollin turned his back. I hurried as much as I possibly could and felt ten pounds lighter when I finished. I'd thankfully remembered tissue paper and had a bunch in my pocket.

Rollin stopped walking about halfway back to where his men waited.

"We are going in a few hours after the camp quiets for the night. I'll send a man in first to locate our men. If they are found, we will get them out as quietly as possible. We will kill anyone who tries to stop us and when we leave, it will be faster than when we came in. Tell me if you cannot keep up."

"I promise," I told him. I did not want to be responsible for the deaths of his men. Will I be going in with you?"

"You will stay glued to my side. Use your sword if you need to."

I nodded.

I couldn't help the admiration I felt for Rollin when he spoke to his men. They looked to him with absolute trust. It reminded me of Captain Dickson. I was still coming to terms with him as a werewolf. Once more, my life was a lie.

When Rollin finished speaking, he sent one of his men to investigate the camp.

He returned two hours later. They began shifting to their werewolf forms.

"Are you going to shift?" I asked when Rollin didn't remove his clothing.

"No. I will stay in human form."

It seemed strange but I didn't ask why. Now was not the time.

Rollin signaled the men and we moved toward the camp. We ran into two dead guards outside the camp perimeter. Mule, my ex-friend, stepped out of the shadows and led us to the tent where the prisoners were kept. The smell got to me first. Unwashed bodies, urine, and feces were the first signals that we were close.

Two additional guards stood on the outside of the tent. Rollin's hand developed razor claws while the rest of his body remained human. I had no idea werewolves could do that. Rollin and one of his men killed the guards quickly and quietly.

I entered the tent with Rollin and there were two men chained to upright posts. The chains were thick, and I couldn't see how we would get them off.

"Find something to remove the chains," Rollin whispered to one of the men behind me.

The smell was worse inside the tent. One of the prisoners stirred. He was covered in weeks of grime with blood mixed in.

I knelt beside him.

"We will get you out," I said softly.

"Tara?"

I would know that voice anywhere.

"Captain Dickson?" I asked in shock.

"The one and only." He coughed and moaned slightly.

Through the grime, I could see bruises covering almost every inch of his flesh. His midsection was covered in blood. He was naked.

"You're going home," I told him.

I'd asked if Dickson was a werewolf but I hadn't asked the most important question. Was he okay? Damn, I needed to sit down and make a list so I stopped feeling so stupid about the prophecy and other important subjects.

"I won't make it," he said. "Leave me behind."

Rollin squatted beside me.

"You'll make it old man. We're taking you both out."

One of Rollin's men walked in with a pry bar that I hoped would work on the chains. It took another twenty minutes to get them free. A minute after the chains were broken, all hell broke loose.

A siren blasted and blocked all other sounds with its high-pitched blare.

"Stay by me," Rollin yelled and picked up Dickson.

Another werewolf picked up the remaining prisoner, and we started running. The men fought anyone who got near us. I held one man back with my sword and stayed as close to Rollin as I could and still get a good swing in.

Grunts and shouts were all around us when the alarm stopped sounding. There were too many human soldiers. A man crashed into me and sliced my arm with a knife. I had just enough momentum to run my sword through him. Pulling the sucker out took a few extra seconds.

"Tara," a man shouted.

I registered Mule's red hair a split second before he rammed me, and I flew several feet away. Gunfire roared and he took the bullets meant for me. He fell, and I jumped to his side.

"I'm sorry, kid," he whispered with a gurgle.

I was jerked upright, and I raised my sword to strike. It was Shep.

"Run," he yelled over the noise.

"Mule," I shouted back.

"He's gone," Shep said.

I looked down, and Mule's green eyes stared vacantly at the night sky.

"Run," Shep repeated.

Chapter 54

The enemy killed my friend. I gathered power while I ran, connecting with the scrub brush and weeds surrounding us.

"Duck low," I yelled as I pulled the plants to me.

There was little to work with, and I didn't care. A wall of nearly dry brush began building between us and the soldiers. It wouldn't stop bullets, but it would give us valuable time.

Over the grunts and shouts, I heard engines turning over. We couldn't outrun jeeps mounted with sniper rifles. I stayed low until we hit the first hill surrounding the camp. Rollin spotted me and moved closer as I ran. He still carried the captain.

"Can you keep up?" he asked.

"They are sending the jeeps," I said.

Rollin's smile was full of menace.

"My men put sand in all the gas tanks," Rollin said, his stern eyes grounding into mine. "I'll ask again, can you keep up?"

"Yes, I'm good. How is he?"

"We can't worry about it right now. We need to put space between us and the camp. They will call in reinforcements."

Thirty minutes later, we heard helicopters in the distance.

"Take cover," Rollin shouted.

There were only a few scraggly trees to hide beneath. When the choppers spotted us, we were dead.

The ground beside me spit dirt up about two feet away, and Hax's head popped out. Stunned was not the right word, but I didn't have a better one.

"Crawl in," Hax said.

"Is there room?" I asked.

"For everyone. You'll be safe."

Rollin saw Hax and ran over to hand the captain to him. He remained unconscious. Hax went into the tunnel, and Rollin handed me down to another guttybrew. It took only a few minutes for everyone to crawl in. In less than five minutes, the helicopters passed over us.

I went to Captain Dickson to check on him. He was awake and grimaced when he saw me.

"You're bleeding," he said.

"You're bleeding worse," I told him.

We had to find something to stop the blood flow. He was losing too much too quickly.

"Do we have anything for the wound?" I asked Hax.

"Use this," Rollin said and handed his shirt over.

I folded it and pressed it into his wound. The captain's breath hitched, and he let out a low moan. He was too thin and I could see deep bruises wherever his skin showed. As the blood slowed, I used my magic. I could heal him with enough time. This was mostly an untested part of my powers, but I didn't say anything while I worked.

The tunnel, about three feet around, was big enough to walk hunched over in but not big enough to carry the wounded.

"How are we getting out of here?" I asked Rollin.

Hax grunted, and I looked at him.

"The tunnel system we made leads back to where you left the trucks," he said. "The wounded will be carried above ground. When we hear helicopters, we'll tunnel up, and they will jump in until the danger passes."

Rollin grunted.

Between Hax and Rollin, there was no way I was getting out of the tunnels until we reached the trucks. Rollin handed the captain to one of his men and stayed beneath ground with me.

We traveled for what seemed like hours. Maybe it was. We moved slower than we had when we came.

"What were you planning to do if Hax hadn't helped us?" I asked Rollin while we crawled through a very narrow section that had crumbled earth falling on us as our shoulders squeezed through. It was worse for Rollin and his men due to their larger bodies.

"Hax said he would be here. With your safety on the line, I knew he would do as promised."

"You planned this with Hax?"

"Yes, though he wasn't supposed to come this close to the camp. He and I will discuss it when we're safe."

"Good luck with that," I said.

I'd learned that Hax did what he wanted. Rollin was dreaming if he thought he would change the guttybrew's stubbornness.

Twice, the guttybrew had to tunnel upward to bring those above the surface underground. They were also collapsing the tunnel behind us as we moved forward. I had no idea how they maintained the integrity of the structure, but they managed.

"It's nice to have them on our side for a change," Rollin said after the second time they rescued the men above us.

Someone in front called Rollin's name.

"Stay with her," he told the man standing closest to me.

I glanced up. Shep and Leo stood hunkered over me.

"Are you okay?" Leo asked.

He was in his animal form, but I would know him anywhere. It was slightly strange to see him with fur covering his head when in his human form, he was bald.

I remembered Mule. My anger over their betrayal was gone. Sorrow replaced it.

"Mule," was all I managed to get out.

Leo pulled me close, and I leaned against his hairy chest. It tickled my nose. I needed his arms around me. Leo had been the more affectionate of the trio when we'd lived in the military camp together. He gave good brotherly hugs when I needed them. Shep's warm hand landed on my shoulder, and he offered his own comfort.

A low growl sounded in front of us.

"Tara," one of the wolves said. "Back away from Leo slowly."

I peered through the dark, which wasn't easy for my human eyes. Had the enemy soldiers found the tunnels? An oversized werewolf stalked closer. I recognized Rollin in his animal form. His eyes were on Leo.

"No," I shouted and placed my hand out, blocking Rollin from coming closer.

"These are my brothers," I said frantically. "They have kept me safe for years. Put your pants back on and act like a grown man. I will not put up with your shit."

Rollin growled again, his eyes wild. I would not allow him to injure Shep or Leo.

I took two steps forward and punched his nose as hard as I could. His attention finally zeroed in on me. Maybe that wasn't a good thing.

"Rollin," one of the men said cautiously.

He didn't touch me but he moved closer, rose above me and blasted the two men.

"Stay away from my mate," he roared.

I put my face up to his massive jaws. If we'd been standing upright, I would never have reached him in wolf form.

"They are my brothers," I repeated. "This mating crap stops here. If you touch a hair on them, I'll run you through with my sword. If you survive, I'll do it again. Have I made this clear?" It was my turn to growl.

Rollin's huge arm came around my shoulder, and he pulled me close enough to feel his warm breath.

"I will enjoy your punishment," he said.

"I will enjoy yours." I would not be cowed by his Neanderthal tactics or at least I would not give away that I was scared shitless.

Chapter 55

Shep and Leo survived Rollin's wrath. Captain Dickson and the other injured wolf survived the trip. I somehow made it to my room, removed my clothes, and hit the shower. I fell asleep almost as soon as the warm water fell over me and I didn't wake up until it went cold. I crawled out, fell into bed, and didn't leave my room until the morning after our return.

Rollin knocked on the door and entered when I called out that it was unlocked.

"I'm glad to see you awake. I'm sure you're hungry."

My stomach growled at the mention of food.

"Starving," I said.

He was dressed casually in his normal jeans and tight T-shirt. This shirt was light brown and molded to his arms. His muscles were overly large but perfectly proportioned. It angered me that I even noticed.

Apparently, the others had eaten, and it was only Rollin and I at the table. The same woman served us. She was middle-aged, plump, and wore a green apron with pockets that had assorted utensils sticking slightly out. I had no idea if she was a werewolf or not. The ones I'd seen were all under forty.

"Hi," I said and held out my hand after she placed a plate in front of Rollin and before she headed back to the kitchen for mine. "I'm Tara. Thank you for the amazing meals you've provided."

She placed her hand out but didn't smile.

"The name is Babs." She quickly pulled her hand away and returned to the kitchen and came back out a few minutes later with my food.

I was served fried potatoes and some kind of delicious stir fry with crisp veggies that made my mouth water. I hadn't exaggerated about Babs cooking. The food was better here than at Blade's and that said something. Vamps didn't eat human food, but obviously wolves valued taste. Too bad they stuck to their carnivorous ways. The thought of them going vegan made me laugh internally and to keep it from breaking free, I shoved more veggies into my mouth.

"What do you find so amusing?" Rollin asked because nothing got past him, dammit.

During previous meals, him and his men ate with methodical intent and rarely uttered a word until the meal was finished.

"I tried to hide it," I said.

"That doesn't answer the question. Is something wrong with your food?"

"No," I bit down on a carrot to prove it. "I was thinking about vegan werewolves and if it were possible."

His expression was priceless. He glanced at my plate, and a green cast crept into his face.

"That will never happen. We are carnivorous predators." He plopped a chunk of meat into his mouth to prove it. "Without a large amount of protein, we are unable to shift. A meat-deprived werewolf is one who cannot defend himself or activate our healing capabilities."

That explained why the captain hadn't healed when he was kept in the military camp. They hadn't fed him enough.

I would be happy my need for vegetables was taken into consideration and keep my mouth shut from now on. Since this was a speaking meal, I decided to push my luck with something that had been bothering me.

"Why are there no women in your camp except Babs?"

I hadn't seen a single child either and I waited for his answer.

Rollin took another bite of meat, chewed then placed his knife and fork down before he answered.

"These cabins," he waved his hand at the walls, "were once rentals for humans. We have several places like this tucked throughout the mountains. Our children have been hunted for decades. Women are the last line of defense. Our males are dangerous but there is no comparison to a she-wolf protecting her cubs or even a grandmother protecting her grandcubs.

"What if a woman decides not to have children?" I asked.

"Our survival has not been easy. We must create the next generation. Every man, woman, and child wolf knows this."

"Okay, where are they?"

"Do you consider yourself my mate?" he asked with blinding focus.

"No," I said honestly.

"When that changes, I will tell you."

Not if it changes but when. He was entirely too frustrating but at the same time, I understood. The children were the future and when humans first decided to purge the werewolves, they targeted the young. Too many died.

"I would like to train today. Is there someone who could offer me time with a sword?"

"I would be happy too." He went back to eating.

***

I stood in the clearing that Alaric had shown me before. Rollin, minus his shirt which I swear he did on purpose, stood across from me with a sword in hand. He warmed up with a few circles of his wrist.

"Are you any good?" I asked.

"You'll need to find out." Humor sparked in his eyes.

I lifted my sword and the fight was on. He was good and had added strength and a longer reach. I was still better and faster. We didn't try to land body strikes just simply attacked the other's sword. The sound of metal on metal ran through me. I'd missed this.

We danced until sweat dampened my hairline and covered Rollin's chest. I noticed the lines of every muscle. Blade had my heart but I was not dead.

"Had enough?" Rollin asked about five minutes into our break as I gained control of my breathing.

"I can sword fight for hours," I said honestly. "I don't want to keep you from your work, though."

He smiled and picked up his sword which was resting against a tree.

"You are my assignment for the day." Lust flashed in his eyes. "I thought we should spend time alone."

It wasn't a good idea. At least not with his bare chest eating all my good intentions.

Another hour and my arm felt as if it would fall off. I'd tried switching to the opposite stance but Rollin couldn't keep up with his left arm. In sword fighting, he had a weakness. It might be the only one connected to his fighting skills.

"There's a small lake about a mile from here. The water is cold, but there are some large rocks that you can lay on after you swim."

This was not good.

"I never learned to swim," I said. "I'll shower at the cabin." I'd used the pool in Blade's garden, but it was shallow and no danger to me.

"You need to know how to swim," he said with an evil smile. "Chicken?"

No. Yes. Deep water terrified me.

"Lead the way," I said.

I had no idea where his men were today. I had only seen Babs.

The lake was further than a mile but it wasn't a hard hike. The trees grew thicker and shadowed the sky with their leaves. We followed a path that had roots and fallen branches on it. I had to keep a close eye on my footing. Sunlight suddenly bathed me and I looked up.

The blue water was breathtaking but I had another problem besides no swimming experience. I lacked a swimsuit. I should have thought of it sooner.

"I have nothing to wear," I said.

Rollin's hands went to the clasp of his jeans and without a word, he pulled them down. Commando. Damn. I turned around quickly but I hadn't missed the size of him and he wasn't even erect. Damn. Damn. Damn. I should be afraid to see him hard, but oh, I wanted to.

"If you don't want to take off your clothes, they will dry on the rocks with you in them after our swim."

The boulders were about twenty-five feet away and did look inviting. I was hot though and the water looked better. I heard a splash and turned around.

Rollin's head came to the surface and he rose half out of the water and threw his head back and then forward. A shower of cold water hit me, and I squealed embarrassingly.

"I'll come in but only to my waist. Turn around while I undress." I really wasn't shy, but his gaze had zeroed on me and its intensity made me nervous.

He turned without so much as a smile, which was the only reason I could undress to my underwear. The sports bra covered me, the panties not so much. They were tiny and usually, I liked them that way. After years of military issue underwear, Blade had provided beautiful underthings that I had grown accustomed to.

With Rollin's back still turned, I waded into the freezing water.

"You didn't say it was arctic cold," I grumbled.

He reached out and pulled me against his warm body before I could stop him. I squealed again, much to my shame. He began walking deeper into the water.

"No," I told him sternly.

He didn't stop. I faced away from him, and he walked until the water was at his shoulders which meant it would be over my head if he wasn't holding me up.

"Don't you dare let me go."

"Then you better turn around and hang on," he said with a laugh and a slight push.

I spun and clenched my arms around his neck, our bodies molding together.

"I told you I can't swim."

"And I said you need to learn." There was a breathy quality to his words.

Instantly, I knew why.

The hard length of him pressed against my belly.

Chapter 56

"I love Blade," I said. His hold loosened, and I didn't want to drown, so I clung tighter.

"Why do you love him?" Rollin asked.

It was such an off question. Why does anyone fall in love?

"I just do," I said. My teeth were starting to chatter with the cold. Rollin didn't appear angry, just curious.

"Blade turned you over to me. Is that love?"

Was it? Where was my anger at Blade for giving me to Rollin? I wanted to hate him but being apart for several days had squelched my anger to some degree.

"My feelings are hard to put into words," I said truthfully. Rollin's hands grasped the sides of my hips, and I was lifted, so our bodies aligned, and his hard length pushed against the juncture of my thighs. I was about to push him back when I was tossed into the air and thrown several feet away. Into the deep.

I had enough time to suck in a breath before the water closed over my head. Rollin hauled me to him before I totally panicked.

"That is your punishment for swatting my nose when I was in a mating frenzy."

"I didn't swat it, you asshole, I punched it."

He ignored my anger.

"You will learn to float first and then swim," he said with laughter in his voice while I stuttered to get words out.

My body had adjusted to the water's temperature, and my teeth weren't chattering.

"You have my word that I won't toss you again. If you are to learn, you need to trust me."

Water dripped from my eyes, and the panic of being underwater did not fade.

"You threw me in," I yelled. "Why the hell would I trust you now?"

His expression changed from fun to deadly serious.

"I've given my word."

His dark eyes ground on me and made breathing difficult. My first reaction was to cower. My second reaction was to hit him upside the head with a rock for trying to overpower me with his gaze. I searched deep and found control. The underwater plants were attuned to me. I stopped them from pulling him under.

"Okay, fine. Do your worst."

His laughter filled the area. The throaty sound sent shivers down my spine. Those shivers had nothing to do with the cold.

"It won't be that bad," he promised.

"Said the spider to the fly," I muttered, which only made him laugh again.

He was right. It took thirty minutes for me to float. The delay was mostly a trust issue on my part even if he had given his word.

"I'm floating," I said when I finally mastered the weightlessness. I immediately started sinking.

"Straighten your body and relax," he reminded me.

I did as he said and kept my face out of the water without his arms under me.

"I'm cold. Can we do the swim lesson another time?" My teeth were chattering again.

"Swimming will warm you up." I could hear the grin in his voice.

"So will the rocks." I started to go under again, and he grabbed me.

"You win," he grumbled. "I can't hear the surrounding noises over your chattering teeth, and that puts us in greater danger."

What an ass. I was freezing. He carried me out of the lake and strode to the rocks.

"You can put me down," I told him.

"I could."

He infuriated me.

When he stood on the boulders, he dropped my lower half slowly so his nakedness rubbed against my body. It was sneaky and underhanded. I knew he wouldn't rape me now and I could play and win his game. My sports bra unzipped in the front. I took it off, removed my almost nothing panties and laid them out on a smaller rock. I lay back, placed my hands behind my head, and closed my eyes to absorb the sun. I heard a groan.

"You are cruel," he grumbled as he stretched out beside me.

The heat felt wonderful. I had lived with men in the military. States of undress were common. Men had walked in on me while showering plenty of times, and I'd gotten over most of my shyness. Shep, Leo, and Mule had put a stop to the shower trespassing when I had told them, one night after a few rounds of tequila.

Mule. The thought of him mentally forced the sun behind a cloud, and I saw only darkness.

"What's wrong?" asked Rollin.

I whispered Mule's name, and Rollin's hand inched over and clasped mine, gently squeezing my fingers.

"He was a good man," he said.

"I had been so angry at Mule, and I never told him he was forgiven. He died saving me." Tears ran down my face.

Rollin didn't bring me closer or say anything while I cried. We lay in the sun in silence with only the sounds of nature around us.

"Do you hold funeral services for your fallen?" I asked.

"We do. There will be a gathering this evening."

"Can I be there?"

His fingers squeezed a bit harder.

"Of course."

"Tell me about your family?" I said at last.

"My pack family or my birth family."

"Whichever you would like to tell me," I said.

I needed to face my guilt over Mule's death and put it to rest, but I wasn't ready.

"You and my mother would have liked each other. She died ten years ago."

"I'm very sorry, is it hard for you to talk about her?"

"Her life, no. She deserves the honor. She died protecting pack cubs. Rage fills me when I think about it."

It was my turn to squeeze his hand. In another life, we could have been friends. Grief had filled his voice, and it had been ten years.

"Do you have siblings?"

"I did. They are gone now too. My mother watched her two youngest children die over a hundred years ago. My father, her mate, died a year later. She never mated again. She led the women into battle and she feared nothing. The pack hasn't been able to replace her."

The words hung in the air. Was I to be her replacement? I hoped not because I wouldn't stay. My heart belonged to Blade.

"It's time to go," Rollin said sometime later.

I must have fallen asleep.

"The sun will be down by the time we reach the cabin," he added when I didn't immediately move.

The sun was sinking below the surrounding mountains and a chill had entered the air.

Rollin handed me my dried underwear and the other clothing I'd left behind before going into the water.

"What time is the gathering for Mule?" I asked.

"An hour after the sun goes down."

My heart hurt, but I wouldn't miss it. Leo and Shep would want me there.

I hoped.

Chapter 57

The gathering was located a short distance from the cabins, surrounded by trees with a small stream on one side. I didn't see Leo or Shep and simply stood silently because I had no idea how their burials were performed. Over one hundred men arrived and stood as silently as I did.

A few minutes later, Leo and Shep walked in carrying a stretcher with Mule's body, which was covered by a large gray wolf pelt. They placed the stretcher on a raised platform that was about four feet off the ground. When they finished, they walked over and stood on the other side of Rollin without looking at me.

Did they blame me for Mule's death?

Everything was different now. I thought they were my friends, but I was a job to them. Would they be interested in friendship now?

Rollin stepped forward and turned to face everyone. Babs was the only woman. She wiped her eyes with a giant wad of tissue as Rollin spoke about Mule's life and his dedication to the pack.

"When he was sent to protect The Promised," Rollin said solemnly while looking straight at me. "He promised to keep her safe. He fulfilled his duty, and in the end, he saved her life. He will be remembered by our pack as a hero."

Guilt ate at me, but I didn't cry. I had no right to cry. He died saving me, and he hadn't known how I felt about him.

Something brushed my shoulder, and I turned to see Shep standing beside me.

"Leo and I will locate a final resting place for Mule. We would like you to come with us?"

Rollin, who now stood beside him, was looking at me. My eyes must have conveyed the question because he nodded. The fingers of his hands pumped into fists and released over and over. He wasn't happy. Shep and Leo walked to the stretcher and lifted Mule's body.

They left the clearing, and I looked at Rollin.

"Go," he said. "If you don't follow them right now, I will stop you."

It was the mating thing. It wasn't a bond because, in my opinion, that took two people, but Rollin did feel something. I hurried after the two men. We'd spoken in the tunnel, but that was when we were in danger. They'd had time to think now. I caught up and walked silently behind them, wondering if they could forgive me.

Chapter 58

We walked for miles. The half-moon allowed me enough light to see. The forest smelled differently at night, and I breathed deeply to hold the scent in my lungs.

"What about here?" Leo asked and looked at me.

I glanced at the vegetation surrounding us and nodded my head. They lowered the stretcher and stepped away from Mule's body.

"I am so sorry," I said. "He died saving me and he never knew how much I cared about him."

Shep took my hand.

"He knew, kid. We are sorry that we could not tell you who we were."

Hearing my nickname felt good. What if they had told me what they were? The old me would have freaked out. My father had ingrained a fear of vampires and werewolves deep inside me from my earliest memories. I would have blown their cover. How many men would have died?

"You couldn't tell me," I said looking between him and Leo. "I understand that now." My gaze went to Mule's body. "He enjoyed teasing me. He always had a smile." The first tear slid down my cheek, and I looked back at the two men. "Do we dig now?"

"No," said Leo. "He belongs to the forest, and the forest will take him."

Leo placed his arm around my shoulders and hugged me. Shep hugged me next.

"We must return," Leo said.

We looked one final time at Mule. He was now at peace but there was still a war to fight.

"How was your time with the vamps?" Shep asked after we had walked for about twenty minutes.

"Not what I expected," I said honestly.

"Did he feed on you?" he asked.

I considered the question invasive, but my friends had never shied from interfering in my life before so I answered.

"He did, and I loved it. I love him. I didn't want to come here, and I don't understand why it had to be this way. I will never love your alpha. It isn't possible."

"Never say never," Shep insisted.

He had teased me like Mule but not as often.

"We love our alpha," Leo said. "You need to open yourself to the idea. Mule died to protect The Promised. That is the weight you carry in this world. Rollin tried to deny the prophecy for too long and it got us nowhere. Whatever brought us to this point is stronger than all of us even the vampires."

"Do you hate the vampires?" I asked.

"I did, but I no longer feel the burn to kill them," Leo said. "I gave my loyalty to Rollin, and it means I follow him unconditionally. If we do not side with the vamps, we will not defeat the humans."

"Why do you love him?" I asked.

It was Shep who answered.

"He would die for any of us," he said. "He holds compassion and enough power to bring us out the other side in this fucked up world. He cares deeply for his people and feels each death like it stabbed his own heart. Everything inside him screams when you are outside his line of sight. He knew you needed to be with us tonight and he let you go. He was crazy while you were with your vampire, and none of us understood how he could allow it."

"He tried to kidnap me," I said in defense of my feelings.

"That was one of the crazy times," Leo said.

"The dangerous times," Shep muttered.

"I can't simply love him because he or you want me to," I told them, feeling more guilt sweep through me.

"Give him time. He grows on you," Shep said.

"Do you live near the main cabin?" I asked.

"We are in a guard barracks about a hundred yards from your room."

"I don't have friends," I said. "Is that a role you can fill?" I needed them in my life.

"We never stopped caring, Tara. You are our sister."

"I'll hold you to that. I have no idea what I'm doing."

Shep laughed. "Your power kinda kicked the meeting room's ass and shattered all the windows when you told it to."

"I didn't mean to cause that much damage." A ten-feet section of the roof had to be replaced. "I will, however, rephrase. Between Blade and Rollin, I have no idea what I'm doing."

"If you decide the vampire needs to die, we're your guys," Shep said.

Even with laughter added to the statement, he wasn't joking. We continued walking but this time in silence.

When I returned to the main cabin, several werewolves sat at the large table where we ate meals. They had a few bottles of alcohol and an assortment of meats and cheeses. There was a bowl of grapes and other cut fruit which I nabbed. They looked at me then went back to talking about Mule. I listened for a few moments while eating the fruit. I had missed dinner.

Rollin wasn't here, and there was no way I would hunt him down in his room, though it wouldn't hurt to ask his whereabouts. I waited for a break in the conversation.

"Does anyone know where Rollin is?"

All eyes turned in my direction.

"He's out," one of the men said.

I didn't know his name. He was shaggier than the other men with an unkempt beard and long messy hair. If it were red, he would remind me of Mule. Even with his rough exterior, the artistic lines of his face and beauty of his muscle only added to his overall good looks.

"Out?"

"In the forest."

"Is anyone with him?"

"No."

I placed the fruit bowl back on the table and went outside. For the strangest reason, I was worried about Rollin.

I stood still in the quiet night. My magic sparked, and even without knowing if it would work, I asked the trees to guide me to Rollin. A slight breeze stirred up leaves and they rustled. A crackling sound came from my right, and the plants moved aside enough for me to walk on the path they made.

I heard him before I saw him.

Crack. Crack. Crack.

I stepped closer and stopped. His broad back was to me, his shirt off and his muscles bulging. His fists hit the tree again and resulted in another loud crack. The moonlight did not give me a clear picture of his hands, but I knew fighting a tree must hurt.

Crack.

"The tree is crying and needs you to ease up," I said softly.

He turned.

I saw such raw emotion on his face that I stepped back.

Something dripped from his hands, and it didn't take much for me to figure out that it was blood. Had he crushed his knuckles?

"You shouldn't have come," he said, his voice so rough his pain engulfed me.

I took a step forward and then another. Grief shadowed him. I could see it in every line on his face. I reached out and cupped his cheek.

"I'll stay here and cheer you on while you punch the tree if it will help."

"I thought it wanted me to ease up?"

"It's decided you need it worse than it needs bark."

He gave me a very small grin. Then his expression changed and something else flickered in his eyes.

"I'm not safe to be around."

The storm brewing in his gaze said he wanted to murder someone.

Chapter 59

I disregarded Rollin's statement and peered down at his hands, which were hanging loosely at his sides. Blood covered his swollen knuckles, and they appeared misshapen. I didn't stop to think; I grabbed his wrists and lifted his arms so I could see the damage.

He stood very still.

"Why?" I asked.

"One of my men died, and my mate went off with two other men. This solution was better than the other one."

"I'm not your mate." It was an automatic response.

"That's another problem." It was said so low and growly; I wasn't sure how to respond.

His hands were warm within mine. They had started healing, and I realized he continued pummeling the tree because he wanted the pain.

"Other than agreeing to be your mate, what can I do to help?"

He searched my eyes.

"Sit with me," he finally said.

We sat with our backs against a large tree. I listened to his breathing, which slowed until it was even. He wasn't asleep, just relaxed.

"If you could have anything, what would it be?" His breath whispered against my hair.

I didn't even need to think about it.

"My mother and father alive."

His head tilted against mine.

"I'm so sick of death," he said. "I want our children safe and for our women to live with their mates instead of staying hidden. I've known Mule all my life," he continued. "He saved me more than once. He threw himself into every dangerous situation he could find. He was deadly in a fight, and he fought like one of the berserkers of legends. It's why I chose him to guard you at the military camp. It wasn't just that, though. I knew he would befriend you and make your life better. Now he's given his life for yours."

"I'm so sorry."

He lifted my hand and brought it to his lips. Their warmth touched me in a soft kiss.

"I would give up the life of every man in this camp to keep you safe. I shouldn't be alpha right now. I'm not thinking of the good of my people. All I can think about is you, and it's making me crazy."

"Why did you allow me to go on the rescue?"

"I knew I could watch over you, and no matter how hard I tried, I couldn't leave you behind."

He loved me. I hadn't considered this complication. Was that what mating for werewolves was about? It made this entire mess harder.

Rollin looked away. After a minute, his shoulders gave a small shake and then another. Hell. He might be crying. I wasn't sure what to do.

I leaned into his side and simply offered comfort. He never made a sound, but I could feel the small twitch of his chest as grief took over. His humanity caused a small fracture in my heart. I wasn't sure what it meant. Rollin was a good man. I felt it deep in my bones. Was Blade a good man? I wasn't sure. I knew he loved me, but I'd seen him twist the neck of one of his vampires the first time we met. Did he care about his people like Rollin or did he just care about me?

An unexpected coldness settled in my stomach. I had to stop these thoughts. Blade should never have sent me to Rollin. It might be the mistake we both regret.

Chapter 60

The first two weeks of my time with Rollin went quickly. I carried the mental reminder of Mule with me and tried to simply be happy with the life I had at this moment. Shep and Leo were great, but they had to be covert, and thankfully, Alaric helped. He was Rollin's right hand, but I think he hoped having Shep and Leo in my life would keep me from doing chores.

I tried to help in the kitchen, but Babs had no trouble throwing me out. I didn't take it personally; I just would have liked another woman to talk to. Hax helped too, but he pestered me non-stop about mine and Rollin's relationship. I spent most days working with my sword with Alaric and sometimes Shep and Leo if they weren't busy. I ate breakfast with Rollin but rarely saw him again until dinner. Hax felt I should go out of my way to be with Rollin. Some days the four-foot man needed to find a tall tree to leap from.

The prophecy was the most important thing to the guttybrew. They had dedicated their lives to seeing it progress.

"How can you learn more about him with only an hour a night?" he demanded. He was speaking of the walk Rollin and I took after dinner each evening.

"If he wanted to spend more time with me, he would make the time," I said stubbornly.

Hax grumbled.

I hated to admit it, but I enjoyed the hour Rollin and I walked together. We spoke about our childhoods and other things that taught us more about each other. He even told me about the pain of losing his brother and then taking over the pack. He blamed the death on the war and not personally on Blade. He held my hand, and I enjoyed the touch of his skin on mine. He had no problem throwing in sexual innuendos when I least expected and he would laugh when I became flustered.

"You do it on purpose," I said during our walk that night.

We were a mile from the cabins. The forest was denser here, and it wasn't as easy to navigate. There was no moon, and I had finally figured out that Rollin enjoyed helping me stay upright and not trip over roots and downed branches.

"Did what?" he asked innocently.

"Your hands keep straying to improper places."

"I don't want you to fall," he said.

"Then we should have stayed on one of the main paths," I huffed.

He stopped and faced me. His hands went to my waist, and I didn't stop him. Slowly he pulled me closer.

"Have you wondered what it would be like to kiss me outside a dream?" he asked in a voice too husky for my good.

My dreams of him caused me endless embarrassment. Thankfully I hadn't had one since I arrived in the forest.

"I learned in the dreams that you weren't a good kisser, so the thought hasn't entered my mind once."

"Liar," he breathed against me.

He was so close, and the look in his eyes showed the wildness of his animal.

"If you must, kiss me, and I'll see if you've improved."

He moved closer still, the front of his body an inch from mine.

"I'll kiss you when you're ready," he said and moved back.

I'd leaned in closer and given him permission. Damn the man was infuriating.

I longed for Blade. I missed him so much. A single kiss from Rollin would have been okay, and maybe for a moment I could have forgotten Blade.

I fell asleep thinking about my vampire.

The blare of an alarm startled me awake, and I sat up in bed.

Sounds could be heard throughout the house. A heavy knock sounded at my door right before it opened. Hax walked closer to the bed.

"Their women and children are under attack," he said.

"Who is attacking them?" I asked over the incessant alarm that hadn't stopped.

"Human soldiers."

"I'm going." I jumped out of bed, took clothes from a drawer, and shouted, "Grab my sword. Can you make a tunnel to their location?"

"It will take too long, though I will have it started as soon as I know where they are."

I closed the bathroom door behind me and tore off my nightshirt. I dressed in record time and gathered my boots.

Hax was gone, and Rollin stood holding my sword.

"I'm coming with you," I said.

He nodded while I laced up my boots.

I had put on leather pants and vest for the first time since arriving at the cabin. These were my fighting clothes and offered more protection than jeans and a tee. I stood, and Rollin handed me the sheath with my sword. I pulled it over my head and took a moment to situate it.

"Are we going by foot?" I asked.

"Yes." Rollin was too angry to do much more than grunt.

"If I can't keep up, leave me behind," I told him.

"I'll put Shep and Leo on you. We are leaving now," he said as I rose.

The men waited outside. Their eyes were wild with fear and anger. We set off at a fast pace, and I knew I wouldn't be able to maintain it for long. This was nothing like the run to save the captain.

"How far," I asked Shep who was in front of me with Leo directly behind.

"Ten miles," he said.

Fuck.

Shep's hand came up in the universal stop signal so I didn't run into him.

"Jump on my back."

I did as he said, and he started running again as soon as I secured my legs around his hips and my arms around his neck.

"Why doesn't Rollin have helicopters?" I asked as my head bobbed up and down with his gait.

"They killed most of our pilots over a year ago," he said. "They found the camp and demolished our air patrol."

"I can't believe this happened under my nose and I never knew anything about it."

"Most of the fighting these past two years has taken place in the east," he said without even the slightest change in his breathing after carrying me for five minutes. "Rollin is the future and we know it. Our children are the future too."

"Do you have kids?" I asked.

"No, Leo and I are single, but Mule did. Twins, a boy and girl. They are toddlers."

Dammit, another reason for guilt.

"How would humans find the camp with the children?"

"We are unsure."

"Do they have someone on the inside?"

"No," they said in unison.

"Very few people knew the location of our women and children," Leo said. "Rollin changes it every few weeks. We suspect they are using infrared cameras sent in on drones. We've destroyed several over the past two weeks."

"What will the human soldiers do to the children?"

"Kill as many as they can," Shep said.

I didn't want to believe they would kill women and children, but I remembered the hatred so ingrained in the human military.

"Will they take prisoners?"

"No."

We needed to go faster.

Chapter 61

We heard gunfire when we were a mile from the women's camp. A hundred yards closer, several women stepped out with children. Shep let me down, and I ran up to where Rollin was speaking.

"Take the children to the backup camp," he told them. "Alaric is preparing it for you. If you don't make it before the sun rises, hide until we find you. If the military knows about your camp, they may know about ours, and we won't be returning."

The five women took off running with twelve children. One of the women held an infant. Two had toddlers in their arms. I had no idea if they were Mule's children.

"Was that all of them?" I asked.

"No. Less than half," Rollin spat out in anger. He turned and signaled his men. "Keep your eyes out for other women and children. We split up here. Team one, you will come in from the north."

Half the men were in wolf form. The other half removed their clothing and shifted. Rollin did too.

"This will be bloody," he said out of his oversized jaws.

My hand rose to the pommel of my sword.

"I hope so." My wielder power was sizzling beneath my skin and it needed an outlet.

So many questions went through my head. Would the military find the new camp? Would the human soldiers actually kill little children and babies? I knew the answer to the last one. Fear drove them and yes they would kill what they considered monsters. But who were the real monsters? I hadn't seen vampires or werewolves going on a terror campaign to kill children.

I barely managed to keep up with Rollin, but I was too close to him to jump on Shep's back again. I wanted Rollin to focus on the coming battle and not the so-called mating bond.

Two children stepped from the bushes. They looked to be around ten and twelve. Both female.

Rollin spoke to them while I caught my breath. He turned to me.

"I know you want to be part of the main fight. I need you to stay with them so I can send more in your direction if we find them. Your job will be to keep them alive."

"I've got them," I said. "Go."

Shep and Leo stayed with me. They carried rifles and put them at the ready.

"I'm Tara," I told the girls.

"Jannie." Jannie had huge brown eyes.

"Marley," the other said. She was the youngest, and her eyes were green. "Should we shift?" she asked.

"You can shift?" I didn't know the most basic thing about werewolf children. I was that stupid and wanted to kick myself.

"Yes."

"Will you feel safer if you shift?" I asked.

"Yes," they both replied in unison.

"Then do it quickly."

I looked at Leo, who was closest to me.

"Why did they not shift already?" I whispered.

"First," he said with a slight grin. "They can hear you." He held up two fingers. "We've learned that humans dislike killing human children in most cases. If they are not in animal form, it's impossible to tell that they are weres. They are trained from birth to control their shift and to never do it in camp."

I was unsure why this made me so damn angry. Even their children couldn't be who they were meant to be.

Another child, a boy, about eight, named Mathew showed up within thirty minutes. He shifted as soon as he saw Jannie and Marley without asking if he could.

We found a cropping of trees with dense underbrush, and my mini pack of wolves started digging and making an area for us to hide. Once we burrowed in, I called to vines and branches to give us more coverage. Leo and Shep walked into the distance so they could stand guard and not give away our location if they were spotted.

I lifted my finger to my lips to silence the children from talking. I felt bad about it, but I was too afraid they would attract the wrong kind of attention.

The wait was interminable. We stayed put and watched from our hiding place for the enemy. We heard a helicopter, automatic artillery fire, and then an explosion. The children's wolf expressions never changed. Gunfire slowed down and so did men's screams.

I had time to study the children. For the first time, I didn't see monsters at all. They were actually cute though I would never say it aloud. If you took a wolf cub and stood him on his hind legs giving him versatile fingers with two-inch claws, it wouldn't come close to describing the miracle of their existence. Their fur looked softer or maybe fluffier was more accurate, and though I wouldn't ask, a child-wolf hug would be wonderful.

"Rollin is coming," Leo said sometime later.

Rollin entered my line of sight, and I crawled from our hiding spot. There were about twenty women with him and even more children. The look in his eyes told me everyone did not make it.

"We can't stay here," he said. "They will gather reinforcements and come back. They were stupid to have limited air support."

"Will Hax be meeting us?" I asked.

"No. Hax is going to the new camp. He insisted he needed to be there."

It seemed strange after my conversation with Hax earlier. He must have discussed it with Rollin while I was dressing in the bathroom. I trusted him to do what was right. He knew I could take care of myself.

We traveled for an hour. The children were exhausted, and Rollin called a halt so they could rest.

He walked from one child to another and asked how they were doing. They looked at him with worship in their eyes. I heard one little girl ask if I were The Promised. I didn't hear his answer but she turned to me and gave me the same worshipful smile.

One of the younger boys was injured. Rollin held him in his lap while his mother treated his wound. The boy stopped crying as soon as Rollin took hold of him.

One moment I was standing, and the next an explosion sent me flying.

Chapter 62

I gained my feet, but the explosions came one after the other, and I almost fell again. The wolves quickly formed a perimeter around the children, their guns and claws ready. Smaller children cried, and the older ones held them. The women had joined the men in their defensive position.

My magic charged through me stronger than I'd ever felt it. I pulled at the trees, and they curved downward. A chopper with mounted artillery came in for another bombardment. I released several trees, and one slammed into the helicopter.

"Run," I said. The chopper blades would kill us, and I'd had no idea my plan would work so well.

A second copter came in but not low enough. I focused my power on two specific trees and waited. Again, the helicopter stayed out of their range, but the tops of both trees snapped off, and six-foot projectiles flew into the helicopter. This taught me something else about my power and what it could do. We stopped running fifty yards away as small pieces of debris rained down around us. Both helicopters were out of commission.

I glanced at Rollin's people. They stared at me in wonder. Rollin took my arm, and I turned to him.

"They are not hurting these children. If they send more, I'll take them all out," I said.

His stunned expression changed into a slow grin.

The attack was over for now. We didn't run into more human soldiers or their aircraft. I was barely staying upright when we entered the new camp. It wasn't as nice or as large as the other. There were only five small cabins.

Hax stood next to a hole in the ground. Relief washed over me, and I walked to his side.

"The women won't enter the tunnels," the guttybrew told me instead of the greeting I expected. "It's the only way to guarantee they are safe. Talk to the werewolf."

Hax was at the end of his rope. Building a place big enough for his people and Rollin's couldn't have been easy. I, for one, was thankful to have the guttybrew on our side.

I left him and went to where Rollin stood speaking to one of the women. She held the two toddlers. They were the ones I had seen in the first batch of children who found us.

"The women will not enter the tunnels Hax built," I said when Rollin glanced at me.

Before he could answer, the woman spoke.

"Mule was my mate. These are his children. Are the tunnels safe?" she asked.

"Yes. They are our only chance if we're attacked again. I'm tired and hungry, and my power won't hold up to another strike tonight."

"I will persuade the women to enter the tunnels," she promised.

She spoke to different groups of women, and they remained unsure, but Mule's mate carried her toddlers to Hax, and he had the three of them lowered into the ground. The two girls who had stayed with me when Rollin went to the women's camp walked toward Hax too, and thankfully, more followed.

Rollin smiled at me again. I really liked his smile.

***

We stayed in the tunnels longer than we wanted to. Rollin sent scouts into the forest, and they reported sightings of soldiers. With Rollin's command not to engage unless necessary, they all made it back safely to give the intel.

The tunnels with a few small cave areas were not the ideal habitat, but the children didn't seem to mind, and the guttybrew enjoyed the kids. The guttybrew and adult weres weren't as fortunate, and Rollin put out several proverbial fires between the two factions.

Hax looked haggard from calming his people.

Each night Rollin found his way to me and fell asleep beside me. I always woke up half on top of him. His erection was evident, and I tried not to be mortified. We were safe inside the tunnels, and that was what mattered or so I reminded myself.

"Where will we go?" I asked Rollin late on the third afternoon. He had just spoken to one of the reconnaissance teams.

"I want to appropriate the military camp you lived at," he said. "They won't expect an attack, and they have higher-level weaponry that we need."

"You want to attack my old camp?"

His gaze stayed steady on mine.

"Yes."

I inhaled slowly trying to give myself time. The men I cared about were here with Rollin. The humans in the camp would have killed me if they discovered my power. There wasn't a day that I hadn't asked myself *what if* when I lived there. To them, I was a monster.

"What about the city?" I asked.

"We don't want a major battle there, and if we go there with so many of us, it will eventually attract the wrong type of attention."

"Okay, I'll help."

"Would you be willing to enter the camp to look around so we know the best way to get in with the fewest casualties?" he asked.

I didn't need to think about it this time.

"Yes."

"We'll leave in a few hours. Get some sleep if you can."

The sun would be going down soon, and I was still tired from the night before. I had attempted not to sleep on Rollin and it kept me awake most of the night. What little sleep I managed ended up being on top of him so avoidance was a wasted effort.

I ate a small bowl of veggie soup made by the guttybrew before I wandered to the area I'd claimed for my bed. I stretched out on the sleeping bag that was given to me the first night and fell into a deep sleep.

"Tara," Rollin whispered in my ear.

My eyes cracked open. He was sitting next to me fully dressed.

"We need to leave."

"Did you sleep?" I managed to croak.

"I'm good. You have five minutes."

I grabbed my sword and followed him past his sleeping werewolves. He climbed from the tunnel and lifted me out with one arm. I didn't see anyone else.

"Where are your men?" I asked.

"Those on guard are hidden."

I tried again. "Who is going with us?"

"No one. It's just you and me. We have a better chance of getting to the camp alone. I'm your bodyguard until we get there and also once you get out. The guttybrew will leave today and head to another location to dig backup tunnels."

"How long will it take us to get to the military camp?"

"A day. You'll be inside for a day, and we'll travel another day to return here."

Three days. I would be alone with Rollin for three days. I wasn't sure if it was a good idea but it was too late now. We needed that camp.

We kept to a light jog that I could easily handle. We each carried a backpack with food and a change of clothing. I recognized an area two miles from our destination. We decided to sleep there and go to the camp in the morning. Rollin would stay behind and wait for me.

We had only thin blankets to lay on, and it wasn't comfortable.

"Come on, you've done it every other night."

"So gracious," I muttered and stayed where I was.

"You have pushed my control to the limit, and I've kept my hands off you. Come on."

His whispered words sent chills through me.

"It's different," I whispered back. "We're alone now. What could you do with everyone sleeping in our general area?"

"You have no idea." He chuckled softly, and I wanted to hit him.

"Okay," I agreed, "but keep your erection to yourself."

Chapter 63

Rollin's low laughter filled my ears as he pulled me on top of him. I had to be honest with myself. Over the past few days, seeing Rollin's compassion with his people and the guttybrew had been eye-opening. He helped everyone he could. He took time to reassure the children. He helped with the injured and stayed with one woman who barely escaped death due to a gunshot wound to her heart. She'd lost too much blood for her wolf magic to work. I swear she hung on because of his insistence that she would make it.

He'd look haggard like Hax, frustrated that he couldn't do better for his people, and also in his element. I admired him. Then there was his rock-hard body. I was as attracted to it as I was attracted to the man. I thought of Blade, but his memory was foggy with all that was happening. Blade sent me to Rollin, and I was falling in line with his expectation that I would have sex with Rollin and produce a child. Was I to go back to him afterward? More than anything, I was confused about my feelings for both men.

"What are you thinking about?" Rollin asked after I settled on him. Should I be truthful? "I was wondering what Blade thought would happen when he sent me to you."

Rollin stayed silent for a full minute. "I know he loves you," he finally said. "He fought the prophecy just as I did. Once we accepted it, we had to wait for you. When you turned eighteen, we made the pact, and I thought I could live with it. As you were growing closer to coming into your power, it got harder for me not to go to you." He paused again. "I'm not proud of scaring you. Something came over me and I couldn't fight it." He paused again. "I don't understand why he didn't kill me. I wanted him dead and I wanted you with me."

Nothing he said helped the questions floating in my head. Only Blade could answer them.

"I had dreams of you and Blade before we met. They had been going on for years and it was very confusing." Rollin's fingers ran up and down my back as I spoke. "What happens if I can't love you? The prophecy will destroy the world if I don't."

He inhaled deeply before he spoke again. "No one can force love. I will respect your decision at the end of the month, but it won't be easy, and the best thing will be for you to return to Blade if that is your wish." His hands had stilled, and his fingers clenched. "He will protect you from me. I will fight this war until I'm dead. The humans in the city must be protected along with my own people."

"But you need Blade to win," I said.

"I need you alive more."

He'd told me he shouldn't be alpha because I came before his pack. I hadn't understood the danger but now I did.

"You must sleep," he said.

I closed my eyes and inhaled his scent that I had become familiar with and it lulled me to sleep quickly. I woke as sunlight peeked behind the horizon. I was still on top of Rollin, and from his breathing, I thought he was asleep.

I leaned away slightly and simply looked at him. His strength showed in every line of his face even when relaxed in sleep. Without thought, my finger ran over his skin on the side of his neck, up across his jaw and stopped.

He grew hard beneath me.

"You're awake," I accused.

He bit my finger.

"Ow," I said though it hadn't hurt.

"I'll lay still while you run your hands over me anytime," he said, his lips curving up slightly.

"It was one finger."

His hands clamped my waist, and he rolled so I was beneath him. He was at least gentlemanly enough to keep his upper weight on his forearms. His finger went to my face, and he ran it across the same pattern I had used on his.

"I love you," he murmured. "I haven't forgotten what I said. You need to know that losing you will destroy me, but I will let you go. I've made love to you in my dreams too many times to count." His voice had dropped, and the sound went clear to my toes. "Those dreams will carry me for the rest of my life, but I want something deeper. Give me one night. The two of us and a soft bed. I don't need your answer now. I want you focused on getting in and out of the camp. When you decide, let me know."

I rested my head on his chest, and we lay like that until the sun was completely up. My decision was made, but I wouldn't tell him until we were together again.

Chapter 64

During the long jog the day before, Rollin and I had come up with a plan for me to enter the camp. I walked in like I owned the place. A sense of déjà vu came over me. The canteen was active even this early, and that's where I headed. Soldiers watched me, but they stayed away. I wore jeans and a dark blue tee with my hair hanging loose around my shoulders and down my back. I went in without my sword or any other weapon. There were a few scrawny trees in the camp, and I called to them as I walked. I also felt weeds under the dry dirt that were waiting to pop free into the light. I gave them a small push that wouldn't be noticed by anyone around me.

The canteen looked and smelled the same. The large canvas shelter was old and weathered, in need of replacement. The same bartender stood behind the counter. I held up one finger.

"Tequila," I said.

He splashed some into a shot glass and slid it toward me. "Haven't seen you here in ages," he said.

"Just walked in," I told him.

I carried my shot to the table we'd used when I was with Shep, Leo, and Mule. I placed the glass on the table and sat down to wait. The front flap opened, and four armed men entered, looked around, and headed in my direction. I threw back the shot and enjoyed the sweet burn.

"Gentlemen," I said, casually. They spread out around me.

"You are to come with us," a large man with a square jaw and slightly crooked teeth said.

"I was hoping for another shot," I told him. He grabbed my arm, and one of the other soldiers grabbed me on the other side. Talking was at an end as far as they were concerned. I took longer than normal strides to keep up with them so I wasn't dragged on the ground. They led me to the tent that the general used. I couldn't possibly get this lucky.

I didn't. I had never seen the officer who sat behind the desk. A captain like Dickson. He wasn't in the least handsome, and he didn't so much as smile. His thin hair was combed over and not the tight cut one would expect. His brown eyes were sharp like a rodent scoping out a garbage can.

"Tara Lott," he said.

"Have we met?" I asked. He stared at me so long it turned creepy. I wanted to fidget before he spoke again, but I managed to control the urge.

"We've heard interesting things about you. You were sent into the city for information, and you disappeared. Where have you been?"

"I was attacked by vampires," I told him. Rollin and I had decided to keep his pack out of my story. "The local gang helped me go underground until I was safe. The vamps have looked for me since." I placed my hands out in a what-the-hell manner. "I returned as soon as I could."

Red suffused his cheeks, but that was the only outward sign that he didn't believe my bullshit. I remained calm. I had a backup plan.

"Did you stay with the vampires?" he demanded. "I just told you what happened." He looked at the man I named square jaw. "Place her in a tent with two guards." He looked back at me. "Let me know when you're ready to tell the truth. We'll try no food and water before we move on to other proven methods."

"You're making a mistake," I said. "I came back here because this is my home."

"Get her out of my sight," he ordered.

A few minutes later, I was sitting on a cot in a desolate tent on the far side of the camp. I'd eaten before I came, and I could go a bit without water too. I would be gone before I became desperate, regardless of how airless the tent was. Two guards parked themselves outside the flap. Another guard placed an empty bucket inside the tent. They were not giving an inch, and it wouldn't help me gather the information I needed.

The good news was they didn't know about my magic. I waited two hours before I requested I be taken to the captain.

"I'm angry," I told him when I was standing in front of him again. "I was sent on a false mission and almost died. I want to understand why. I have information that can help us."

"There is no us," the captain said. "You were never a member of the military, and we are not here to accommodate you."

"Then why send me on a fake mission? I had never caused trouble. I am loyal. Why?"

"The command came from higher up, and I am not privy to the information. I received orders that you were an enemy of the people's army."

Awe, the "people's army" had a nice ring. By people, he meant human.

"If I were the enemy, I wouldn't have returned," I told him as earnestly as I could. "I've heard rumors too. I heard the vampires were set to attack." I had his interest, though he still didn't believe me. "I also know how to find them."

"And how is that?" he asked.

"I want information first," I told him. Before I got my question out, the captain interrupted.

"You will make no demands on us. We have a team leaving in the next few days to attack the monsters up north. I have no time for your bullshit."

He'd just given me the information I came for.

"Men, hold her," the captain commanded.

I was grabbed and held by square jaw and his comrade. The captain stood, walked from behind his desk, and planted his fist in my stomach. I only stayed upright because the men didn't drop me. The air left my lungs in a rush, and I couldn't breathe. It would pass, but my magic didn't like it. The trees and plants responded, but I mentally held them back.

"Have you been with the vampires?" he barked after oxygen returned to my lungs.

"No." One-word replies were easiest right now.

"Where were you?"

"Gang hangout."

He pulled a knife from his belt and lifted the sharp blade. He ran the dull side of the point down my face.

"I know exactly who you are because I knew your father," he whispered. Every thought in my head froze. "Did he suffer?" the captain asked. He'd also just told me exactly who he was. My father died in my arms after somehow dragging himself home, and this was the man who killed him.

"You will die," I bit out through gritted teeth.

"This is what a traitor looks like," he told his men. "You know what we do with traitors?"

I didn't intend to wait around and find out. My backup plan was the trees. Their size wouldn't matter. I would return for the captain when he least expected it. A loud noise came from outside.

"I think we're under attack," one of the men said when the sound of soldiers yelling filtered into the tent.

"Hold her," the captain yelled and rushed outside.

"We're sitting ducks," I told them. "If we're under attack, we need to at least take cover."

"Why would we hide?" square jaw asked.

"If you aren't fighting or running away like a coward, the only other alternative is to hide. The captain's desk will give us a bit of cover depending on the size of the artillery." He looked undecided, but another loud thump came from outside. A man cried out. That would be the weeds which were now four feet tall. They pulled their roots back as they grew and made pits in the dirt. Those pits were perfect for breaking ankles. The trees were doing their own thing. Branches were flying and lifting the dust to decrease visibility.

"Look, if the two of you want to die in here, fine. At least allow me to hide behind the desk."

"Go ahead," square jaw said.

As soon as I was beneath the desk, I called to the remaining trees. Everything they had now hit the tent. Both men yelled as the tent came down on top of us, and branches from the closest tree pelted the canvas. I rolled from under the desk, pried up the bottom of the tent and continued rolling until I was free. The camp was in chaos. I had to make it back to Rollin. His people had to attack before the unit pulled out, or they would return and discover us after we took their camp.

Chapter 65

I made it back to Rollin with a little luck and a lot of help from plants and trees that did my bidding. The earth hadn't stopped trembling until I was clear.

"They are sending a team north to help kill your people. We must attack in the next forty-eight hours or that team will return after they don't find you. If we don't see and stop them, they'll notify another unit with your new location."

"Can you run?" he asked.

I started running in the direction we came at the fastest pace I knew I could maintain. An hour in I slowed a fraction.

"We'll do better if I carry you."

I didn't argue and climbed onto his back in the same piggyback carry I'd suffered through before. Undignified but we had to hurry. Rollin picked up his pace like he wasn't carrying a full grown woman on his back.

"Have you heard of using shortwave radios?" I asked as the steady jar of my head began to make my neck sore.

"Our communications are intercepted and we stopped using them unless it's an emergency."

It made sense, and I should have asked a week ago when it started bugging me.

"We have jammers, and when we attack, they won't have a signal to notify others," he continued.

"If the military discovers you've taken the camp, they will attack. How will you hold it?"

"Shep and Leo will be put to use. We'll give them weapons and send them with others to act like they are the strike team from the camp. It should buy us some time. If we must, we'll confiscate and evacuate to another location. It would be easier if we could stay there, but I'll do what's safest for my people."

"If the guttybrew dig tunnels for the women and children, we can acquire some military uniforms and look like we belong after we take it."

"I like it. Tell me about the guttybrew?" he asked.

There was so much I didn't know, but I told him what I had.

"They are loyal to you and not the vampires?" he asked.

"Yes."

"They've been a tremendous help."

We made small talk for another hour before I fell into a light sleep due to exhaustion. Rollin made it back to his people in half the time it took us to get to the military camp.

Two women would handle the children and travel underground. They would miss the heavy fighting because it would take the gutty-brew longer to dig. It would keep the children safe, though. The other women were fighting with us.

I was tired, and I knew Rollin had to be exhausted.

"Have dinner with me?" he asked after the plans of attack were settled.

I agreed. I expected we would find privacy in his room, but he'd planned our meal for outside. He carried the food in a sack and set about making a fire when he found the spot he wanted. The area was overgrown, but somehow he knew there was a place for us to prepare the meal and eat. I carried a blanket over my arm and spread it on the soft grass.

"How did you know this was here?" I asked after I sat down and watched him gather wood.

His smile was pure sin.

"I have my ways," he said huskily.

I watched him prepare the meal. He kept my vegetables away from his meat. The sizzling smell of my veggies was amazing, his food not so much.

"When are we leaving?" I asked.

"In a few hours. We want to hit them before the sun rises."

"You're not taking me?" I wouldn't be able to keep up if they were moving fast enough to make it by dawn.

"Shep and Leo will carry you."

I'd seen him talking privately to the two men.

"Will that bother you?"

He looked at me, and his eyes changed. They said he wanted to devour me like I was the perfect meal after weeks of hunger. In his mind, I was his and his alone. He didn't want any other man touching me. The answer wasn't with words, but I got the point.

We ate in relative silence, each aware of the other. My nipples ached for his touch, and I kept pulling myself back by thinking of Blade. My dreams of sex with Rollin encroached on my thoughts of Blade.

"You need sleep," I said after we cleaned up our makeshift picnic.

"Stay with me here, and I will sleep," he told me.

"That's bribery," I said.

"No, actually it's coercion."

"I see. Can I trust you?" I asked, knowing my voice had dropped.

He grabbed me and laughingly, I didn't fight.

"Will you give me one night?" he asked, his warm breath sending shivers through me.

I looked into his dark eyes that had a faint ring of amber around the pupils. I rolled and stood. Some of the light left his gaze at my abrupt departure.

"Stay here for a moment," I told him.

He nodded without a word.

I walked into the forest and traveled far enough away that I could remove my clothes without him hearing the rustle of material. I then walked further into the woods until I found another perfect spot, this one with taller grass.

I ran another twenty feet to the left and called out loudly, "Find me."

I knew when Rollin drew close because the insects stopped chattering, but I didn't hear him move. I had hidden myself among the tall grass like in one of the sex dreams I'd had of him.

"Is this your answer?" he asked from behind me and I startled.

"You found me," I said as I watched him remove his clothes. For the oddest reason, I couldn't directly answer his question, and I conveyed it the only way I could.

When he was naked, he went to one knee beside me. The skin of his leg touched my hip.

"I remember this dream, little rabbit." He said it in little more than a whisper. He pounced, and his hands locked on mine, drawing them above my head.

"You know what I like," he said against my lips. I strained, and he didn't release me. "I need you to say the words out loud, though. Tell me you want this."

"I want this." My words were low too. I wanted him so damn badly.

His legs spread mine wider. His erection rubbed against me. His lips began their own exploration while his hands held mine tightly.

"I want to touch you," I groaned. Every muscled valley and inch of taught flesh cried out for me to touch him.

"Soon," was his velvet reply.

His lips moved further down while my fingers clenched and unclenched. When he found my breast, I inhaled sharply. He moved to the other and sucked until my toes curled. I moaned.

"Quiet." His tone almost undid me. "The big bad wolf is at your door."

My body bucked beneath him when his knee pressed against the neediest part of me. He chuckled softly.

"You must be still, little rabbit."

Each touch traveled like a beacon to my sex. I once more breathed in the musky scent of an aroused werewolf. His warm breath slid over my skin. A small nip here, teeth there. My flesh sizzled with unfulfilled desire. I couldn't get enough air into my lungs.

He continued to play and drive me half mad. When he released my hands, I wound them through his hair. His fingers found me, and I wreathed. One then two pushed in and out of my slick passage. His mastery over my body was learned by dreams from our past. We'd been here before. My body remembered this aching burn. I needed him inside me, and finally, I whispered my desire aloud. He peered into my eyes, his face inches from mine, his grin one of pure ownership. Before I understood what he was up to, he flipped me to my stomach and drew me up to my hands and knees. This was not our dream. I wanted to object. I wanted so many things.

He entered me, long and hot, thick and hard. I pushed back against him and groaned in pleasure.

"Shh," he whispered against the back of my neck, his breath warm, the sound fucking hot. He pushed in and out like his fingers had, every inch of him going deep and turning me into a hot mess. His hands found my breasts, and he pinched my nipples in time with each deep thrust. My gasps came quicker, and he increased the pace. His breathing became as ragged as mine. The grass tickled my flesh, and I didn't care. My only thought was Rollin inside me, driving me crazy.

The world stopped as my orgasm shook from my toes to fingertips. My internal muscles clamped his cock with pulsing need as the delicious sensation went on and on. He groaned and pushed deeper, released my breasts, and held my hips in place as he came inside me, his hot seed filling me. My body wouldn't release him, and waves of ecstasy continued until I could no longer stay on my hands and knees and collapsed.

Rollin's warmth came down on me. We were both slick with sweat. He pulled out, fell to my side, and moved me closer to him.

"Thank you," he whispered.

I felt split in two, mentally and physically. I loved Blade, and I was very afraid I loved the man beside me.

Chapter 66

We took the military camp the next day. It was bloody, but we came out on top. Two of Rollin's men died. I found the captain. As much as I would have liked him to suffer, I made it quick.

"Why did you kill my father?" I demanded.

"There was something wrong with him. He was a monster." His eyes held defiance.

"My father was a good man, but his daughter is the real monster," I said and sent power to my sword so the blue flame rose larger than I'd seen it before.

The captain lay on the ground looking up. He screamed in horror. Now he saw the monster in my eyes. Very slowly, I pushed the sword into his flesh clear through his heart.

After the captain died, his men gave up. Rollin held the prisoners in tents with guards. Coop had been the first to tell me that human boys as young as ten were conscripted. The prisoners we'd taken were not all adults, and it infuriated me. They would be moved to the city where they weren't a danger to Rollin's plans. Hopefully, the boys would welcome a life with the monsters.

I took five minutes to charge my sword in the ground. While I held it, I saw my father's smile in my mind. I had avenged him, and now I could let go.

Rollin had one pilot for two helicopters. We needed more but would be thankful for what we had.

Shep and Leo took off with a group of werewolves in military fatigues to act as the unit assigned to locate the werewolves.

They were gone for a week while we redesigned the camp in strategic ways. We now had firepower and weapons, including over one hundred anti-aircraft guns and several anti-tank guns. Rollin explained that the city had an ample supply of weapons that would also be called into play for the final battle. I had no idea when that would be but we would move to the city before it happened.

Staying at my old stomping ground was strange. The guttybrew built a large enough area underground that the men who were not on guard stayed down there too. If we were attacked at night, they would find empty tents.

All but one.

I stayed with Rollin each night. He made love to me, and I couldn't get enough of him. I did think of Blade, but it was in the abstract. Rollin's people accepted me as his mate, and they thought I had accepted him too. I wasn't quite there, and Rollin didn't ask. I felt his love in every good morning, every meal he handed me, and every thrust into my body.

Weeks went by. Shep and Leo returned from their mission. It hurt that they stayed clear of me.

"Rollin would kill us," Leo said after I made it known that I was angry by their treatment.

I asked Rollin about it.

"They understand mating," he said after a slight hesitation. "I'm volatile and seeing the men close to you makes my head boil. It's like me coming after you when you were with Blade." We hadn't mentioned Blade once since the night we first made love. "I lost control and right now I need to be focused on strategy. Leo and Shep understand what's at stake."

I got it but Shep and Leo's rebuff still saddened me.

I spent most of my time underground during the day. Mule's wife, Clarissa, and her children filled a void in my heart. I needed and wanted friends.

Jannie and Marley, though young, were also my friends and slowly, their mothers sat with them and spoke to me. For the first time in my life, I was part of a large family. I found strength in the women, and we worked drills together. They could fight, and they would kill when the time came.

The largest battle was on the horizon, and we would need everyone but the children.

And then there was Hax.

He had looked at me with knowing eyes after the first night I spent in Rollin's tent.

"Not one word," I said. "My emotions are all over the place, and I need time to figure this out."

"Humph," he said and left me alone about it.

But he watched. They all watched. I saw covert smiles on the women's faces when Rollin did something endearing, like ruffle my hair when he walked past.

Two weeks turned into a month and then two. The weather changed and gave us relief from the heat. I sat in on war plans and offered advice. I wasn't the only woman. Several who had fought with us to take the camp sat in too. What shocked me more was the men listened and often changed plans with our suggestions.

Drake, Blade's right hand, arrived one night to represent the vampires. He nodded but never spoke to me directly.

In our meetings, I sat beside Rollin but, in order to stay focused, we never touched. I was unsure what Drake thought and what news other than war plans he took back to Blade. I would have sought him out, but I was worried it would set Rollin off, and I didn't want friction between the two men.

The entire camp was on edge while the vampire was there.

I partially understood.

Many of the men and women had been alive during the worst of the vampire-werewolf war and lost family members. I hoped one day their distrust could be put aside.

Two and a half months after we took the camp, we left for the city. Rollin had a place there. I sent for Mika and Coop. Even though Blade had assured them I was okay, they were frantic.

"I'm fighting with you," Coop told me after he had spent several days under Rollin's roof. "I'm a bigger fan of the weres than the vamps, but I'll fight with both to defeat the human forces."

I wondered how all of this fit into the prophecy. Something I couldn't put my finger on bothered me. I had a feeling I didn't actually want to know what it was because it would be bad. Very bad and once more, I felt as if I didn't ask the right questions.

When we arrived in the city, Rollin took me to meet with the gang leader, and I saw Murdock again. He hadn't changed, but I could see the respect he had for Rollin. The humans in the city had amassed weapons and would fight.

"We've prepared all we can," Rollin said after loving me on our fourth night in the city. "If we don't attack now, they will attack us here." He dipped his head lower so we looked into each other's eyes. "I have a favor to ask," he said.

I wouldn't like it. I could see that in his expression.

"Ask."

"Go to the vampires. Blade will have you protected during the battle. You can take Mika and anyone else you want."

"No."

He rolled, took my hands, and held them above me.

"I need you safe."

"I can help."

"You can also die." His eyes had gone amber.

"You can die too."

"Do this for me."

"No." There was nothing he could say that would detour me. The prophecy wanted me to fight or so I thought.

Three days later, everything changed.

Chapter 67

Mika, Clarissa, and the twins, plus Captain Dickson, came with me to Rollin's compound to sit out the battle. The captain volunteered, and Blade agreed. The guttybrew were a main component of the attack. They would move troops underground while a smaller force moved above ground with heavy equipment. Several women along with the children were once more in hiding until the end of the battle.

I fought tears and hugged Hax tightly when I said goodbye.

My parting with Rollin was worse. He didn't think I would return to him. I could see it in his eyes. For two nights, he lay beside me, and we didn't make love. The night before I left, he pulled me close, said, "fuck it," and proceeded to make me scream. I didn't care that the entire house heard. Rollin loved me, and I wanted the world to know.

I worried that not telling him my final decision would cloud his focus during the battle. Even though I knew I wouldn't change my mind, I had to see Blade first.

The ride to the vampire compound was faster than I wanted it to be. I was worried about facing Blade, but I had to see him.

We arrived at night, and Drake greeted us. Ambrosia gave me a long hug then showed the others to their rooms.

"Is he here?" I asked Drake, my hands held tightly in front of me because they were trembling.

"Yes."

"Please tell him I'll be in the garden," I said.

"As you wish." Drake bowed slightly and left the room.

I didn't need to remember the twists and turns of the halls. The garden knew I was here and led me outside. The sweet scent of flowers filled me, and the power of the well-tended plants swamped my senses. I laughed with pure joy and spun around. When I opened my eyes, Blade stood in front of me.

The first sight of him was painful and joyful at the same time. I understood the prophecy as much as it could be understood though there were still holes. Blade had not betrayed me. He loved me, and it shone so bright I couldn't look away.

He wore a white shirt with those ridiculous sleeves, leather pants that fit him like latex, with perfect hair, and a body that still gave me pause.

Love, hope, compassion, worry. He allowed every emotion to show.

"I'm pregnant," I said. It was the exact opposite of what I had planned to say.

Pain flashed in his expression but then it was gone, and a soft smile appeared.

"I love you," he said.

"I love you."

The words hung between us.

"I think I also love Rollin." I never took my gaze from Blade's.

Pain flashed again.

"I'm glad for you."

I landed on the bench I'd used so many times before and covered my face with my hands. I could no longer hold back tears. I'd discovered I was pregnant three days after I told Rollin I was going into battle. I hadn't told him of the pregnancy when I changed my mind.

He didn't know, and I was sending him into battle not knowing about his child or my decision.

The tears turned to sobs, and I couldn't seem to stop once I started. Blade lifted me in his arms and sat on the bench holding me, my face against his shoulder.

"The hardest thing I've ever done was let you go," he whispered against my cheek when I finally quieted. "I knew you would need to love Rollin to make a child. It's who you are." He moved my hands from my face and tipped my chin so I was looking at him. "Does Rollin know you love him?"

In his mind, my love for Rollin was not a maybe. It wasn't a maybe in my mind either, and I had to admit it to Blade.

"I don't want to lose you, but I love him too much," I whispered in a raspy voice, the pain unbearable.

"Neither Rollin nor I will share you. It had to be this way, but you must know, I will love you through time. His hand slid to my stomach, and my heart felt as if it stopped. "I already love this child as if it were my own."

More tears poured from my eyes.

"It's so unfair," I breathed.

"What will you name her?" he asked.

"Her?"

"The prophecy says a female heir will rule."

Hax hadn't told me this.

"Werewolves don't have female rulers," I said.

"The dawn of man and all their rules has come to an end. The prophecy was given to right the imbalance. It's now the dawn of women and that reign begins with you. The werewolves won't stop you. Everything will change now. Our baby was the missing key."

"You knew I would stay with him?" I asked.

Blade smiled down at me without answering. He bent low, and his lips took mine. It wasn't a gentle kiss. My heartbeat sped up, and a flush of heat rose inside me. This wasn't a betrayal to Rollin. It was the only way to say goodbye.

He released my lips and looked deeply into my eyes.

"I am going into battle with the werewolves," he said.

All at once I was frantic with worry for both the men I loved.

"I'm coming with you."

"No. Your place is here." He touched my stomach again. "You hold the future."

I wanted to argue. I wanted to kick and scream. Blade was right. I would wait for his return and then I would go back to Rollin, and we would start our life. I loved two men but I couldn't have them both. The love I felt for Blade was different now.

"When do you leave?"

"Tonight. Drake will stay here. I'm taking half my fighters. The baby will be safe regardless because there is a fierce wielder protecting her."

He was right. No one would hurt my child.

"Coop is fighting with you and Rollin," I said. Worry had filled my voice.

"I will protect Coop. He will come back for Mika."

"Thank you."

"I will even watch over that pain in my backside Hax. I've missed him."

I smiled through my tears. Hax missed him too.

"The guttybrew have kept us alive. With their help, you can't lose."

"I'm tired of war and fighting," Blade whispered.

Rollin had said these same words.

I pulled my locket from my pocket.

"I want you to have this," I said. "It holds the images of my mother and father."

"No," he said and shook his head.

"Yes. You changed my world. Part of my heart will always be yours. The locket is also part of my heart."

His look was one of sorrow but he took the locket from my hands and held it.

"Stay safe," I said through teary eyes.

He kissed me one last time, more gentle than urgent, and walked away leaving me alone in the garden. I lay on the grass, my misery deep. The plants began working their magic. Power wrapped around me and I glowed.

Tomorrow the battle would be in full swing. It could be a week, even two, before we knew the outcome. With everything I'd been through with the prophecy, the vampires and werewolves united, and Hax's help, I still worried. Even so, I couldn't make a backup plan. Rollin would return. He had to.

***

When Rollin entered my room, I had known for three hours that we had won the battle. Additional information was in short supply.

Drake stood with me, his shoulders back, his eyes on the werewolf. Something was horribly wrong but Drake refused to tell me.

"Wolf," he said.

"Vampire," Rollin acknowledged.

"I will leave you and go see to the returning men and women." He did the slight bow thing and left us alone.

"How many did we lose?" I asked.

"Too many."

"Hax, Coop?"

"Safe. They came here with me."

"Blade?"

Rollin stared at me.

"He told me of the child," he said.

I couldn't smile.

"I don't know why, but I needed Blade to know first," I explained. My hand went to my stomach. I looked straight into his eyes. "I told him I loved you."

"He said that too. His final sacrifice fulfilled the prophecy, and we are free."

"What are you saying?" A tightness formed in my chest.

"The man you chose would rule by your side. The other man would give his life for you and the child."

"I wasn't there," I said shaking my head. I knew what he was saying but I couldn't accept it.

"He saved my life and changed the tide of the battle. Without him, we would have lost."

"No. Where is Blade? I need to see him." Frantic terror was taking over.

Rollin grabbed my shoulders and pulled me against his chest. His scent enveloped me but it wasn't enough. I had to know that Blade was okay.

"It was daylight and the vampires were down in the tunnels. Coop and Hax were with me when explosions went off around us. We were waiting for the next barrage when a team of their best soldiers located us. Blade sprung from one of Hax's tunnels and attacked before they opened fire. He saved all of us and without his sacrifice, we would have died."

"No," I whispered. My heart couldn't take this.

Rollin lifted me and carried me to the bed. My eyes were dry because I refused to believe Blade was gone. I lay frozen, and I wanted to go back in time so I could tell him I loved him again.

"He was too far gone from the sun, but I was able to speak to him before he died. He said you would know where to find his final goodbye."

I stared at nothing.

"He told me to return this to you for our daughter."

The locket rested in his hand and that was when I knew Blade was gone forever.

"Where is Blade's letter?" he asked.

There was only one place it could be.

"In the box my father gave me. It's in my bag." I said it with no emotion.

Rollin stood and retrieved it.

"I will leave you alone to read it." He handed me the bag and left.

I wanted him to stay and I didn't. I wasn't strong enough to read the letter.

I located the piece of wood and pulled it out. My hand smoothed over the surface. I used a needle from the bag and pricked my finger. The wood changed to a box in my hand. I had placed his first note back inside the box after I'd read it. The paper was newer than that of the letter from my father which was also inside. The newest note, beige, rested beside Blade's first note which was white. I lifted the beige paper, unfolded it, and read.

Tara, my love,

I know you are filled with sadness. I do not want that for you. When I sent you to Rollin, I knew this outcome. I planned for it because my plans would make life easier for you. Lizbet is my successor. She and Drake are together. He will guide her until she is ready to stand on her own. Men have fought in wars for thousands of years. Our time to rule is over. Our daughter, and yes, I include her as yours, mine, and Rollin's. She will come of age in a changed world. It will be one of peace. It is her inheritance. Love does not stop in death. Your stories of me will keep me alive in our daughter's mind. I regret that I will never hold her, see her smile, or hear her laugh. She is a child of love and she will be spoiled and headstrong and perfect. Think of me with a smile. It's the image of you I carry into death.

Yours through eternity, Blade

I didn't know I was crying. Wracking sobs shook my shoulders and I cried out in agony. Rollin must have waited outside the door and heard me. I was in his arms with little awareness of how it happened. I don't know how long I cried. He rubbed my back and soothed me. I fell asleep in his arms, the note crushed in my fist.

Epilogue

Our daughter was born in the spring. I had given birth in the vampire garden among the soft grass that had cradled me many times. Macos delivered her. Rollin and I looked at her red-splotched and beautiful face with smiles and tears. Rollin took her and lifted her toward the sky.

"I name you Blade," her father said and lifted her higher.

Plants moved up his legs until they touched our child, and I hadn't called them. Light glowed from our baby as soon as the connection was made. Then, it traveled throughout the garden, into the trees, flowers, and plants. She began a new generation of wielders.

Rollin pulled the baby close to his chest and held her while I looked on. I wished Blade could be with us, but I felt him. His ashes had been collected, and I spread them throughout the garden. He was here. He would forever be a part of my child's life.

Rebuilding our world wasn't easy. We began work before the sun came up and we ended long after it set. Mika was now in charge of the city with Coop by her side. Adjusting to women in power was easiest for the werewolves. Their women had always had a say. Rollin was right about their fierceness too. You did not mess with a mother's cubs without deadly consequences.

Lizbet and Mika met with me weekly to discuss our plans for the future and to iron out current problems. Mika moved into the vampire compound to stay with me when the birth was near. There was no one I trusted more than Macos to deliver my baby.

Was our world perfect? Not by a long shot. But, we had time to fix the problems. I had no idea if women would make the change the prophecy promised, but I planned to do everything within my power to ensure it. Women held the gifts of the elements, and we wouldn't be giving them up. I held earth magic along with the magic of werewolves which was air. Lizbet held fire and Mika held water. When we came together, we were an unstoppable force for peace. We would protect it.

Mika stepped forward and rested her hand on the baby's head. Energy flowed from her to our child. Lizbet was next, and she did the same. After her gift transferred, she turned to me.

"You passed on your elemental gifts when she was conceived. Now, with ours, she is one with all of them."

Naming our child was something that strangely enough, Rollin and I had never discussed and no one had ever asked. People left the garden, and we were alone.

"Blade?" I asked my mate.

"Did you have something better?" he smiled at me and handed our daughter over. She was wrapped in a soft blanket and so tiny, holding her made me nervous, but once she was in my arms, the world righted and she was exactly where she was meant to be.

"You know that naming her Blade will make her a handful?"

"I can only hope," he said.

He sat on the side of the bed, leaned over, and kissed my temple.

"She is beautiful and fierce. She will rule far longer than you and I."

"Do not," I said sternly, "bring that damned prophecy into this special moment."

No one could ever show me the prophecy even though I threatened them with spitting fire. I couldn't do it myself but I had a plant that produced oil when burned and could. Hax swore that with Blade's death and me being pregnant there was no more. Dare I believe him?

What I did believe was that I loved my mate and our child. Blade. Her name was Blade.

"Blade won't just be a handful, she'll be a demon in disguise. Maybe we should talk about this."

"She will be the blade of legends and it's the perfect name."

He took my hand and kissed the back of my fingers.

"I love you," he whispered.

Our child was the Blade that would rule the world.